T0038511

EX-WIFE

EX-WIFE

URSULA PARROTT

WITH A FOREWORD BY ALISSA BENNETT
AND AN AFTERWORD BY MARC PARROTT

McNally Editions

New York

McNally Editions
134 Prince St.
New York, NY 10012

ISBN: 978-1-946022-56-1
E-book: 978-1-946022-57-8

Design by Jonathan Lippincott

5   7   9   10   8   6   4

To H.

FOREWORD

I'd never heard of Ursula Parrott when McNally Editions introduced me to *Ex-Wife*, the author's 1929 novel about a young woman who suddenly finds herself suspended in the caliginous space between matrimony and divorce. The first thing I wondered was where it had been all my life. *Ex-Wife* rattles with ghosts and loss and lonely New York apartments, with men who change their minds and then change them again, with people and places that assert their permanence by the very fact that they're gone and they're never coming back. Originally published anonymously, *Ex-Wife* stirred immediate controversy for Parrott's frank depiction of her heroine, Patricia, a woman whose allure does not spare her from desertion after an open marriage proves to be an asymmetrical failure. Embarking on a marathon of alcoholic oblivion and a series of mostly joyless dips into the waters of sexual liberation, Patricia spends the book ricocheting between her fear of an abstract future and her fixation on a past that has been polished, gleaming from memory's sleight-of-hand.

It's been nearly a century since *Ex-Wife* had its flash of fame (the book sold more than one hundred thousand copies in its first year), and as progress has stripped divorce of its moral opprobrium, it has also swelled the ranks of us ex-wives. Folded in with Patricia's descriptions of one-night stands and prohibition-busting binges are the kind of hollow distractions relatable to any of us who have ever wanted to forget: she buys clothes she can't afford; she gets facials and has her hair done; she listens to songs on repeat while wearily wondering why heartache always seems to bookend love. My copy is riddled with exclamation marks and anecdotes that chart my own parallel romantic catastrophes, its paragraphs vandalized with highlighted passages and bracketed phrases. There is a sentence on the book's first page that I outlined in black ink: "He grew tired of me;" it reads, "hunted about for reasons to justify his weariness; and found them." The box that I have drawn around these words is a frame, I suppose; the kind that you find around a mirror.

For all its painful familiarity, it's easy to get caught in the trap of *Ex-Wife*'s nostalgic charm; there are phonographs and jazz clubs and dresses from Vionnet; there are verboten cocktails and towering new buildings that reach toward a New York skyline so young that it still reveals its stars. If critics once took issue with the book's treatment of abortion, adultery, and casual sex, contemporary analyses have too often remarked that Patricia's world cannot help but show us its age. "Scandalous or sensational?" wrote one critic when the book was last reprinted, in 1989. "Times have changed." Yes and no; released in the decade between two World Wars, and just months before Black Tuesday turned boom to bust, *Ex-Wife* probes the violent uncertainty of a world locked in a perpetual state of becoming.

Lurching toward sexual revolution but still psychologically tethered to Victorian morality, women of Parrott's generation found themselves caught in the freefall of collapsing convention. The seedy emotional texture of *Ex-Wife*'s Jazz Age debauchery reflected the panic felt by women across the country who had glimpsed freedom but remained ill-equipped to navigate its consequences. Almost immediately following the book's publication, the press began a guessing game that sought to identify who was being shielded under its mantle of anonymity; was *Ex-Wife* a confession, a fantasy, or the indictment of a culture shifting too rapidly to acknowledge the inevitable casualties we leave in the wake of change? By August of 1929, conjecture had correctly zeroed in on Katherine Ursula Parrott (née Towle), a journalist and fashion writer who seemed to bear an uncanny resemblance to her bobbed and brushed heroine.

Considering the book in the context of what we now know about her life, one cannot put much stock in Parrott's suggestion that Patricia was a composite figure. Instead, *Ex-Wife* seems to have been a place to record injuries too personal for her to claim as her own. Born in Boston to a physician father and a housewife mother, Parrott decamped to New York's Greenwich Village shortly following her graduation from Radcliffe College in the early 1920s. Her first marriage to journalist Lindesay Parrott Sr. ended in divorce in 1926, the year he discovered that the childless marriage he had insisted upon was not so childless after all. In 1924, Ursula had learned that she was pregnant and left the couple's London home for Boston, where she gave birth to her only son before depositing him in the custody of her father and older sister. It was a secret that she managed to keep from Lindesay and their glamorous circle of friends for an astonishing two years. Marc Parrott, whose afterword concludes this book, would never have a relationship with his father. He was nearly seven years old when his mother finally acknowledged her maternity and assumed responsibility for his care. It was 1931 by then, and Ursula had become one of a handful of women who would find her fortune writing escapist romance tales under the pall of the Great Depression.

Marc Parrott's recollections of his mother paint a vivid portrait of a spendthrift who often worked for seventy-two-hour stretches in order to meet the deadlines that would keep her (and her lovers) in furs. Parrott swanned through the 1930s publishing short stories and serialized novels in women's magazines, her name often mentioned alongside the Hollywood stars who were attached to her screenplays and cinematic adaptations. Although I never once found her son mentioned in the many news items devoted to her work and her persona,

Parrott was occasionally found in the company of a pet poodle improbably named "Ex-Wife"; in more ways than one, it would seem, her greatest scandal was also her most stalwart companion.

Though *Ex-Wife* was initially framed as the writer's endorsement of a dangerous new cultural model, Parrott herself was painfully aware of the double standard that continued to condemn "girls who do." Divorced for a second time in 1932 and a third five years later, the writer openly mused about her vulnerability in a world where marriage no longer insulated aging women from "man's urge for variety." Parrott called divorced women like her "Leftover Ladies," a term that implies both surplus and rejection. Her abandoned woman is doomed to a battle that offers neither victory nor surrender. I think of Patricia examining the phantom lines that have begun to etch themselves across her face. I think of her cold creams and her lipsticks, of her awareness of a clock that never stops ticking. "The Leftover Lady is not free to get old," Parrott wrote the winter after *Ex-Wife* came out, "for she has entered the competition, in her work and in her social life, with younger women. And that competition is merciless."

By the early 1940s, as a serial divorcée who wrote stories with titles like "Love Comes but Once" and "Say Goodbye Again," Parrott found herself a target of increasing mockery in the press. No longer young or glamorous enough to rate in the world she knew, her name would soon be attached to a series of scandals that could not be dismissed as the product of invention. In December of 1942, she was arrested and charged with helping an imprisoned soldier to escape from the military stockade in Miami Beach where he was being held on suspicion of trafficking narcotics. Michael Neely Bryan was a twenty-six-year-old jazz guitarist who had found some notoriety playing in Benny Goodman's band before enlisting in the Army; the heady mixture of drugs and sex led to a high-profile 1944 trial and brought a swift conclusion to Parrott's fourth and final marriage. Under headlines that read "Novelist Seen Making Love in Army Stockade," the writer was described as a matronly woman who, following a lurid encounter, drove through a checkpoint with her lover hidden in the back seat of her car. The two enjoyed one night of freedom at a hotel, where they registered under the name Artie Baker, then turned themselves in to the police, each making a tearful confession. "I looked at him and knew how badly he wanted to go to dinner," Parrott said, "So I decided to take a chance for him."

Though Parrott was ultimately acquitted, the trial marked her. No longer welcome in the pages of magazines that catered to "respectable" middle-class women, Parrott published her last story, "Let's Just Marry," in 1947, by which time she had completed twenty-two novels, fifty short stories, and four original film scripts, in addition to the eight novels that were adapted for the screen. She would surface in a fresh scandal in 1950, when she was arrested in Delaware after skipping out on a $255.20 bill following a six-month hotel stay. Friends said that she'd gone to Delaware to gather material for a new book, but would note that she'd spent much of her time walking her dog and very little of it in front of her typewriter. Newspapers suggested that she'd been undone by too much success, as though the tale she'd told two decades prior had finally proven to be a cautionary one. Parrott endured one final humiliation that definitively ended her career and any illusion she had of a return. In 1952, she was accused of stealing $1,000 worth of silverware from a friend who had allowed her to stay in his house under the premise that she needed a place to work on a new book. A warrant was issued for her arrest, and she spent the remaining five years of her life in hiding. She died, at the age of fifty-seven, in a charity ward.

It seems easy from here to understand that Parrott's career as a writer was usurped by the drama of her scandals. Like many women whose early lives and work are defined by rebellion, Parrott's indiscretions ceased to appeal once they were no longer deemed youthful ones. Her legacy endured one last condemnation when her work was framed by history as "women's literature," a term that was a tombstone in the days before it was understood as an industry. It became a ghost, like its author, neither married nor divorced, resigned to a perpetual now. Drifting around without a future, she drinks and shops, she goes on dates, and she wonders what else can possibly change in a world that no longer seems to have any rules. "Men used to buy me violets," Patricia remarks with brutal resignation. "But now they buy me Scotch."

Maybe I feel protective of Patricia because she feels so familiar to me, proof that time doesn't always change us in the ways that we would like to believe. If the book was once too far ahead of its day and later too far behind, it seems now somehow just right, as though we have rounded the circle again and finally found synchronicity. Wedged between Edith Wharton's constrained society girls and the squandered glamour of Jean Rhys's doomed wanderers, *Ex-Wife* was received by an interstitial America still negotiating who and what women were allowed to be. Once caught in a cultural riptide, the book now reads as a shockingly anticipatory account of what it means to want and what it means to be left; we live in a world now where most of us know the feeling of both. I think of the letter Patricia sent to a lover who could not love her back in the way that she needed him to, of the loneliness she felt when day turned to night and back again. "I shall be long dead," it reads, "of waiting for a telegram saying you are coming home."

Alissa Bennett
New York City, 2022

EX-WIFE

I

My husband left me four years ago. Why—I don't precisely understand, and never did. Nor, I suspect, does he. Nowadays, when the catastrophe that it seemed to be and its causes are matters equally inconsequential, I am increasingly disposed to the belief that he brought himself to the point of deserting me because I made such outrageous scenes at first mention of the possibility.

Of course, during the frantic six months that preceded his actual departure, he presented reasons for it, by dozens. I remember some of them. At times he said I had lost my looks. At other times he said I had nothing but looks to recommend me. He said I took no interest in his interests. He said also that I insisted on thrusting myself into all of them. He said I was spiritless, or temperamental; had no moral sense, or was a prude. He said he wanted to marry the woman he really loved; and, that once rid of me, he would not marry anyone else on a bet.

In the four years since, I have listened to the causes given for the dismal ends of many marriages, and have come to believe my husband's list as sensible as most.

He grew tired of me; hunted about for reasons to justify his weariness; and found them. They seemed valid to him. I suppose if I had tired of him, I should have done the same thing.

But I was not tired of him; so I fought his going ruthlessly and very stupidly. I was sure that if I fought I would win. I have never been as sure of myself since, as I was then, when I was twenty-four. No stirring of any ethical scruples about possessiveness, or idea of the futility of coercing emotion, complicated my efforts to keep what I wanted.

At first, I think, I pretended to high motives—"stay for the sake of our families," and so on. Later, as I grew panicky, I experimented with argument, rage, anguish, hysteria and threats of suicide; and refused to admit to myself, until five minutes before he left, that he really might go, in spite of everything. . . .

While he finished packing, I sat, beginning to believe it. I tried to think of some last-minute miracle to manage: considered slashing my wrists so that he would have to go get a doctor, and then to stay until I recovered. But I recognized, in a world that had suddenly become an altogether incredible place, that he might just walk out and leave me to die of the slashes.

I hoped I looked devastated; I hoped I looked lovely. Then I remembered that the armchair in which I sat was a wedding present from his Aunt Janet, and wondered what one did with a husband's relatives' wedding presents when a husband left. (In New York, one sells them to impecunious young-married friends, ultimately.) The lamp beside me was among the first of the modernistic ones. I remembered that Wanamaker's had not been paid for it.

The sound of trunk lids closing, stopped. He came in.

He stood there, looking handsome and stubborn and unhappy. I was assailed by recollections of how good-looking I had thought him—first time we met, a house party at New Haven, four, no five Springtimes. . . .

"I'm going to get a cab for my things," he said.

"Peter, don't go," I said.

"What's the use of that?" he said.

We regarded each other. And suddenly, after six months in which I had always managed to find one more protest, relevant or otherwise, there were no more.

I ached. We had loved each other for three years, and hated each other half the fourth. It seemed such a long way to have journeyed from a gay and confident beginning.

Apparently, he had a few last words to offer, if I could manage none. He suppressed two or three beginnings.

"When will you divorce me, Patricia?"

I said, "On the far side of hell."

He shrugged. He was not even angry. He just looked tired.

"Have it your own way, Patty." (He had not called me "Patty" for months. "Pat," casually; "Patricia," furiously.)

Then he said, "Well, don't mourn me long, old de-ah." He came and patted my hair, and went out.

My last and silliest inspiration arrived. I thought, "If he doesn't get his trunks, he can't go," and I bolted the apartment door. He came back with the cab driver, and knocked. I sat very still. He shouted, "If you don't open that door, I'll break it in." He would have done it. So I opened the door. He threw his keys on a table. "I shan't ever need these," he said.

I went back to sitting in the armchair. Trunks and bags and taxi man and husband departed, noisily. I thought, "This is the end. Why don't I cry or something?"

II

In that lazy space on Sunday, between late breakfast and time to dress for a cocktail party, Lucia, with whom I was sharing an apartment, tried to define "ex-wife."

"Not every woman who used to be married is one. There are women about whom it is more significant to know that they work at this or that, or like to travel, or go to symphony concerts, than to know that they were once married to someone or other."

She looked at me, reflectively. "You're an ex-wife, Pat, because it is the most important thing to know about you . . . explains everything else, that you once were married to a man who left you."

"You're one, too, by that definition. That you once were married to Arch explains most things about you," I said.

"Yes, but I convalesce somewhat. One isn't an ex-wife if one's in love again, or even if one never thinks about one's husband anymore."

"How many years does it take to get to that stage?" I asked. I had been to dinner with Pete the evening before, and knew that I would be miserable for a week.

"There, there, child," she said, "you'll feel better tomorrow." She began again. "An ex-wife is a woman with a crick in the neck from looking back over her shoulder at her matrimony."

I contributed. "An ex-wife's a woman who's always prattling at parties about the joys of being independent, while she's sober . . . and beginning on either the virtues or the villainies of her departed husband on one drink too many."

"An ex-wife," Lucia said, "is just a surplus woman, like those the sociologists used to worry about, during the war."

"Nobody worries about an ex-wife though, except her family—or her husband if she is one of those who took alimony," I said.

"We don't need to be worried about that, yet, darling. We're too much in demand. Wait 'til we're forty . . . if we're not dead of insufficient sleep, before then."

"I'll be dead of drinking bad absinthe," I announced, resignedly.

Lucia protested. "I really wish you would stop drinking that stuff. It will hurt your looks."

But her voice was languid. We were just talking. Pretty soon it would be time to make up one's face, and put on a velvet frock, and things would start happening fast again. It was not a bad life, while things happened fast. And they usually did.

I tried one more definition. "Ex-wives . . . young and handsome ex-wives like us, illustrate how this freedom for women turned out to be God's greatest gift to men."

We laughed. The winter sun came warmly in over our shoulders. It was pleasant, sitting there. Peter and I had fought like hell the night before.

"Don't think about him," said Lucia. "I can always tell when you are; it does horrid things to your mouth." She talked about ex-wives again, abruptly.

I felt bitter. After a while I said, "An ex-wife is a young woman for whom the eternity promised in the marriage ceremony is reduced to three years or five or eight."

Lucia: "Brought up under the tattered banners of 'Love Everlasting' and 'All for Purity' we have to adapt ourself to life in the era of the one-night-stand."

Then she remembered that she was trying to make me feel gayer.

"Darling, what's the difference. . . . We are awfully popular, and we know endless men, and we go everywhere."

"They all want to sleep with us," I said. "So soon as they get here for dinner they begin arranging to stay for breakfast."

"And that isn't very important, either, Pat. You know it isn't. You are just feeling flat today. . . . What are you going to wear?"

I told her, and went to dress. When I came downstairs again she had mixed two Martinis. I felt better, when I had mine.

After that Max came. We gave him a Martini and he said, "Here's to crime and other pleasures." He always said that for a toast. Then he inquired about our health and our jobs. I suppose because jobs seemed important to him.

They were not to us. We both did advertising. Lucia was in an agency. I was fashion copy-writer in a department store. We averaged about a hundred dollars a week apiece, with odds and ends of freelance writing. We had what we called a garret, on Park Avenue. The rent was a hundred and seventy-five dollars a month, and we spent most of the rest of our money on clothes. We never saved anything.

Lucia said she used to save money when she was married. So did I. Once I saved five dollars a week for a year, for a rug that would be "nice enough to keep when we had a house." After Peter left, I sold the rug for forty dollars, and bought a pair of shoes and a hat with it.

While I was married, I saved money and made plans for the next fifty years and so on. Afterward, I did not make plans for the month after next. It seemed such a waste of time.

When there didn't seem to be much else to say to Max about our jobs, we took him along to the cocktail party. He loved observing the younger generation. So he said.

We did not know many Jews. He was one of the nicest. He was old; looked like a Rembrandt portrait; had made about a million dollars in the junk business; and been taken up by people who wanted him to give money to their philanthropies. He had a huge wife whom he adored. One day he told us proudly that she was learning to write. We thought for an instant it was to write books; but he meant a-b-c's.

He was not one of our set. But it was not a set; just unmatched pieces. The names in my engagement book for the first year post-Peter show well enough the sort of people we knew. (I can't remember for whom some of the initials did stand.)

"Dinner—Richard" . . . he used to be Sunday feature editor of a newspaper. He went to Hollywood on one of those three month opportunity contracts. I've heard he's writing sports in San Francisco now.

"H. R. G.—8 o'clock" . . . author of one play that was a hit, and two that flopped. I went with him to the opening of one of the flops. It was not a gala evening.

"David—Sunday breakfast" . . . who was David? Some vaguely unpleasant association. Oh yes, that was the night I actually did get out of a cab on Eighty-Sixth street in a rage and a snowstorm. David imported sausage casings from Russia. Odd occupation, that.

"Hal—to go beer-gardening in Hoboken" . . . he was just an ex-ambassador who thought he was very, very young at heart.

"Leonard—at the Russian Bear—8 o'clock" . . . he was rather sweet. A former Rhodes scholar working for thirty a week on a tabloid.

"C. L. C.—the Ritz—7:15 o'clock" . . . *the* younger generation novelist. He always admitted it without being asked.

"Dominic—to dine at the Cecelia" . . . such a solemn young Italian surgeon, he was; and danced like an Argentine professional.

"Gerard—the Brevoort—6:30 o'clock" . . . he was minor Wall Street.

"Ken-Ken-Ken" . . . at least three times a week through most of that year. When I see his name, I see lights of Harlem dance halls glittering across the most golden hair I ever saw. He might have been the greatest art director in the movies. He and I had the loveliest time imaginable. But he never once kissed me.

"John—Samarkand—9 o'clock" . . . painted murals for gas-houses, and Elks' clubs and places like that.

"Ned—his house—6:30" . . . he did something in publishing; collected Napoleon—and served endless quantities of marvellous cognac.

The men were like that. I didn't have many engagements with women.

III

That conversation with Lucia about ex-wives was a year and more past the night Peter left me sitting in his Aunt Janet's armchair.

I sat there four and a half hours. I know exactly, because when I heard Pete's taxi start, I looked at the banjo clock my grandfather gave us. It was ten minutes past six.

There was an unopened package of cigarettes beside me. I tore two or three of them in opening it; lighted one; and tried to realize that there was no more Peter. But instead, I began to remember things we had done. They slid through my head like moving pictures that were being run off much too fast—except that these were vividly coloured, not black and white and grey, and they had sounds of voices and fragrances of things in them.

Winter in London. (We spent every penny of our wedding-present checks on four months in England and a Springtime in Paris; because, after that, Peter would have to work hard a long time and get to be a star reporter. Or, I suggested, a dramatic critic, because I liked the theatre so much.) After luncheon we used to rush to Brown-Shipley's on Pall Mall to get a check cashed; and then hurried down the Strand to Romano's American bar, so that we would get there before it stopped serving at two-thirty. We usually reached the door, breathless, at two twenty-five.

Peter ordered enough double Scotch and soda all at once to last the afternoon. A little of the fog filtered in. I could remember the smell of the fog; the smoky fragrance of Scotch; the lights glancing off little bottles of Schweppes, spread all across the table; Peter's deep voice saying gay things about how pretty I was, and what fun we would have, and the strange places to which we would travel someday soon when we had money— Moscow and Buenos Aires, and Budapest and China.

Or, over the third highball: "I'm teaching you how to drink properly, Patty darling. Most men's wives drink so badly. Good Scotch . . . it'll stand by you, Pat, in the days you have great sorrows. . . . But I'm not ever going to let you have any great sorrows.

"No great sorrows . . . and no baby, at least no baby for years and years. You are too young and nice-looking, and I don't want you to be hurt."

We did have a baby though after we got home, when Peter was earning forty-five dollars a week. He was so disturbed about it. When he was not worrying as to how we'd ever support it, he wondered if it was going to hurt me much, and whether I would ever be pretty again.

He was twenty-two years old, then. I was twenty-one.

Our families were letting us struggle, because that is supposed to give young people a sense of life's realities. They did think they were letting us struggle on seventy-five dollars a week though: for we had told them that was Peter's salary.

After I got used to the idea of having a baby, I thought it might be rather nice . . . a small son something like Pete.

He said: "Where in hell will we put it in a livingroom-bedroom-and-bath? We'll never be alone again. It'll take all your time. They have to be washed and rocked and fed incessantly."

I said: "Maybe it can sleep in the kitchenette, and I'll let it spend long visits with my family, so you won't get tired of it."

"Oh, God," he said, "they cry all the time, don't they?"

"I don't know. Pete, do I look very awful?"

"Of course not, and anyway I expect you'll get over it."

I went home to Boston for the baby to be born. I felt that whatever happened to me would be more easily endured if I did not see Pete looking miserable and trying hard to be helpful.

The baby was a boy. He had enormous dark blue eyes and a fuzz of light hair like Peter's, and weighed eight and a half pounds. I was crazy about him; in intervals between feeling that I had neither energy nor interest for anything, and never would anymore.

Pete came up to look at him, of course; but was so delighted that I was thin again, that he did not talk about the baby at all, except to say, "Call him Patrick, because your name's Patricia; and because, by the time he grows up, Patrick will be such a rare name that it will be in good standing again." So I did. I thought it was entertaining to have a baby called Patrick.

After I had stayed at home with Patrick for three months, I went alone to visit Pete for a week, to find an apartment where we could have the baby. The kitchenette solution did not seem adequate, now that he was born.

The baby died, the second day I was in New York.

When I went back to Peter, we were frantically hard-up. He had borrowed money to pay my hospital bill, for we had not wanted our families to know we could not pay that. He expected to get ten dollars more a week, and got only five.

We were not very happy. Sometimes, when he was tired, he grew exasperated because I cried so much about the baby, and I was always vaguely resentful that he did not seem to be sorry about the baby at all.

Things grew better, after a time. Our families, who had begun to realize that we were very poor, sent us checks for our birthdays, and those paid our debts. We moved to an apartment toward the western border of Greenwich village. It had a roof, where we sat, hot August nights, and talked again about places we would go and things we would do, fairly soon (but not so soon as it had seemed the year before).

A man across the street played Chopin gloriously. I used to sit with my head against Pete's shoulder, listening; feeling tranquil.

One day: "Patty, we have to adjust the budget to include one pair of shoes for me. These split at the side and wore through a sole simultaneously."

"It's a major tragedy, Pete. I haven't had the iceman and the laundryman placated at the same time for a month. How much do men's shoes cost?"

"Darling, what I used to pay for mine, and what I can get a pair for now, are things altogether different."

Next day: "I saw a pair for six dollars that don't look too hellish. Can we hold out three dollars this week and three next, my child?" He was cutting out cardboard to put in the sole of the one that was worn through, and being very cheerful about it.

I felt altogether sad. Poor Peter. He had always been so well-if-casually dressed.

The new shoes became the event of those two weeks.

The night before the second pay day, he came home gaily. "Uncle Harrison wired me at the office, he'll be at the Brevoort at seven, to take us to an enormous dinner, Pat. Hurry and dress. I wish it were tomorrow and I had the handsome shoes." They had grown from "not too hellish" to "handsome" in a fortnight of anticipation.

I dressed. I had one or two things left over from my trousseau that were quite possible. But, "Pete, which do you prefer, a stocking with a large run down the inside, or a medium-sized one down the back?"

"My God, dearest, are all your stockings worn out?"

"Seem to be."

We chose the pair with the run on the inside, and had a most beautiful meal with his uncle.

Next day, he came in looking rather self-conscious. I looked for the lovely shoes, but he was not wearing them. He was carrying a small package. "I bought you a present, Patty," he said. He had bought me three pairs of stockings.

The next week he got a ten dollar increase in salary; and the month after that I answered an ad in the *Times* for a copy-writer, and lied about previous experience, and got it for forty dollars a week. At first Pete wrote my next day's ads for me the night before, until I learned to do it myself.

We had, suddenly, money for a maid; and for Pete to stop for drinks on his way home; and for us both to go out to dinner every night; and money for gin for parties.

We lasted just a year after that.

Peter and I both drank well; that is to say, he did not get raucous and I did not get giggly; and neither of us was to be found at an evening's end, pale and dizzy on the nearest bed; but that is not to say he did not hold more closely any girl with whom he danced on eight drinks than on three, or that I did not take pretty speeches from almost anyone with increasing interest in the same ratio.

We were still in love, and acutely jealous of each other; but we never admitted the jealousy: it was too outrageously old-fashioned. He encouraged me to go about to dinners and places to dance, places he could not afford, with the occasional old-friends-from-out-of-town who turned up; because he wanted me to have a nice time. And he acquired two or three slightly misunderstood pretty wives, who called him to make a fourth at bridge, or a second at tea. I thought all of that was pleasant for him.

But we were jealous. When I came upon him, once, kissing a pair of charming shoulders at a party, I said nothing but resented it. And, on a night that I was in a trivial automobile accident in New Jersey, and turned up, very rumpled, at five in the morning, he was the calm and amused modern husband in manner, but his eyes were raging.

There is a progression in things of that sort.

While I was at the shore for a week-end, Peter spent a night with one of the not quite happy wives. He told me. He and I were very definitely committed to the honesty policy. I made no scene about it—and I never felt about Peter, after, quite as I had before.

It would have seemed to me incredible that I should ever be unfaithful to him. But I was, two or three months after that episode.

Pete had gone to Philadelphia over Sunday. Rickey telephoned, asking if he could join us for the usual Saturday night drinking, dinner somewhere. I told him that Pete was away, and he said he would take me places and amuse me. That sort of thing had happened dozens of times before—a good many of them with Rickey.

He happened to be Pete's very oldest friend. The same class at prep school, and so on. Rickey was an altogether charming person. He liked me; we danced well together; he usually kissed me once or twice in the course of an evening, and Pete knew it. I do not believe that Rickey had any more definite ambitions about me on this occasion than on any other.

We felt like slumming, and went to Harlem; but it was a warm evening and Harlem was crowded and sticky. So Rickey said: "Come down to my place, and I'll make something cool to drink, and we'll do a symphony on the phonograph. It'll be calmer."

There seemed to be no reason against this. It was fairly early, and I was not sleepy, anyway.

Rickey mixed gin fizzes, and we sat on his window seat admiring Washington Square for a while, and put on some records, and had some more fizzes. We talked about Galsworthy and Wells and Bennett, as I remember. I wandered into his bedroom to put on fresh lipstick; and he came in, and felt impelled to kiss me. I kissed him, too. I liked Rickey very much.

And then—whether it is put down to a summer night or physical attraction or fizzes is not very important—Rickey went caveman. At first, I was just startled. Then I was angry, and said: "Rickey, stop this instant." The instant, specifically, was when he had stopped kissing my mouth and begun to kiss my throat.

He stopped, and stood for a minute with his arm around my shoulders. I looked up at him—he was about a foot taller than I—a pleasant brown-haired young man.

"Sorry," he said.

"Don't have such a tragic face, Rickey de-ah. I don't feel complimented by making anyone look like that." He laughed then, and kissed me again; and in a moment, it was all to do over.

But in that moment I had lost the wish to do much about it. Curiosity? Desire? The feeling that Pete experimented and why should not I? The thought that it would be an adventure? I cannot remember now. So many things have intervened.

I woke at six. Rickey, sleeping, looked very peaceful. From whatever angle I regarded that personable head, I could not make it look much like a villain's.

I thought about Peter, and I thought I was going to be sick. So I got up very quietly, and took a shower, and dressed. Rickey was still asleep. I left him a note. I remember it.

It read: "Rickey: I'm not having hysterics, but I know I could not think of anything to say at breakfast. Call us up soon."

As soon as I got home I did have hysterics. All the ghosts of my ancestors who had been good women sat about and damned me. Then I considered the Peter problem. I had more hysterics. I was very hungry, so I went to Alice McCollister's Coffee Shop and had a large breakfast.

Peter was to get home at six in the evening. It was about four when I discovered that I was afraid to tell him—that to confront a theoretically modern young husband with the actual fact of his wife's infidelity was just beyond me.

So, what I did about Peter was to bathe again. Then I made up my face carefully, and greeted him with tea and muffins instead of a confession. We dined out, and met Rickey by accident; and he and Pete had one of their when-we-played-on-the-same-team reminiscent evenings. I listened and thought that life was not very simple. It was probably the first time that had ever occurred to me.

Also, I realized, that if I did tell Peter, I could not tell him that it was Rickey. The wife-and-the best-friend pattern was so particularly dreadful. Besides, Peter might feel that the man who had led his wife astray should be beaten, in the conventional manner; and he probably could not beat Rickey, who was so much bigger. That would just add to Pete's humiliation.

I know it all sounds absurd—as if I thought then the thing should be played as a farce. I did not. There was anguish and regret and bewilderment. But they have faded. I only remember my surprise that all the theories about the right to experiment and the desirability of varied experience—theories that had seemed so entirely adequate in discussing the sexual adventures of acquaintances—were no help at all when the decision concerned Peter and me.

Also surprise that, though I had been married to Pete for more than two years, I did not have the faintest idea how he would take this. I thought it conceivable he would shoot me—more likely that he would not, but would leave me forever—and just possible that he would understand how fortuitous the whole thing was.

A week went by. I bought a hat Pete admired; wrote copy in the daytime; danced about evenings; tried being "good" to him, having things he liked for breakfast, and suggesting the restaurants he preferred for dinner.

And I thought, every time that he kissed me, that I should cry.

That was why, at the end of the week, I told him. I did not wait for a suitable moment. It never would have arrived, of course. I told him while we were finishing an amiable leisurely Sunday breakfast. At the point where anything that might happen seemed no worse than to go on as if nothing had, I was even relatively cheerful.

I finished my waffle. (I'd made waffles because Pete loved them.) I thought, "I bet I never eat another waffle in my life." (I never have, either.)

Pouring Pete a second cup of coffee, I thought, "My hands are cold, but they don't shake." Lighting a cigarette, I thought, "It is nice to have a breakfast room."

And, looking at Pete and myself in the wall mirror—Pete, blond and lean and fit and comfortable in an aged purple silk dressing gown, myself small and dark-haired and white skinned, relatively decorative in a turquoise satin negligee—I thought that we both were definitely charming looking.

I can see us sitting there now, but not as if it were Peter and myself. As if, through a dusty windowpane, I regarded two strangers in a doorway across a wide street.

I managed flippancy. "Peter, I want to put on a wife-confesses-all show."

He looked unworried. "My God, darling, have you bought a fur coat and charged it?"

"Worse than that."

"You've lost your job, and we'll have to go back to honest poverty?"

"Don't be funny, Pete."

His voice changed. "Sorry, Patty, what is it? . . . Don't look so worried. I won't beat you, you know."

I drew a long breath. "I've been unfaithful to you." ("Unfaithful" . . . what an odd word it was.)

I could not look at him, and then I had to look at him. I always had admired Pete's poise. Now he was sitting absolutely expressionless . . . but how dreadfully still.

"Patty . . . is this a joke by any chance?"

"No." What had I loosed . . . what was he thinking?

"How did it happen?" His voice was very quiet.

I could not tell him about Rickey. I had not planned what to tell or not to tell; had not thought what he would ask. Well . . .

"I was drunk, Peter." That was thin; he knew I did not get as drunk as that.

He let it go. "Who was the man, Patty?"

(Play for time. Maybe someone will telephone or something and I'll get time to think.)

"I didn't ask you the name of the woman you stayed with." I had known anyway, of course.

"That has nothing to do with it."

And it did not, if he did not feel that it did.

(Must not say "Rickey." . . . Is there anyone who has just gone away? . . . No, must not name anybody.)

"Tell me who it was Patty." He had known Rickey fifteen years . . . he cared more about Rickey than anyone, except me. I did not care about Rickey. I did not care if he went and died somewhere really, but I could not humiliate Pete so dreadfully.

He took my hand: "Don't look so frightened. I'm going to try to understand about it, darling." What an *old* voice.

"But you must tell me who it was. I shall have something to say to him."

(Get time . . . get time to think.)

"You've gone conventional, Pete."

No good, that.

"I expect I have. Will you please not be evasive?"

I lost my head. Like the traditional tabloid murderess, I then heard a shot fired, it seemed.

I heard myself saying, "There's no use in that. You see . . . it was more than one man."

He knocked his coffee cup off the table.

"Sorry," he said. "That was awkward of me. Go on. . . . What were you saying?"

"Peter, you don't know, but sometimes on parties when I've had too much to drink I just get pretty vague . . . and I don't seem to have much control, and this has been going on for some time" . . . (I can't have him checking up dates) "and I've wanted to tell you but I haven't dared . . . and of course I'll go home or give you a divorce or anything you like." (Oh, let him believe me, no, let him not believe me.)

He moved his mouth as if it hurt him. "Don't talk so fast, Patty."

I stopped talking altogether. He was going to believe me, all right. He always had. I had never lied to him before.

He stood up. He said, in a completely impersonal voice, "And I always thought you were the cleanest person in the world."

I began to cry, not because it would do any good—because I could not help it.

"Don't do that, Patty," he said, again very gently. "Listen, will you do something to please me?"

I said "Yes."

"Will you sit down and read a book for a while, like a nice child. . . . It's all right . . . I just want to be by myself."

I sat down. He went into the bedroom and closed the door. I shed tears over all the rotogravure pictures; and knew that was a silly thing to do.

Suddenly I thought, "Maybe he'll kill himself. I must tell him not to." I opened the bedroom door softly. He did not hear me. He was lying face down across his bed, sobbing.

That was the only time I ever saw Peter cry.

I did not dare go in. I went back and stared at the living-room wall. It was cream-colour. It needed redecorating, but not badly.

After a while, I heard Peter taking a shower. He came in, looking all right, or pretty nearly.

"Listen, Pat, I have a short speech to make, and don't interrupt, darling. You're an enormously desirable young woman, and I've never taken the least care of you. I have encouraged you to drink and that sort of thing. This show is my fault. We won't talk about it anymore. Only . . . you won't do it again, will you?"

"No, no, no," I said. "Never. But it wasn't your fault, you trusted me."

"More to the point if I'd looked after you a bit. . . . Well, my dear, go take a shower, and dress, and I'll mix cocktails, and we'll have a couple and then go calling. Might find out what Rickey's doing."

I dressed, we had two Manhattans apiece, and went to see Rickey. He mixed highballs. After my first, Peter took my glass away. "The child's cutting down on liquor, Rick. It's bad for her nerves," he said. Rickey looked surprised, but said nothing.

He and Peter got pretty drunk, and talked about football.

After two weeks I said to Peter, "Look here, if on second thought you want me to go home or anything, because of that show, tell me."

He said: "Forget about it, angel. I have." He had not, but I did not speak of it again.

Then we had three very serene months. Small things were different. Peter censored what I drank; and when Bill Martin, whom I had known in Boston, came to town and asked me to go roof dancing, Pete said he did not want me to go.

I did not mind at all. I had loved Peter before all this and I loved him twice as much after. I thought he was so marvellous about it. I still do.

I thought: "I will try to make it up to Pete by being good-tempered always, and looking as pretty as possible, and following all his stories, and not being extravagant anymore." I felt very grown-up.

One day Peter said, "You know, you are turning out the loveliest person to whom to be married. Just a perfect wife."

Then I was really happy again.

It was the week after that that Hilda Jarvis came to New York.

Any estimate I give of that woman's character will necessarily be inaccurate, I suppose. She told me once, when she was being kind and explaining why I was so bad for Peter, that I had no moral sense, and so could not understand people who did.

And I told her that might be so, but that I had more sense about men in my left thumb than she did in her whole hundred forty-five pound body.

All our conversations became as irrelevant and vicious as that. We never had talked the same language. That had not mattered, all the years we lived around the corner from each other in Boston, because we only talked about books, clothes and her struggles with her Aunt Genevieve. She was wonderful to her Aunt Genevieve.

Let me try again. . . . Hilda was a little rigid in her joints, likewise in her soul. She was well built and had capable hands and feet. She had smooth long brown hair, blue eyes that would have looked deeper if she had rouged her cheeks under them, but she would not. She was a very pure girl. She should have married some simple soul, and made him an amiable wife. Of course, she would have got very fat, after a couple of placid children.

Yes, I do dislike her. She convinced me of the relativity of virtue: i.e. if a woman has been asked into twenty beds, and managed to stay out of nineteen of them, on a purely percentage basis she is a good deal more virtuous than a woman who has only been asked into one, and went.

She had not married, because her invalid aunt would not let her go about and meet any men. She was unpaid nurse, companion, secretary and housekeeper for this aunt. She had a boring life, and was extremely pleased with the idea of visiting us in New York for three months, when I asked her. (The aunt had been invited to Florida, and Hilda was not.)

Pete and I both had salary increases, and actually achieved an apartment with an extra bedroom. So I could ask her. She was our first and last house guest.

In the beginning she disapproved of us both somewhat—our cocktails, cigarettes and conversation—and Pete was a trifle bored with her attitude. But after we had taken her to a couple of amusing Italian restaurants, she had decided she was seeing life. Over two glasses of red wine she just bloomed. I thought it was rather sweet and a trifle pathetic—so revelatory of the very little gaiety she had ever had.

Pete discovered one evening that she read French poetry superbly, and was delighted. It was one of his passions. I could read French, but my teachers had been bad, and my pronunciation was awful. So they had a lovely time, beginning with François Villon, and going on from there, two or three evenings a week, while I worked. (I had taken a couple of free-lance advertising accounts that occupied evenings, temporarily, to make money for a beaver coat.)

Hilda fell in love with Pete, over the French poets. I thought that was understandable, and nothing to worry about. She had never seen as much of any man as she had of Pete, and he was utterly charming. He liked her by now—she was so placid and amiable and well-mannered.

I meant to do something dexterous about her—considered who among the men we knew would be likely to find her attractive and not too dull; and planned to have him about a good deal, and see if the transfer of affection from Pete could be effected with no damage anywhere.

But I was extremely busy, and tired all the time, and let the thing slide. I knew that she was growing increasingly absorbed in Pete, because she began to be definitely rude to me. She was always objecting to the amount of lipstick I used, or the lowness of my décolletage, or the shortness of my skirts. It irritated me somewhat, but I was too busy to bother.

One rainy Friday evening I had a choice of intruding on a poetry session of Peter and Hilda, or dining with Rickey, who was the only person at this era with whom Pete was willing to have me dine. That was logical enough. Rickey was his oldest friend, and the person he trusted most.

Rick and I had already adjusted any embarrassment there might have been between us. In ten minutes, when the occasion offered, he told me he was sorry that it had happened, because of Pete. He did not know what, if anything, I had told my husband; but, on the basis that what had happened was a regrettable accident, he and I were at ease with each other.

With a choice of being audience at a poetry evening, or dining with Rick, therefore, I decided on Rick. I telephoned Peter that I would be home at eleven or thereabouts. He took Hilda to dinner.

By eleven Hilda had pulled my life about my ears, and felt she had performed her Christian duty in so doing. Though I maintain that she used unscrupulously a weapon put into her hand at that dinner, to effect what she wanted.

Pete got drunk. He began to talk about me. Hilda grew patronizing about me, as an impulsive and unstable person. Peter, to be comforted by this stable and "good" girl for the terrific and unhealed hurt I had dealt him, grew confidential, understandably enough.

He told Hilda that I *was* impulsive and unstable; so much so that I had been unfaithful to him, with four or five different men.

Well—Peter had never met Hilda's Aunt Genevieve.

He did not know that Hilda had been brought up to believe in good and bad women; black and white; right and wrong;

vice and virtue; and that her life had contained no experience to modify her confidence in absolutes.

She said: "Poor Peter. She's an utterly worthless and promiscuous woman. I'm pretty sure she had four or five affairs with men in Boston before she met you. Perhaps she can't help it. But you—you understand honour and keeping faith. You should put her out of your heart before she lets you down again."

(It might be labelled footnote to a life. Maybe Hilda believed what she said, since on Pete's statement I was "bad." But it was not until two years later, at one of our rare dinners together, that Pete explained what Hilda had told him.)

What she told him was not true. I had never had any affairs before I knew Peter.

I went home that Autumn evening in '25, feeling tranquil, feeling gala, to a Peter who was through with me; and I was never to know why, while the knowledge could conceivably be useful.

I let myself in. The apartment was dark. Undressing, I said to Peter, who stirred restlessly, "Rick and I saw an awfully amusing show."

He said, "I don't care what you saw."

I thought, "He's very cross . . . probably fed up with evenings with Hilda. Must do something about that." And went to sleep.

Next day when I came home, Peter asked me for a divorce. Just like that, with no introduction.

I said, "This is rather surprising. Why?"

He said, "Because I want to marry Hilda." (Hilda had absented herself for the evening.)

I thought one of us had gone mad, and did not believe it was I.

I said, "Why do you want to marry her, all of a sudden?"

Pete said, "Because she's pure, and you haven't the least idea what that means."

All this was before I had taken off my hat or coat. I did not take them off. I walked out. I went for a long walk, along the docks, and tried to think.

I decided Pete had told Hilda about my infidelity and that somehow she had used it. I decided also that I would have left him months earlier, if he had wanted it; but that I would not leave him now because of any little girl from home who offered him aphorisms about virtue versus vice, and did not know what it was all about.

I decided to make a fight for Peter. But I did not know what I was fighting.

I bought myself some dinner in a Coffee Pot, where a couple of dock-workers tried to talk to me. I did not realize that they were there until an hour or so later, when I remembered it.

Hilda was at home when I got there looking pure, and like a cat gorged on cream, and asking me if I had a pleasant walk. Peter looked uncomfortable.

How badly I managed it!

I was brief. I said, "Hilda, you are going home tomorrow. It's not convenient to have you anymore. Pete's had three weeks of your life, and some three years of mine.

"You and he seem to have developed a great love for each other. All right. I won't keep you apart forever. You go home. Pete stays here. If, after six months, during which I'll try to convince Peter that he's quite insane, you and he feel about each other as you do now, I'll divorce him with no further protest. If you don't give me six months, I'll never divorce him. Whatever my faults, and I'm not admitting any to you, he's condoned them and he cannot divorce me. Take it or leave it. Good evening."

I went to bed. Pete spent the night in Hilda's room.

I lay in bed, and said, "I'll fight this. I offered to pay the check for what I did, and was told I need not. That's that. I won't give up Pete to this woman. I know her better than he. First time he's drunk and comes in saying, 'Everything spins, my dearest, but it spins so felicitously if you let me put my head against your shoulder,' and puts his head there like a tired child, she'll speak to him severely about the evils of drink. She doesn't know what he's like, or what any complicated person is like. And I want Peter, and won't lose him to a stupid woman like her."

Next day she went home, after making the speech to me about my lack of moral sense. Pete said to me, "You get your six months. Much good may they do you. I'm taking a chance that you are telling the truth, for once, about divorcing me at the end of them. It seems to be my best chance to get rid of you, relatively swiftly."

I said to myself, "This is incredible. But I must keep my head, and not get angry. After all, he finds me desirable; he's used to me; there are things on my side. And I have six months."

I worked; I bought pretty clothes; I kept my temper. And I found soon, that Peter was never going to kiss me again—when he was sober.

I said to myself, "That too may go past," and kept my head.

He never joined me for dinner. He never told me where he went. If I asked, he laughed at me. Sometimes for days he did not speak to me—read a newspaper at the breakfast table, and stayed out until after I had gone to bed. Occasionally, I tried having guests. Usually then, he did not come home; although I had told him they were coming. If he came, he was polite to them and never spoke to me, through long evenings.

She had got him to promise to have nothing to do with me.

He forgot about that though, when he came home drunk. He would sit on the edge of my bed, and say, "Patty the complete slut. So pretty, too bad you are a slut. But you are a lovely one."

I would think, "I shall scream, I shall go mad, I can't bear this." And he would sit there, cool from a shower, smiling, strange. And I would put my arms about his neck.

I would pretend that everything was as it had been, once. Next morning, he would not speak to me.

Peter had always been an angel about money. Now, he stopped giving me any, at all. I was faced with paying rent, the maid, the iceman, and the telephone and electric light bill, and Pete's tailor and my cleaner, on fifty-five dollars a week.

We fought then—incredibly sordid and stupid fights about money. One morning the iceman came, wanting two dollars. Pete was shaving in the bathroom. The maid had not come.

I found twenty dollars in my purse, and nothing else. So I took two dollars out of Peter's wallet, and paid the iceman. Pete came out of the bath. He had a hangover. He said, "I'll teach you to go through my pockets for money or anything, you bitch." He struck me across the mouth. It bled.

I thought, "This is a bad dream. Things like this just don't happen to people like Peter and me. He has gone crazy, and I have to stand by until he gets better. He would do that, if I went crazy."

He used to go to see Hilda week-ends. When he came back, he was always much worse. He sat and read. I sat and read. I thought for half an hour of something amusing to say. When I said it he sometimes threw his book at me.

She wrote him every day. He took her letters out at night, and read and re-read them in front of me.

Rickey gathered, as all our friends did, easily, that Peter and I were coming to an end. Rickey struggled, through some weeks, to decide on the correct attitude. Apparently, he weighed his fifteen years' intimacy against one night . . . and the decision was easy. He never came to see us, anymore, but dined with Pete at the Yale Club, two or three times a week. That was logical, too.

Hilda had gone two months, when Peter asked her to New York for a week-end. She stayed at a hotel for women on Gramercy Park. She and Pete went to a party together.

I guessed she was in New York—he was so especially mysterious about his goings and comings through those two days, and so much more sullen than usual afterward. But I knew nothing specifically until Rick telephoned me on Tuesday at the office.

He said, "Pat, I'm trusting you not to repeat this conversation. I'm crazy about Pete, but I think that Hilda wench is awful. This may be useful to you. On Saturday at the Hilles' party, she made a minor scene because Pete danced three times with another girl, and because he was tight. It's too soon for her to try the managing-him-for-his-own-good attitude, but she hasn't brains enough to know that. Sit tight. You may pull through. Good luck."

So I had a little hope.

After another month, and a few days of dizziness and headache in the mornings, I gathered that I was pregnant.

I refused to believe it for weeks. I thought, "It's too awful and I can't face this with everything else. Maybe if I just don't think about it, it will turn out not to be so."

After another month—of dragging days writing copy, and horrible quarrelling evenings with Pete, increasing headaches and dizziness, and comments from my friends and Pete on how badly I was looking, (Pete phrased it, "You look like hell nowadays; you aren't even pretty anymore") I knew it was so, all right.

I remembered the first time it had happened, how shy I had been about telling Peter; and, although he thought then that the pregnancy was most unfortunate, how kind he had been to me, bringing me gay boxes of liqueur chocolates that I could not eat, and flowers and things. That was two years before, though.

This time, I said to him, "Would you mind stopping reading for a moment? I have something to tell you."

He looked up: "Hurrah, you've got a new sweetie."

"I'm ten or eleven weeks pregnant."

He did not say anything for a minute. Then, "By whom this time, or don't you know?" . . .

I got up and screamed at him, as if I were a washerwoman and he were a teamster. My voice sounded awful, even to myself.

I said, "By you, by you, damn you and you know it."

"Stop yelling, and go look at yourself in a mirror," he said. "That ought to stop you quicker than anything."

I did go look at myself. I looked horrible, red-faced and distorted, and about thirty-five years old. And I hated Peter, as I had never hated anyone. I forgot all about how we had got to this place; I only knew that he was a person who said dreadful things in a disgusting calm voice; and that he had turned me into a person who looked like a hag, and that I hated him, hated him.

"Well, you are an attractive object to have about, aren't you?" he said, behind me. I turned. My voice had got quite steady.

"All right, we'll let 'by whom this time' ride," I said. "Now would you be interested in knowing what I'm going to do about it?"

"Yes indeed. The workings of your mind are always entertaining."

He lighted a pipe, watching me over it. I stood there and said words very slowly. My throat hurt so.

"I'm writing to your father and mother tonight telling them we're having another baby, and that I'm giving up my job instantly, of course. I'm writing Hilda the same thing. She's so 'good' I'll give her something to be good about. Then we'll have the baby, and you'll take care of me and it. That'll be all about Hilda."

He got up, slowly. He put his pipe down. He stared at me. I was afraid.

He said, "Will you get out of this room this minute, before I kill you? If I have to look at you ten seconds longer, I'll strangle you." Then he came close, suddenly, and put his hands around my throat.

But I hated him more than I was afraid of him. I said: "You won't kill me. You'll just do as I say, from now on."

He did not kill me. He just picked me up and threw me through the glass door of the breakfast room. Then he went out.

I lay on the breakfast room floor, and thought vaguely that things like this did not happen. I seem to have spent a good deal of time, off and on, thinking that.

Then I noticed that my left arm was bleeding. I got up, and went into the bath, slowly. The whole left arm of my dress was in shreds, where glass had cut it. Apparently I had put my arm in front of my face, instinctively. My face was not cut. I felt a little faint, but not very.

I took off the dress. My left arm had seven cuts on it, but all but one were just scratches. I bathed the arm carefully. One cut was deep and I could not stop the bleeding. So I bandaged it as tightly as possible, and put on a sleeveless dress, and changed my slippers to match the dress.

I knew Pete had a flask of Scotch in his dresser, and hunted around for it, and poured myself a drink. In a detached sort of way, I wondered if he would strangle me when he found out I had taken some of his Scotch.

But I did not hate him anymore, or love him, or feel anything about him at all. I felt tired. There was not the slightest chance that I would attempt to hold him, by going through with having the baby. It would not work. And anyway it was just too much trouble.

My arm kept on bleeding. I remembered that next day I had to do the *Sunday Times'* ad on Paris imports. So I thought I had better go to a doctor and have my arm fixed.

I knew a doctor who lived on Waverly Place. I had been to him for colds and tonsilitis and things like that.

When I went out to find a taxi, the cold air was amazingly pleasant. It was nine o'clock and the doctor's office hour was almost over. I did not have to wait long.

He was a polite blond young man, very dependable-looking. When he asked me what had happened to me, I told him calmly that my husband had thrown me through a glass door. I could not think of anything else to say. He gasped, but did not make any further inquiries.

He had to take one stitch in my arm. When he was through, he said I had better sit down and have a cigarette, and he mixed me some spirits of ammonia. He asked me about my work—he remembered I did advertising.

I interrupted him. "By the way," I said, "I have to have an abortion. Will you do it for me? And how much does it cost?"

He did not look shocked. "Better finish that spirits of ammonia. And would you mind telling me why you must have an abortion, if you actually are pregnant?"

That was easy. "Because my husband's leaving me any day now, and I have no money, and must keep my job."

"But—I don't want to ask you about your private affairs—having a child has been known to bring husbands and wives together, you know."

I laughed and laughed. I just sat there and laughed. "Pete was so pleased when the baby we had died, Doctor."

"Steady," he said.

There was a pause. I caught myself on the verge of telling him, as a fact of extreme significance, that the baby Patrick . . . dead more than a year, now . . . had the longest eyelashes I ever saw.

He said, "I'm sorry for you. But I can't perform an operation of that sort. Never, in the six years that I have practised . . . the ethics of the profession do demand—"

I stopped him. I knew all about the ethics of the medical profession. My father was a doctor.

"All right. You won't do it. Tell me someone who will. I have acquaintances who would give me some physicians' telephone numbers, but I don't know how good they would be. And dying by an 'operation of that sort,' as you describe it, seems so messy."

He said, again, "Steady."

I said, "You are a nice man."

He said, "You aren't likely to die. The dangers are only of infection; or if the physician is the sort who depends on that class of practice for his income, perhaps the night before he may have been drunk and his hand isn't quite steady. . . . Well, there is no need of frightening you. How old are you, anyway?"

"Almost twenty-four."

"You look nineteen."

He hesitated. "Sometimes physicians of the type that perform this operation, say that it is necessary whether it really is or not. . . . If you would be willing to have me make an examination—"

Later: "You shouldn't delay unduly. You seem to be nearly three months' pregnant. There is a man whom I could recommend, who was in my class at medical school. I hear that he has a very scientific procedure. However, because he is compelled to deal with women who are frequently somewhat hysterical he is, a little—what you might call hard-boiled. I would go with you, if it would make it easier for you."

"Well, Doctor, if you could make the appointment for Saturday morning, I could arrange to take the day off."

"Would your husband go with you?"

"I think not."

"Then you can depend on me. Telephone me tomorrow, and I shall have made the appointment."

I felt very grateful to this capable young man.

Pete and I had no more conversation, between then and Saturday. I managed to get an advance on my salary, by a few engaging lies to my publicity director.

Saturday.

I dressed with extreme care, with the feeling that I might be turning up a corpse before sunset, and that did not matter very much; but I would prefer to be a well-groomed one.

Bath salts were pleasant. Very beautifully tailored glove silk underthings were pleasant against the skin. Life had been full of rather nice sensations like that, once, and why not enjoy what remained of them? The Doctor was calling for me at ten o'clock. Peter had gone to work.

I had said to him, "I'm having an abortion this morning."

He had said, "Your show. Hope it's not too bad."

I wonder if those are last words from Peter in this life.

Well—be a credit to that extremely kind young doctor. Cold cream, skin food, astringent, rouge, powder, lipstick. Enormous grey eyes I have, fringed with thick black lashes. And an awfully white skin, considering how black and straight my hair is.

Wonder if it is true that my great grandfather found romance with an Indian girl, and that that accounted for the straight, very black hair. Wonder if he was nice to her.

Black hair, black eyebrows, lovely shoulders, very white. And a lot they had got me, first and last. More than anything else had got me, though, at that.

"A woman five feet one, weighing a hundred nine pounds" . . . would I be a paragraph in various newspapers among the day's casual deaths? Probably not.

Be a credit to that young doctor, who was taking a good deal of trouble on my account. Wear the Jane Regny original that the manufacturer sold me for a song and a couple of ads for Women's Wear. Soft grey tweeds, a grey wolf collar and deep cuffs, a cream-coloured blouse. Its scarlet piping matches the close fitting hat, and the shining flat purse. Brilliant scarlet and blue scarf, grey mocha gloves that matched my stockings, precisely, and black lizard sports' shoes. A small, slim, scared, extremely smart young figure.

"I may not be pure, but thank heaven I look immaculate."

Five to ten. Find a handkerchief that exactly matches the blue in the scarf. Is that important? What is important? That dead baby Patrick, little and fragrant and toothless and rosy-lipped. To die when his mother had gone away and left him. Sentimentality, that. Well, this one would not live to die.

Put some perfume on handkerchief and hair. Just a little essence of gardenia, faint aroma for daytime.

Peter, Peter.

Doorbell ringing. The maid will answer. "The Doctor, ma'am."

"Tell him I'll be in in a minute, Nora."

Purse, money, gloves.

"Good morning, Doctor."

"You are looking very well. I hope you don't feel nervous."

(Hell. I just feel dead.)

"Not at all, Doctor, shall we start?"

In the taxi. "You are going to survive this, you know. You are the healthy, glandularly normal sort that can survive a great deal with no ill effects. I should be interested in seeing you do it. This may sound rather—unethical—but I do wish, if you and your husband separate, that you would let me know, from time to time, how you are getting along.

"You are very young, and life holds a great deal for you."

(Isn't he sententious?)

He went on: "I should appreciate the privilege of taking you to dinner sometime, when you've forgotten about this whole—unfortunate—affair. Do feel free to telephone me at any time, it would give me great pleasure."

(A nice young man. Rather attractive. Peter, Peter, are you thinking about me at all? In the midst of re-writing *City News* copy, are you thinking about me—five minutes?)

"Doctor, do you mind if I ask—does this take very long?"

"At most—twenty minutes. I strongly advise against gas, if you think you can maintain your poise, at all. The heart—"

"Whatever you advise, Doctor." (Did I want this baby? No sense to wonder about that now.)

"You are being extremely kind, Doctor. I am appreciative. I shall look forward to telephoning you one day, soon, and ask if you are free for dinner?"

He beams. Well, it is a lovely tweed ensemble, and I am clear-skinned enough to wear a bright red hat.

"Here we are. Now remember, I'll be close by, and it will be all over within the half hour."

(Be a corpse by then, maybe? Oh, don't lose your nerve, Patricia. A thousand a day in the city of Chicago, they say.)

Dingy waiting room. Green plush livingroom set. No magazines. Patients can contemplate their thoughts, I suppose. Drawn curtains, a desiccated potted palm.

My doctor is holding my hand, in an entirely impersonal and very helpful way. A man and a girl come in. Her clothes were bought on the Bowery, but she is a lovely, gentle-faced blonde child, and so amazingly young. Seventeen at most.

She looks at that boy as if he were her saviour. He is a nice boy, too, blue eyed Jewish. Waistline coat. Maybe he is as old as twenty-one.

"Doctor," (very softly.) "That girl is nothing but a child."

"I noticed. These places depress me. Ah—Dr. Cohen."

"My patient."

The Paris tweeds impress Dr. Cohen. What a hard face he has, but efficient, clean hands.

"Come this way."

(Office is camouflage obviously. Operating room looks very sanitary. I'll say that for it. Room with five beds in back. Nurse. Isn't she pretty? Sort of lavender kimona, she gives one. Wonder if the colour is symbolic, or if they got a lot of them at a sale. Give the nurse five dollars. She is pleased.)

"Now don't be frightened, madame. I hear your doctor advised against gas. That's sensible, really."

"May I hold your hand, nurse?"

"Of course, dearie."

Set one's teeth. Now.

Bed feels very comfortable. Here is my doctor. I have to think of something to say to him, something appropriate? Would it do to say, "Well, I lived through it and I don't care if I did?"

"Don't try to talk. You are a courageous young woman." (Just because I would not cry in front of that disgusting doctor who made a joke about the price of pleasure.) "I'm going to give you a hypodermic. Try to sleep, and I'll be back to take you home in a couple of hours."

He is gone.

Just to rest—not to think. Here is that young blonde child getting into her lavender kimona, slowly. She wants to talk.

"Listen, does it hurt much?"

(Give the little girl a hand.) "It's not bad, my dear, and soon over."

What a brilliant yellow chemise she has on. Amazing. And what a pretty undeveloped figure.

She is very scared. Undressing so slowly. She wants to talk some more. Maybe I can stay awake.

"Gawd, I'm scared. But my boy-friend's worse. He's sitting in front wipin' sweat off his forehead."

"I saw him. I thought he was very handsome."

"Say, that boy's grand. He gave me this chemise. I wore it to make me feel brave."

Poor little devil.

"It's soon over, you know."

"Him and I'd get married in a minute, and I wouldn't have to do this, only his ma's orthodox Jewish and she'd die if he married a girl who wasn't kosher. He's good to his ma."

The vivid yellow chemise comes off. The kimona of sorts goes on. The child takes my hand. "It isn't very bad, is it?" The nurse is calling her.

"No, really. Hold your breath and say, 'I can last another five minutes.' Good luck."

She smiles, gallantly.

The door of the operating room is ajar. That hard voice, "Are you paying for gas, young woman?"

Her ardent, rough young voice, "Why . . . why, I guess so. My boy-friend said for me to have all the trimmings." The door of the operating room slams.

Sleep, sleep now. Patrick, Peter—wonder if this one might have been a daughter . . . well, better to sleep.

"All right?"

"Quite convalescent, Doctor, thank you. I'll dress now."

The blonde child is asleep, looking altogether tranquil. Never see her again. Like to give her a present. That cloisonné compact. Slip it in her hand, that closes on it, like a . . . like a baby's.

"Will you tell her, nurse, I wanted her to have this?"

"Yes, madame."

"Good-bye. You'll feel better tomorrow."

That night Peter said, "I'm sorry you feel so badly . . . could I make you some soup or anything?"

"Thanks, no."

"Look here, Pat, I'm sorry about you and me, but it would be easier for you if you could let go . . . if you didn't try to hold on so hard."

It is worse when he is kind. Fight it through. One might have some luck. "Only nine weeks of servitude left, Pet-ah." He said nothing. He went out.

All insane, all ridiculous, all horrible; but fight it through. Committed to that. Cannot think anymore; cannot feel much; but play for a little more time. Hilda is stupid. She may be stupid in time to save me.

Another week, and another, and another. He kept all her letters in the top drawer of his desk. The drawer was not locked. Curious that he could place such dependence on a decent up-bringing. He could, too . . . but if I knew what she was writing, what they were planning, perhaps I could think of something to do.

Meanwhile I was grateful for the advertising business. The Christmas rush. Two more weeks gone.

Peter twisted my wrist one night when, overtired, I did a parody of Hilda explaining why she was pure. I thought my wrist was broken. He left me crying, raging, pleading. That had got to be chronic. As soon as I began to protest, anything, he left for the evening. Sometimes for the night.

I had a curious suspicion that he sometimes went to see Judith, just-divorced wife of a well-meaning dullard. Judith had always looked avidly at Pete. That was odd, if he went to see her now. But too complicated for me to evaluate, along with Hilda. Those letters. My wrist throbbed, most painfully. If I knew what was in those letters . . .

I only read a sentence or two of the top one.

It said: "If you continue discouraging Pat's advances, she'll soon take another lover, and then you and I are rid of her, Peter my dearest."

I put it back in the envelope carefully. That girl—that girl did not know what she was doing. She would not last a month, with a Peter who had recovered sanity. But—at that, she might last long enough to finish Peter and me.

When he came home that night, "Peter, I suggest you take those letters of your dear love and lock 'em up. If I read any more of her advice on how to handle me, I might take 'em to a lawyer. Also—I don't care what I said before—I'm not going to give you a divorce to marry that woman, ever, ever, ever."

I thought he would strike me. I did not care now. The first time I had wandered about with a bruise on my mouth, it did something rather permanent to my soul, or whatever I had like a soul. After that, I just jested about falling against a table in the dark. No one believed me. It did not matter, whether they did or not.

But he did not strike me. He took the letters and put them in his pocket and said, "I'm leaving a week from Saturday, Pat."

It was a week from Saturday now, and I had been sitting a long time in the wing chair, remembering irrelevancies. I hunted about for a cigarette. There were no more. I had smoked the whole package.

The apartment seemed almost unbearably still. I thought that it probably always would be, now. No more Peter, to come in gaily, flinging coat on one chair, and hat on another, and gloves on a third, calling eagerly, "Patty, Patty, dearest. Oh, most delicious young woman, a husband is home for the night, thank God."

Yes, it probably always would be desperately still, without Peter. It occurred to me, as a very surprising fact, that, since I was only twenty-four, I might well live forty or fifty years, with no Peter. How many nights was that? An appalling number of thousands.

I stood up. I wanted a cigarette. There was a package Peter had left, on the mantel, with just two or three in it. That fool woman upstairs was playing sentimental ballads. This was "What'll I Do?" God-awful idiotic song. "You-r lips an' my lips were joi-uned in a ki-i-sss, a ki-is with an *un*-happy en-nnding . . . Whaddl' I dooo with jest a mum-o-ry." Would she stop her phonograph if I telephoned her? What's the use.

I will telephone the doctor. That will be entertaining. Won't he be startled? And why not? The number is in the book.

I looked at the banjo clock. It was twenty minutes to eleven.

•

"You said you'd be interested in knowing what happened after? Well, I've been deserted at last."

(He remembers me all right. His voice was very cheery and decidedly non-professional.)

"That's cause for celebration. May I come over and offer felicitations, and take you dancing? . . . In half an hour? Splendid!"

Gold brocade dress and rose slippers, rhinestone necklace and rhinestone embroidered bag. Very bright lipstick. Rose velvet wrap. I half forget what the doctor looks like.

If I do not stop aching I shall cry in public, and disgrace the man. Hope he brings some Scotch. That will see me through— "to stand by you in the days you have great sorrows." Someone said that once, to someone a lot younger than I.

All ready, and five minutes to spare.

There was a long old mirror between two windows. I regarded myself. Not bad, not bad at all. Straight black bobbed hair that shone, grey eyes, a straight nose, a red, red mouth, very soft and warm-looking, pointed chin, lovely shoulders, slim waist, straight legs, small feet. It was no good to me, no good any of it, with no Pete to make it come alive; but all I had for the next forty years or so.

There might have been a baby—like Pete, like me. Never now. What of it? The nights of forty years had to be got through. The door bell ringing—this would fill the first of them. "So nice to see you, Doctor. So you're one of those men who turn out to look five years younger in a dinner jacket, and so much less awe-inspiring. Do have my last cigarette."

IV

March sunlight came palely through the window that was dingy with the drippings of two-day old snow, and shone along the crinkled counterpane on Peter's bed. Under the crisp blue and whiteness, the doctor slept, peacefully. I could touch his shoulder, by sitting up and stretching out my arm, but I did not want to, at all.

Peter said, yesterday, "Don't mourn me long."

In a sense, my dear Peter, I mourned you only seven hours, but I may be going to mourn you all my life besides. The doctor is an efficient person. I do not like him much, though. The way he shifts from professional to passionate manner, and back again, is a bit automatic. Hot water faucet, cold water faucet, hot water faucet . . . He must have been Don Juan of some hospital staff six or seven years ago. But he solved one night for me, and that was what I thought I wanted.

(I wonder if Peter is waking up by himself, or not. Peter.—I could scream and beat my fists against the floor and sob hours and days and weeks to have you back—to have the year 1922, again. And all that would happen, if I began, is that I would wake up the doctor. He would fish bromide tablets out of his dinner jacket pocket, for the emergency, I do not doubt.

He will have to telephone for a cab to get home in those dinner clothes. Wonder if he will sleep all day.)

I did sleep well, extraordinarily enough. One is not supposed to; one is supposed to lie awake biting sheets, or something of the sort, when one's husband deserts. But I was so tired.

It feels remarkable to be a deserted wife when one is only twenty-four. Not what I planned to do with my life, precisely. I planned to be a Red Cross nurse, in time for another war. Was just sixteen in the war, and felt sick because I was too young to marry someone on his last leave, for my-country's-sake, under a flag.

Peter was too young, too. He would have looked marvellous in a uniform . . . naval aviation green. But most of those did not get across. Peter marching with sun shining on his blond hair.

Oh God, if I begin to cry I shall not be able to stop. Better get up, and see what there is for that doctor's breakfast. I want to be all dressed when he wakes.

Left leg out of bed, right leg out of bed, negligee, slippers. I feel very clear-headed. We did not drink much. The doctor probably believes in keeping fit. (I must ask him, I bet he will mention "mens sana in corpore sano." They had that on the wall of the gymnasium in school.)

I believe in keeping fit myself. I shall go do calisthenics in the livingroom, I do not want him waking and watching me. Calisthenics every morning—and nights when there is nothing exigent to prevent, are ten minutes sacred to the memory of an athletic adolescence.

One, two, three, four, five, six, seven, eight. They help. I like touching my toes to the floor over my head. Calisthenics make me feel like a warm, live animal rolling about in a pasture. Liquor makes everything go far off, too, but it makes me feel like a mind wandering freely through space, not like a warm body in a pasture.

Better go look at the doctor. He sleeps on. "After life's fitful fever," no, that is something else. I will have a shower, now. Someone should invent a method for using bath salts in a shower, then it would be perfect.

I am actually hungry. People are not supposed to be able to eat with broken hearts. I feel like an alarm clock wound up too tight. I must not think . . . count sheep jumping a fence . . . no that is for going to sleep.

I will wear my blue jersey dress with white collars and cuffs . . . it looks so chaste. Lord, I have been more chased than chaste. Oh damn, I must get myself together, that man will be waking up. I wonder what his first name is. I forgot to ask. Should I look it up in the telephone book?

I wonder what Nora ordered for breakfast. She is a very good maid. It is a good thing she does not come on Sundays. I shall have to get her another job; Gretchen will snap her up. I cannot keep this apartment. What will become of me? A bad end no doubt—walking Sixth Avenue, and touching Peter on the arm begging for fifty cents—like hell.

This kitchen is nice and sunny. Give the doctor orange juice, of course, it is full of vitamines.

There are duck eggs . . . Nora went to Jefferson Market and bought duck eggs, for Pete's Sunday breakfast because she knows he is absurdly fond of them. I am going to cry, now, only for a minute though. . . . The duck eggs will do for the doctor. There are no others. They are nicest shirred.

"Good morning, Patricia . . . you look very fresh."

"I've been doing calisthenics."

"The *mens sana* idea?"

(Hold everything while he kisses you. Count sheep fence jumping. A kiss does not take long.)

He is a more percipient young man than I thought. "Are you having morning-after reactions? I'm sorry, my dear."

"It's all right. I'm just a bit—what my husband used to call jittery."

"That's understandable. Have you such a masculine accessory as a razor, Patricia?"

"Silly little gold one . . . in my dressing table. I'll get it—can you manage with that?" (Pete used a big straight one . . . that was what I was going to slash my wrists with . . . he packed it . . . the bathroom has gone feminine overnight.)

The doctor talked about medicine, vitamines, ductless glands and things, at breakfast. He was *extremely* percipient. And he liked duck eggs.

He called the Brevoort for a cab. Then, "I'm going to be tactful, and wait for you to telephone me, Patricia, because I don't want you to feel that I'm thrusting myself on you."

I smiled, looking friendly, I hope.

"I'm somewhat older than you . . . and should like to give you a small piece of advice—or warning, if I may?"

"Of course, and I'm sorry if I'm being childish this morning, Doctor."

"Not at all . . . Perhaps you don't realize that as a young woman—and an extremely attractive one—separated from her husband—men are going to consider you the fairest game in the world. You'll get used to it, and adjust yourself. At first it may be difficult." . . . (Well, why doesn't he get to his advice? Is he going to suggest a course in the Psychology of Sex? I should not be so impatient, he has been very kind to me. That must be his taxi man ringing the doorbell.)

"Try to remember that the banality about time healing everything is quite true."

(Is that all the medical profession has to offer me? How much time does it take is what I want to know.)

"Yes, taxi, wait outside a minute."

"Meanwhile, Patricia, don't take things too hard."

He smiled. "It was one of the pleasantest nights of my life," he said quite gravely.

He picked up his hat, refrained from kissing me, and held out his hand. For that last I was suddenly so warmly grateful that I could smile, really gaily, and say what was truth at the moment. "I am glad you stayed."

"I shall hope that you telephone, Patricia." The door closed behind him—a completely comprehending and nice man.

I knew that I would never telephone—that I would never see him again. He understood that, too.

•

The telephone rang. It was Lucia. Very beautiful Lucia was —ex-wife of a man named Archibald. I met Arch once; had known Lucia casually some time, at the Advertising Club. She seemed to be taking more interest in me of late, since she knew I had been having what department store help call "family troubles."

"I hear from a friend of a friend of Rickey's, that your husband and Rick celebrated your husband's return to bachelor life, at the Yale Club last night?"

"I shouldn't wonder, Lucia. He left before dinner yesterday."

A little silence.

"How are you feeling?"

"All right, I guess." (It is going to be awful to have people asking how I feel all the time, as if I were convalescing from typhoid.)

"Come up and have tea with me?"

"Love to."

"And Pat, it's not bad being an ex-wife when you get used to it. I quite like the life."

"Tell me about it at tea."

"'Right."

Ex-wife—ex-wife of Peter puts on a beaver coat and fresh white gloves. I cannot *bear* being ex-wife of Peter.

The late sun of Sunday afternoon shone on ex-wife of Peter walking fast uptown, through the crowds of funny people recovering from too-huge dinners by waddling a few blocks along Fifth Avenue. (I can tell by the expression of men's faces that I am looking well. I look just the same as I did last week, probably, and shall not look much different next week, or for five years, or even then, if I take exercise. In five years or ten, shall I walk, still wanting to meet Peter in the middle of the next block?)

Park Avenue.

Lucia is a red-haired oval-faced madonna in a black velvet dress. She is much slimmer than a Titian madonna though—a sort of a cross between Titian's and Burne-Jones' women.

"Pat, I'm giving you a highball instead of tea."

"Lucia, don't break the news gently, but does one ever get over it?"

She sipped a highball. She held a cigarette in long thin fingers. She regarded me sympathetically, then appraisingly. She grinned a gaminesque grin, that set oddly on her lovely face. She looked as if I were being very funny indeed. She did not answer.

"One doesn't ever get over it, does one?"

She threw her cigarette into the fireplace, impatiently. "I'll make a prophecy, Pat. In three years you won't remember the colour of his eyes."

"That's a comfort."

"Do you think so?" said Lucia.

V

It was time I went home. Lucia, no doubt, had a dinner engagement. But I did not want to leave. I suddenly did not want, ever, to spend another night, another hour, even, in that apartment that had been Pete's and mine.

Lucia said: "Come upstairs, there's something I want to show you." She wanted to show me a small duplex apartment, on the upper two floors. There was a huge room and bath on each level, with an amusing interior staircase connecting them. There was the usual Manhattan view of building operations in progress.

"If you would come live with me," said Lucia, "we could afford this place. I'd like to live with another woman anyway—it would have its advantages, provided there was a relative amount of privacy."

Indifference, that was rather comfortable, descended on me. I would have to live somewhere; Lucia was lovely. Why not?

"But do you make a habit of being kind to dumb animals, Lucia?"

She laughed. "You *will* be dumb for a while, you know, Pat. I was . . . I'm going to put on my hat, because Checko will be turning up. You'd better stay here tonight. There's a fruit-cake for you to eat, or you can go out and get something nourishing. Why go home and wait for your husband to telephone? He won't—yet. I'll be late. . . . The daybed unfolds, or you can sleep on the little couch."

"Have you a daybed by the way, Patricia? No ex-wife's home complete without. A single bed, as decorative as possible, capable of adjustment to meet crises as they occur."

I was not interested in daybeds. "Who is Checko?" I said.

"No one. Just a help on an off-Sunday. He is going to write an epic poem, year after next, meanwhile he's a ghost-writer for a couple of movie stars and a prizefighter. I'll meet him downstairs if you don't mind, because you're his type and he would spend an hour talking to you, and I'm awfully hungry."

"Do you really want me to live with you, Lucia?"

"Yes. We'll have fun. You'll see."

Ringing of the doorbell sent Lucia downstairs. I lighted a cigarette, and began to read, "The Silver Spoon."

Lucia arranged everything. She saw my landlord and got permission for me to break my lease—chose what furniture I would take uptown, saw Nora, and decided we could manage to support her as well as the rent, if she would keep our clothes pressed and lingerie straps sewn on; bought me a daybed.

The day the storage people came to pack was the only time, after that Sunday, when I spent more than ten minutes in my old apartment.

Maple beds with pineapple posts, gold-framed mirror with the eagle on it, that had been my great-grandmother's, Peter's cherished ship bookends, the hangings we had bought at Liberty's in London—all were swiftly mummified in brown paper, and departed.

I found a bottle of port Pete had left and gave it to the moving men.

The apartment would have to be redecorated, before anyone else took it. I wondered if they would have it done in the same colours.

The moving men were through. I was taking the silver to storage myself, in a cab. I left the key and ten dollars with the superintendent. He thanked me, said, "I'm sorry for your troubles, ma'am," and got me a cab.

On the way to the warehouse, I thought I might as well slip my wedding ring in with the coffee spoons. When I got there, I found that the storage people counted over everything, before they made out their receipts. I was embarrassed, when they came to the red flannel case with the coffee-spoons and the wedding ring, and said, "I suppose you think a wedding ring is an odd thing to store."

The clerk who was checking looked up at me over rimless eyeglasses, with old, incurious eyes. "Why, ma'am, we must have two-three hundred of them in the vaults right now," he said.

I was used to green tiles in the bath instead of white, to going downtown to work on a bus, instead of uptown on the subway, to Lucia, unfailingly kind, unfailingly good-tempered, with her manner of treating all things as equally unimportant and entertaining. I had been living with Lucia three weeks.

"You must go places," said Lucia the first day. "You just trotted about with five or six friends of your husband, didn't you; and when the conversation grew dull they exchanged reminiscences about great crew races of 1919 or somesuch, didn't they? Well, we'll go places."

In the three weeks we had been to six parties, three first nights, five speakeasies, four nightclubs, two operas, and a concert where a negro sang spirituals.

"You are amazingly popular, Lucia." It was Sunday again, and we seemed to have an hour with nothing to do.

"You mean, ex-wives are popular, Pat. Most popular class in New York. Anyone can fling a life's devotion at an ex-wife's feet, and she can't do a thing in the world inconvenient about picking it up—at least an ex-wife like you, can't; because she has no divorce. Why don't you divorce Peter?"

"Nobody's flinging any devotion at my feet. I can't talk at parties. You have to tell me what to say."

"I know; do you mind, Pat? You'll get over that, in a month or so when you feel better. Seriously though, you should do something about seeing to a divorce. The sooner the better, it makes a clean break. . . . Have you heard from that Peter person? . . . I don't want to seem intrusive. . . ."

I had heard from him. I had a note. I got it and showed it to Lucia.

It read, "Here is a cheque for the last month's rent downtown. I don't plan to make further contribution to your support. Of course, if you are starving or anything, call me up and I'll send you a few meals. But I imagine you'll get on all right. Your sort does. I am living for the moment at the Wilton Arms Hotel. Better address me at the office, though. How about letting me have some furniture when I take an apartment? Have a nice time. Peter."

"Succinct young man," said Lucia, and hesitated a minute. Then, "I've been hearing this and that about him, Pat."

"All right, tell me," I said. I had wondered about that. During the week or two when we had been moving, Lucia had experimented a bit with a tentative "he might come back, Patricia, you don't want to feel hopeless," attitude; and had then shifted definitely to the "it's all over, but someday you may be glad it is," point of view.

Lucia said: "I made inquiries. That's a long story. Everyone's always advising a woman separated from her husband. Dozens of people advise me. Some were helpful, some anything but. I didn't want to press you into talk about him—it might distress you too much—but I thought since I'd taken you on more or less, I'd better find out what the situation was, if I could, so that I shouldn't advise you badly."

"You are an angel, Lucia. Tell me, really, though, why you bother."

"Several reasons. Wanted to live with someone, knew you'd be fun when you convalesce somewhat, and you are a type that contrasts with mine beautifully. I mean you're black haired and vivacious (normally) and petite, and I'm long and langourous and red-blonde. Beside, someone did as much by me, while I was in the state you're in, and that's sort of a bill I wanted to pay somewhere. . . . All that's irrelevant. You told me all about that Hilda business . . . but where does this Judith woman come in? I found out through a girl who knows a man on Pete's paper, that he's seen about with her every night in the week."

"Something must have happened about Hilda," I contributed. I felt miserable again. I was having a very bad time, trying not to speculate where Peter was, and with whom, and what he was doing, in every quiet half hour I had, anyway.

"You are bright, Pat. Sorry; I don't want to tease you. . . . Anyway, before I heard that, I thought your beloved was likely to get enough of his Hilda in a few weeks, and turn up wiser . . . and content for a while. You do seem to be crazy about him, and in spite of the awful time you've both been having, a great reconciliation scene might well have been managed."

She stretched out an amazingly white arm for a piece of Turkish paste, nibbled it with a few words about thanking God she was thin enough to eat as much candy as she liked, and looked at me to see if I were on the verge of tears or anything.

"That's a nice Chinese kimona you've got, Pat," she went on. I laughed. I was getting used to Lucia's irrelevancies. They meant "If this conversation is bothering you, we'll talk about something else, instantly."

"That's a grand green negligee you've got, darling," I said. "Go on. I don't mind talking to you about Pete. In fact, it helps, rather. I told him I'd never divorce him, but I begin to feel that I'm a rather low person to stick to that, if he really wants a divorce."

"Yes," said Lucia, "we all grow sensible, but it takes time. . . . What I meant about Judith was, that if 'something has happened about Hilda' as you put it, and he's gone on to Jude, instead of coming back to you . . . my child, you may as well go see a lawyer now as next year."

(I thought, "Not yet; I won't let go yet; I can fill in time, while I have hope it's just an entr'acte to be spent, but not otherwise.")

Lucia went on: "Men . . . men are always coming back from little excursion trips—but once they start on world cruises. . . ."

"Judith's no world cruise. She isn't as nice, really, as Hilda, or as good-looking."

"I'll talk about her in a minute. About the excursions and cruises—I mean that a man, really in love with one woman, often can go tripping off blithely but briefly with another, simply because she has a stirring voice or wide innocent eyes. He comes back, then, to *the* woman, no worse off, sometimes improved, even. But once he embarks on a tour, child, he's going to stop at so many ports he will forget perhaps, what city he started from, and certainly what that city had that was unique, among all the scenery he's seen since. Your Peter seems to be sailing on and on, Pat."

"I can't believe it yet, Lucia."

She was, immediately, sympathetic. "Of course not. Don't try, either. I might be wrong, and anyway, the only use for advice is to put it in your pocket and save until, if ever, you feel like taking it. . . . You've met Judith?"

"At the office, several times—she's gone in for being a stylist since she got her divorce, you know. And once on a party."

"Do you like her?"

"No. . . . But I wouldn't anyway, now. I'm afraid I'm a very jealous person, Lucia."

"Everybody is, and everybody poses as not being. . . . I don't like Judith either, but she has her points. Do you mind if I go into that, because I'd like to explain why I think she'll finish you off, to put it very brutally, if Peter has taken up with her?"

"Go ahead." (Peter "taken up" by that hard-faced, young woman. It was just ridiculous. And yet I knew that I was being 1880 about her. She had style, she was amusing.)

"Patricia, be a nice girl and take away this candy. I shall make myself sick. And bring me my cigarette holder, the amber one."

Then Lucia began: "I dislike Judith principally for a triviality, her language, that is. Of course, the use of the vernacular, obscenity, in common speech is just another one-time strictly masculine ceremonial vice, like drinking and smoking, that has, recently, gone bi-sexual. I think, though, there is a difference. Women, attractive women, in spite of the opinion of the Bible belt, actually do not look a bit less feminine, or desirable, with a cigarette in one hand and a cocktail glass in the other, than their grandmothers did, with a fan, held right, and a bouquet, left. The cocktail glass and cigarette are provocative, gayer, that's all. I'm not talking, naturally, about women one sees draped, in alcoholic semi-stupour, about tables in cheap nightclubs. Men of their type are as distressing.

"But about language. Perhaps the vernacular is picturesque, has a flavour, in men's clubs and bars, like the very physiological smutty jokes they now begin to tell us. It remains, though, to me, incongruous in the speech of a woman supposedly well bred. It affects me, when Judith adorns her comments on bad weather, or something as casual, with phrases one sees occasionally scrawled on walls of empty buildings, just as if she appeared in her very good copies of French clothes chewing tobacco and spitting at intervals."

"I know, Lucia. That's why I don't think Peter *can* take her seriously."

"That doesn't follow, at all, Pat. You see, you gave that young man of yours a horrible shock, if you'll forgive me for mentioning it." I winced, she noticed it, but decided to go on.

"Oh, it was a very grand gesture, to tell him of your infidelity, and you'll never be so young, again, as to make another like it. . . . You should have decided never to repeat the incident, and never to mention it. Grand gestures are expensive. How expensive yours was, whether it's to cost you Peter forever, you can't tell yet. But it probably will. You must have knocked all that half-baked young collegiate's conceptions about women, into a cocked hat."

(Peter, a "half-baked young collegiate"? I'd never thought of that. Perhaps he was.)

"Never mind, Pat. I did something as young as that once, with Arch. Tell you sometime. To go on with Judith though. A woman of her sort, with the just-one-of-the-boys attitude, may be precisely what Pete wants at the moment, especially if something has gone wrong with the machinery in the other pure love of his life. Judith has sex-appeal, a deliberate sex-appeal. Of course, not like yours, Pat."

"I haven't any, couldn't keep my own husband."

"Don't generalize from one example and an irrelevant one. You have a practically universal sex-appeal. As soon as you begin to be even a little interested in people, again, instead of just decorative but altogether unresponsive, you'll have dozens of men asking to 'love' (her accent was derisive) you for a night or a month or two or even longer. I worry about that.

"I have very little sex-appeal myself, Pat. Nothing passionate about me except the colour of my hair. My spiritual expression puts men off me, except as a daytime companion. I'm glad too. The other, the evading of incessant pursuit, is so tiring. . . . That'll do for another Sunday sermon though.

"Judith, and women of her type, cultivate sex-appeal because they need to. Women of her type—not really feminine, not pretty, even, actually, succeed by being clever enough to accent what they have. Take her. She has handsome auburn hair, not bad eyes (hazel aren't they?) and a good slim round figure. That's all. Her features are just scattered about her face. Can you remember her nose or hands or mouth or chin? Her knees are much more vivid in my recollection. She always crosses them high. They are quite nice, too. I remember them best, really, and her hair, for she takes off her hat on every possible and impossible occasion, to let the light shine on it. Why do I remember her eyes, I wonder? Oh yes, she narrows them to look at people sleepily."

I giggled. "Wonderful, Lucia . . . Did she ever cut in on you?"

"No, really. Someone like her did, though. . . . The type says, in its startling language, the extremity of its make-up, oh, the way it waves its legs about, 'I am accessible, I am accessible, and I'm very good fun, indeed.' They are good fun, too. They give a man the comfortable feeling of sitting about with no collar on. I'm sure Judith will be easier for your Peter, than either you or Hilda were. He's good-looking isn't he? And the newspaper crowd will amuse her. . . . Patricia my child, she can probably keep him ages, until he gets another attack of grail-seeking, idealism. She may cure him of any further recurrence of that, even. Women of her sort do."

"Lucia, you are the complete Cassandra, this afternoon."

"Let's have a drink—there won't be any at the Stevens'—they have the most amazing Russians who suddenly burst into song, though. Worthwhile, usually. Will you mix it?"

"It will have to be a Bronx. There's nothing but gin and oranges. . . .

"It tastes good. Lucia, do you think I should write Pete and ask him if he still wants a divorce?"

"Why *write* him? That's just obvious indiscretion. . . . Why not telephone him?"

"He'd be at the club, now, probably."

Lucia said absolutely nothing. I went to the telephone, at the foot of the little staircase connecting Lucia's place and mine. On the pad alongside the telephone, were scrawled all our engagements for the week. Lucia had made them all, so far.

"Listen Pat. Plan what you're going to say, before you call."

"That's simple."

"Murray Hill 0003."

I gave Peter's name. Lucia brought me a second cocktail and sat down on the step above me.

I had to wait some time.

"Pat, why not just hang up? There's no hurry," Lucia said.

"It always takes a long time."

"Hello, Peter? It's Pat."

"Yes, I recognized your voice. How are you?"

His voice was quite *gay.*

"All right. I called up to tell you you could have a divorce, if you still wanted one."

A minute's silence.

"Why, thank you. There's no mad rush, though."

"Oh—how's Hilda?" (Lucia prompted that.)

"Very well, last I heard."

What next? "Why don't you come to see me, sometime?" (assist from Lucia, also.)

"I might, sometime. What's your address?" (He knew. I had written him, but I told him again.)

"Well, we might have dinner, and discuss this divorce. . . . What's your telephone number?" I told him.

"Thank you for calling, Pat."

"Good-bye."

"Now," said Lucia, "you'd better have what's left in the shaker. I suppose your afternoon is completely ruined.

"Heavens it's four o'clock, Pat, we have to be dressed in fifteen minutes. Are you very disturbed?"

"I don't know."

"Well, make up down here in my bath and we can talk."

Lucia let her hair down, and started combing it swiftly. I began cold creaming my face. My hair would take only an instant to do.

"I'm glad," said Lucia, "my marriage ended—"

"What?" I asked.

"Long time ago," said Lucia.

VI

It was early Spring . . . time to write ads of "Easter Apparel and Accessories" . . . to get out extra fashion pages, after last-minute buyers' conferences. Rush the art work; rush the cuts; rush copy to the typographer; tell him to rush proofs. The fashion copy-writer left. Then I was fashion copy-writer. The assistant advertising manager was ill—they let me do her work. I was glad. It made the days go fast.

"Get a lizard bag up, an import, to be sketched with those lizard shoes, Miss Thomas," I said. "Miss Hastings's on her way down; she's going to do all the art work in the two accessory columns. Hosiery, gloves, the shoes-and-bag in one, handkerchief, jewelry item, there's one more space. Tell Mr. Johnson the flower and the perfume buyers both wanted to go in the page—and ask him to decide. *I* don't want the one who's left out, discussing why with me. . . . No, we can group the boutonnière and perfume bottle, and use 'em both. They'll balance the shoes-and-handbag. Hastings's good at handling that sort of thing."

A jargon—a jargon I had learned quickly. It paid for the rent and taxis to the office and for clothes—more clothes than I had had since I was married. I had a new Spring ensemble in blue—the dress a Ducharne print, the coat a good copy of one of Vionnet's—"with the intricate simplicity of the original about it"—$89.50 wholesale. The buyer took me over to the manufacturer; I admired his whole line, politely; I talked about advertising; I got his copy to write for Women's Wear; $25 a week extra. Not bad. I got a millinery account the same way, that paid $15. The office paid me $65, since I was fashion copy-writer. I bought two pairs of shoes at once nowadays, and purses to match them, and said it was economy. They stayed looking well longer.

I had plenty of washable suede gloves, that Nora kept beautifully fresh. Silly gay jewelry, to wear a month and throw away. But it must carry out the ensemble idea, meanwhile. A black silk coat, that was not just *a* black silk coat. A black and white Patou frock. Hats and hats and hats—because I loved hats. (The forlorn days when I lived with Peter and hunted about, toward the season's end, for *one* hat for five dollars in a sale.) Lovely expensive powders, and lipsticks and perfumes. (Peter bought me a bottle of Houbigant's *Idéal* once. That is not very expensive, but he must have gone without lunches three days to get it.)

It was seven weeks since Peter left; five weeks since I began to live with Lucia. There was no time, or not very much, to think about Peter—waking, doing calisthenics, having orange juice and toast and coffee in a drug store, taking a cab to the office. No time to think of Peter, from nine to one, or from two-thirty to five-thirty. No time after, walking home fast, two miles in forty minutes, bathing, dressing, going places.

Men told Lucia I was lovely looking, but completely cold. Why cold? I let them kiss me when they must, in cabs, dancing in hot nightclubs, at parties. They were not real. Neither was the office.

Clothes were real. I bought many clothes so that, when Peter called up, I could say "come over instantly" and I would be marvellously dressed. I dressed carefully, always, because I might meet some friend of Peter's, who would go back to him and say, "I saw Patricia; she was looking beautiful." Then he would call up sooner.

The telephone was real. Someday, or perhaps some night, late, it would ring significantly. That would be Peter. He would begin by saying "Patty, it was all—the last months—all a crazy mistake; I'm coming back."

And I would say, "I'm glad."

I would tell Peter about first nights, and the funny tabloid columnist who came in and wrote his stuff on my typewriter when I wanted to go to bed, until Lucia came and took me downstairs to sleep. The columnist looked so disappointed.

I would tell Peter about my arrangement with Lucia, to turn up at Childs at three in the morning when I was out without her; so that I could meet her, supposedly accidentally, and go home with her. The arrangement was made because Lucia said I was not awake enough, yet, to be able to handle anyone. That would amuse him—tell him that I went sleep-walking about, all through the weeks he had gone.

Meanwhile, the days hurried, and the evenings hurried; and, when I went to bed in the daybed that could be adjusted for two people (what had Lucia meant by that, Lucia had no lover), I slept, usually.

Sometimes, when I woke in the night, I began to ache for the feeling of Peter's head against my shoulder . . . and thought "if I could run my hand through Peter's silky tumbled hair— softly, not to wake him . . ."

Then I went downstairs and slept on the little couch in Lucia's apartment. When she woke, she just said, "Hello darling. I have *such* a hangover."

And I said, "You ought to do calisthenics at night, Lucia. They're wonderful for hangovers."

"Oh, don't be such a tiresome athletic lamb. Makes me weary to think of calisthenics. Is it eight o'clock yet?"

One evening when I worked until half past six, I cabbed home, because Lucia and I had a foursome dinner engagement at seven, and I had to be dressed in fifteen minutes.

But Lucia was not in. I looked for a note on the telephone pad, where we always left messages for each other. It said: "Your husband telephoned at six. I told him to call again at seven. Took our two men off. Good luck.

"P.S. Keep your head, darling.

"P.P.S. I'll be home around midnight, if you want to come down."

It was twelve minutes of seven. I dropped hat and gloves and purse and packages (two pairs of chiffon stockings in a shade called "ecstasy" and a net bandeau from Paris) all on the stairs, and sat down beside them. My knees shook, so that they kept hitting against each other, and that amused me inordinately. I got a cigarette and matches from my purse, and smoked and let my hopes run.

(He is coming back; it is all over with Hilda, and he just could not stand Judith; he is coming back. What shall I do with this apartment? I wonder if Pete would live on Brooklyn Heights or somewhere economical so we could save money and have another baby in a couple of years. I always knew if I did not believe it was all over, it would not be. Must be tactful and not too curious about whatever he has been doing. He has just been having an excursion, and Lucia says they come back better for the outing. I must remember that. Should I tell him about the doctor? No, absolutely no. I was sort of crazy; else that would not have happened.)

The telephone rang.

"Peter darling!"

"Oh, is that you, Pat? I wondered if you were free for dinner; we might discuss our divorce."

I could not answer for a minute. (But how stupid of me. He would not admit, instantly, that he wanted me back—it would make him seem so inconsistent. Men mind that.)

"Yes, I'm free for dinner, Pete, if you'll give me three quarters of an hour to get ready. I'm just home, and I have to bathe and things . . ."

"All right. That will be quarter to eight. Shall I call for you or will you meet me? I thought we might dine at the Blue Star."

(Oh, pleasant French speakeasy where we used to dine to celebrate things, occasionally, when we were in funds. That was a good sign, that he wanted to eat there. Better meet him there, he could have a cocktail while he waited. Then he would be sure to feel good-tempered.)

"Suppose I meet you there, Pete, at eight."

"'Right. See you in an hour. Good-bye."

What to wear, the blue ensemble or Patou frock and black coat? I rushed upstairs, started my bath running, took out a crisp pale rose French chemise, that was all beautifully tucked and pleated. Pete loved underthings in pretty colours, and hated lacy stuff.

Then the implications of that—my sureness that he would admire the chemise—made me so breathless that I had to sit down for an instant and have some of another cigarette.

The Patou frock, certainly—it was much more striking— made me look ineffably slim yet sufficiently curved. I bathed and dressed hastily, but efficiently. The great problem was how much rouge? I had so much colour of my own at the moment— but if it faded later I did not want to look wan and forlorn. Better risk a little too much, the lights in the Blue Star were dim, and with a black dress and hat I could stand it.

The dress slipped on. Black marocain with a deep white collar and exaggerated cuffs, cut petalwise. Black satin opera pumps . . . I did not like satin shoes much, but these made my feet look so narrow. An almost brimless black milan hat, with a gold arrow embroidered athwart the front. Pearls—no, the flat gold necklace.

Hunting for the necklace, I found an old ring, a flawed emerald in a curious Italian setting. Pete bought that for me in London, in an antique shop on Oxford Street. I put it on as a good gesture.

Lucia had some Nuit de Noel perfume. Pete liked that. I went downstairs for it. In Lucia's bath, regarding myself in her long mirror, glowing, I was grateful for my looks. They had been useful to me with Pete, and not so long ago. Lucia had written something about "keep my head." I never could with Pete. Never did. But it was reassuring to be looking my best.

In the taxi, being very careful to sit so that the back of the black silk coat did not get mussed and careful not to touch anything that would soil my gloves, I felt a little cold suddenly because I could not remember what, if anything, Pete had ever liked about me except my looks. I would have to think back to find out, nearly two months since I had seen him, and, before that, there was the six months' war. . . (Oh, do not think about that, think about what I am going to say when I see him.)

He sat, in a blue suit that I had not seen, smoking, with an empty cocktail glass in front of him. He looked lean and hard, and a little strange, somehow. He did not see me until I was quite close.

"Oh, there you are, Pat, how are you? What'll you drink?"

"A Martini, I think."

"All right; let's order dinner right away; then we can talk," he said. "You're looking handsome, Pat."

"You, too."

"How's the advertising business?"

"All right. I got a raise. How's the newspaper business?"

"I got a raise, too. Have another Martini?"

"Yes, thank you."

I felt cold and dry, like a Martini. I had sat across a narrow table from Pete hundreds of times before, and felt as close to him as if the lovely hardness of his arms were around me. Now there was a distance compounded of lies and quarrels and separate adventures. I had not known there would be such distance. Perhaps it could be bridged. (Do not hurry him—try to think. I cannot. I want to say, "Take me back; give me another chance, so I'll come alive again.")

I took out a handkerchief, so that I could look at myself in the mirror of my purse. My face was composed. That was good.

"Have you replaced me yet, Pat?" He grinned, a friendly enough grin.

"No." (I have to do something about this. I do not know whether it will be right or stupid, but I have to do something.)

"Haven't you missed me, really, Pete?"

"A person misses anyone that's been around as long as you. I'm convalescing slowly."

I grew a little angry, and knew that I should not. "How's your Great Romance getting on, Pete?"

"Which one?"

The waiter took away the soup. Pete filled my wine glass.

"Hilda-with-the-pure-soul, I mean?"

"Oh, that's all shot to hell; hadn't you heard?" His voice was entirely casual. He ate fish with evident enjoyment. ("The sauces are good here, aren't they, Pat?")

"No—I hadn't heard—What happened?"

"I don't mind telling you. The little girl raised outstanding hell one night I was tight because I kissed someone whose name I don't even remember, dancing. She put on a show next day because I kept her waiting ten minutes and came in smelling beery. Finally, all in one evening, she tried to get me to promise to stop smoking, kissing, and drinking. God, what a possessive woman! So I told her I couldn't make the grade, and she told me you were about what I deserved. Does that please you?"

"Not unduly."

I finished my glass of wine, and drew a long breath. Pete filled the glass again. "You are a grand-looking person, Pat." But his voice was still casual.

(Well, over the top. Nothing to lose; might gain something.) "And where does the exit of Hilda leave me, Peter?"

"As you were."

The waiter brought chicken.

"What does that mean, Pete?"

He smiled, gently, as if it were a matter of no importance. He said, "Through."

Neither of us said anything for a bit—just went on eating chicken. Pete spoke first.

"I thought it would be pleasant to see you, to dine with you. It is. I'm fond of you; think you're charming looking, have a lovely voice and hands and all that. And I'm sorry I put you through such scenes. You can't help being what you are, I suppose. Don't worry about it; it was my mistake in the first place. Have some more wine. . . . And by the way, anytime you want a divorce, tell me and I'll get things arranged. I'm in no hurry myself of course. In fact I begin to feel that the situation, as it is, affords me a certain protection. . . ."

I couldn't talk for a minute. Then, "What do you mean by 'being what I am?'"

"Oh come on, Pat. What's the use of going into that?"

"Why not?"

"I refuse to call you a slut when I'm taking you to dinner."

I was very angry. "No more of a slut than Judith!"

"You *are* well informed, aren't you? Perhaps you are no more of one, but she never pretended to be anything else—to me."

I was hopeless then. This distance seemed occupied by a tangible barricade between us. Could it be bridged? I could not think how. Two tears dropped down into my salad. I hoped Peter did not see them. One had one's pride. No, that was silly. I did not have any pride, because I cared. I just felt I ought to have some.

His voice was elder-brotherly affectionate. "I didn't mean to make you cry, Pat. Don't think about it anymore. Have a cognac and benedictine mixed for a liqueur? You used to like them?"

"Thank you." I looked at him. I stretched my hand to where his hand lay on the table. Perhaps if he let me touch him . . .

He slipped his hand over mine, and then noticed the emerald ring. "Oh God, Pat," he said, "do you remember?"

We talked about London; the first apartment we had had there; dinners for two I had managed to buy for a dollar; things far away and long ago.

When we went out, he tucked my arm under his, and we walked through the Spring evening, looking in shop windows, making each other laugh by remembering things we had done and jested at when we were awfully young.

He was twenty-five and I was twenty-four; and we talked about "when we were awfully young." I asked him—I was shy about it—to come see my apartment. He said he would like to, so we took a cab, and found that we were hanging on to each other's hands rather desperately.

There was no light in Lucia's apartment when we passed. I went straight on up, and locked the door at the stair-head. I did not want Lucia and strange people coming in and talking about plays they had been to, when I could talk to Peter instead.

But I must think of something to talk about. I gave him cigarettes. He was looking at me as if he loved to look at me; and yet, as if it hurt him.

"Peter, I've been meeting playwrights and columnists and a painter who's going to do my portrait, and more funny people . . ."

"Yes, I suppose you would go in for celebrity chasing."

That stopped me. I wished we were somewhere other than this apartment that had nothing to do with Peter and me.

"Sorry, Pat. I didn't mean to be disagreeable."

"It's all right." (He had not kissed me, yet. Maybe, when he did, it might be really all right. It might bridge the distance.)

He walked up and down. He was just a little drunk. I was afraid I would say something stupid, so I said nothing. He began to talk. "Before I was in love with you, Pat, I was rather hard hit by that girl Natalie. Do you remember? I've mentioned her. Promtrotter and so on; I wrote verses to her and she ditched me for Gerard, because he had a hell of a lot of money. It was sensible of her—she was five years older than I anyway, and it was just a case of calflove, as far as I was concerned. But I took it relatively hard. . . . Then I met you. . . ."

I felt tired. Where was this leading?

"You looked so clean, there was something—it's an old-fashioned adjective, but I used to think of you as *dewy,* Patricia."

He stood with his hands in his pockets staring at me; not angrily, not as if he hated me, and certainly not as if he loved me; just puzzled, and as if he were a little tired too.

"Pat, would you mind telling me . . . was I a very inadequate lover? Was that why you slept around?"

I felt as I imagine a man feels when he has been knocked out, and is just coming back to consciousness. What had I done to Peter?

"Peter, my dearest, no!—Could I try to explain just what happened, really?"

I would tell about Rickey—Rickey could go to hell, if it would wipe that look, that *tired* look, off Pete's face.

He smiled a one-sided smile.

"No, honestly, Pat, I'd rather not hear a new version. I wouldn't believe it. You've presented several, in the last eight or nine months; do you remember?"

"But this is the truth."

"They all were at the moment."

He would not believe me, anymore. What was the use?

"Peter, would you please kiss me at once?"

He came over instantly. We kissed. I felt at last as if the last year just had not happened.

Then he picked me up; put me on the new, decorative day-bed; walked across the room; scrutinized a print he had seen before—scrutinized his life and mine, and our generation that everyone had been yelling about since we had grown up, and before; scrutinized his opinions of immortality, for all I know. His expression was sufficiently remote.

He turned. He looked completely unhappy. He said, "Christ, once I thought you were a sort of miracle evolved for my special benefit." He stood staring at me.

I said nothing.

"Well, you remain, the pleasantest woman I ever knew—in bed."

Why protest? Let him say all the things he wanted; if they made him feel better. They did not mean anything—just words.

His voice was unsteady now.

"I want to kiss you again."

"Yes," I said.

•

Was this what I had wanted really, this Peter asleep with his head against my breast like a child—this passion that was supposed to lessen first of all things in marriage, but with us had outlasted everything else, so that it was now the only way we had of talking to each other? No, I did not want this, much. I wanted Peter as he used to be.

Still, perhaps this could be used in recovering the rest. In the morning, we would dress and go to breakfast somewhere, and I would be so gay and amusing at breakfast that Pete would hate to leave, and would come back, tomorrow, or certainly the next day, and then, gradually . . . I felt quite warm and happy. It would be lovely, going to breakfast with Peter.

Judith? Something in me hardened, as I lay with Peter's tumbled head on my shoulder. . . . I survived Hilda, perhaps I could survive Judith too. . . . I went to sleep tranquilly.

But when I woke in the morning Peter was gone.

I did not believe it for a minute; I did not believe that Pete could leave without a word, as if I were some girl he had met in a speakeasy the night before; and not found very diverting. Peter would not do that to me. He had, though, done just that.

I had wanted to go to breakfast with him; I had wanted *so* to go to breakfast with him. I began to cry; and got up and hunted for a handkerchief. Then I saw a note marked "Patricia" on the mantel; and remembered I had left a note for Rickey, once, and cried harder; so that I could not see to read it, for a minute.

It said, "Thanks for hospitality. See you again sometime." That was all.

I went stumbling downstairs to find Lucia. Maybe she could tell me what to do next. I did not know. I showed her the note. I said, "I hate him; I'm never going to see him again. I'm going to kiss so many other men I shan't remember what he was like. He says I'm a slut; I'll be a slut, but never with him, again. Lucia, why did he do this to me?"

"Pat, darling, pull yourself together for a minute. I'm sorry Pat. There isn't anything you can do, you know. There . . . cry as much as you like . . . then we'll talk."

I sat and sobbed. Lucia dressed, saying, "You'll feel better soon, darling" intermittently.

I did not feel any better, but after a while I stopped crying.

"I'll telephone your office, Pat, and say you had to go to the dentist and will be in at noon. I'll stay out myself, too. It's a nice day, and I haven't taken a morning off since the one after the Bordens' sailed."

"I'd like to take a car and drive too fast; race railroad trains to grade crossings, Lucia."

"Yes. Dress, Pat, and we'll go somewhere leisurely to eat."

I dressed, in the new blue ensemble. We went to Mary Elizabeth's restaurant. It was quiet, for late breakfast; and we could look out over the Avenue.

"Lucia, I let him stay, because I thought it was the way to get him back."

"What do you want him back for?"

"Because we used to love each other so."

"Do you love him now, really?"

"At this moment I wish he were dead. But generally I love him."

"As he is or as he was?"

"As he was."

"How are you going to manage to get him back as he was?"

She poured herself a second cup of coffee.

"In a minute Pat, I'll be quoting the well-known source of copy for cigarette ads to you."

"The Rubaiyat?"

"Exactly. 'The moving figure writes and having writ'—what of it? Be like me. Watch people perform and don't get involved yourself."

"The Rubaiyat's just an adolescent's ideal of philosophy, except the parts about drinking."

"Tell me some philosophy that's not adolescent. Self-expression—the new freedom for women-Freud, that Great Excuse?"

"There *is* progress, though, Lucia. Myself, I've progressed, in taste, from Scott Fitzgerald to Ernest Hemingway."

"How much progress is that?"

"A damn long distance on the road to bigger and broader vocabularies."

Lucia laughed. "You see, you're feeling better already, Pat. Did you know I was five years older than you?"

"I didn't think it was as much as that."

"Yes, I'm twenty-nine. Arch walked out on me when I was twenty-five. I tried to manage him too much; wanted to make a success of him, you know. And made scenes about other women. Usual story. As soon as he was successful enough to get a chance to manage his Chicago office, he went; and told me to comfort myself with my love for music, or something to that effect. I forget.

"I used to jump through hoops for him. Used to ache for his visits to New York. I haven't seen him for a couple of years, and I'm glad. He still—there's just a breath's space of disturbance— about the first man you loved—"

She looked very placid, notwithstanding. I ached, but it helped to sit and listen to Lucia.

"By the time you're twenty-nine," she said, "you're likely to have reached—the age of generalizing. I no longer think of myself as *me,* a terrifically important person. I think I'm an interesting example of the unattached woman-about-town. Victim of the new freedom—had it thrust on me willy-nilly. You belong to the same type. But you're younger, and you mind more."

"What's going to become of us, Lucia?"

"Nothing. Whatever 'becomes' of anyone else? Get old, and grey haired, and fat or scrawny."

She could not be as indifferent as all that. "What do you really think about ex-wives, Lucia?"

She grew animated.

"We are *free.* Applesauce! Free to pay our own rent, and buy our own clothes, and put up with the eccentricities of three to eight men who have authority over us in business, instead of having to please just one husband.

"We don't have to be dominated anymore. Twaddle! Grant that a woman married to a brute or a degenerate under the old system, was out of luck. How many of those were there, compared to the women married to average decent men with a sense of responsibility?

"If you and your Peter had been young fifty years ago, you wouldn't have been unfaithful to him once; because you wouldn't have had twenty opportunities for infidelity flung at you in a year; and, if he were unfaithful to you, he'd manage it discreetly, because he'd be socially ostracized if he didn't. And he wouldn't have told you to go your way, blithely; because there wouldn't have been any way for you to go. The principal thing that relieving women from the dullness of domesticity did, was to relieve men from any necessity of offering stability in return for love, fidelity and so on.

"Women used to have status, a relative security. Now they have the status of any prostitute, success while their looks hold out. If the next generation of women have any sense, they'll dynamite the statue of Susan B. Anthony, and start a crusade for the revival of chivalry.

"Freedom from men? Which of us is free who is emotionally absorbed in any man? The choices for women used to be: marriage, the convent, or the street. They're just the same now. Marriage has the same name. Or you can have a *career,* letting it absorb all emotional energy (just like the convent). Or you can have an imitation masculine attitude toward sex, and a succession of meaningless affairs, promiscuity, (the street, that is) taking your pay in orchids and dinner-dates instead of money left on the dresser.

"Women used to be happy if their men were good to them; and, when they grew old, if their children got along all right. They're happy on the same basis now. They always followed their lovers with their dreams, to war or work, but were content enough at home if they were occupied and had a modicum of kisses. The abnormal ones, I suppose, had a rotten time of it, and so they yelled and pushed and tipped over the applecart for the rest of us in the end." She stopped and lighted a cigarette.

"However, Lucia, here we are, with the sun of the new age shining on us; what are we going to do about it?"

"Pat, let's have more coffee and some marmalade. Are you feeling calmer, child? Does the thought of women-in-general make you see Pete and yourself in proportion? I expect not. Give it a couple of years though.

"Ex-wives seem to be doing three things. Some go in for celibacy and business success—one necessitates the other almost always, you know, simply because there is a limit to the amount of vitality a woman has to expend, altogether. Most women can't stand the pace of a career and a great love affair (or several in succession) managed simultaneously. The careerists will be all right, though, in a sense; they'll save money for their old age and so on. But they won't have children, so the problem ends with them. That is class one."

"I don't belong to that class, Lucia. I'm glad—I feel lucky— that I can sling words together, and hold a well-paid job, and get others on the side. But I don't give a damn about it, except that it permits a more luxurious life than if I were a twenty-a-week clerk, somewhere."

"At present, Pat, you're in class two and, I think, on your way to class three, where I am. Class two says 'Love is over, there remains . . . adventuring about.' I'm judging from your before-breakfast-mood of planning to kiss so many people you forget what your husband was like. It will probably give you distance on him; and do you more good than harm, if you go through with that idea."

"Of course, Lucia, there are the scruples that are left over from the way one was brought up."

"Yes. But I think chastity, really, went out when birth control came in. If there is no 'consequence'—it just isn't important. People's ideas—the things they say about *affaires*—begin to shift enormously, and their ideas are half a generation behind their conduct—their experiments."

"The thought of going out and getting me fifty lovers doesn't stir me much, though, Lucia. What'll I have in the end? My memories, I suppose. Hell! Memory may have been some comfort to the Victorians, judging from their poetry; but I don't seem to be able to work the miracle on it. To remember that

Peter adored me in 1923, just leaves me absolutely cold in 1926. I'll have to eat dinner with someone other than Pete tonight, no matter what he once said about forever and ever."

"I know. You'll come to class three in the end. You'll marry again."

"Are you going to marry again, Lucia?"

"You bet, darling, in about another year. The imminence of my thirties makes me believe in the probability of my forties, and do I plan to be a worn-out, irritable female sitting around an advertising office shivering every time they hire a bright kid copy-writer just out of college, and being distressingly polite to an advertising manager ten years younger than myself? I do not."

"Are you in love?"

The serene face looked suddenly wistful. "No. After Arch, no one was ever quite what I wanted. Oh, I experimented, had lovers, not many. Casual lovers, so much more interested in themselves than me, always. Casual lovers are like that. And they felt injured when I'd not live up to the promise of the colour of my hair (with you Pat, it would be the shape of your mouth) and it's difficult to know what to say to them between kisses. I might have cared for someone, again, I suppose, if I had not been always waiting for Arch to come to town. That's the sort of thing you shouldn't do, but no doubt will."

"Whom are you going to marry?"

"You can make raids on any of my men except Sam."

"But he's not good-looking . . . and isn't he dull?"

"I thought that would surprise you. He has more substance (and I mean in character, as well as in banks) than anyone else we know. He's stopped asking what it's all about. He knows a few things that he wants out of the show. I'm one of them."

"I don't believe you'll marry him."

"Wait a year and see. Let's go get manicures."

After we had manicures, I went to my office, and did a full day's work in an afternoon. I knew if I had a minute to think about Peter I would have hysterics over my typewriter; and hysterics, in department store advertising offices, are permitted only to a few, very successful women buyers. I was through at five, and wanted to telephone him. But what was there to say? "You might have taken me to breakfast, Peter?" There was not much sense to that. So I went upstairs to the beauty shop, and managed a facial before the store closed, instead.

Lucia was taking me along to a party given for a woman who had come back from Arabia, the world's greatest authority on Arab love songs.

Lucia and I usually dressed together, downstairs in her room, so that we could talk. "Had a facial didn't you, Pat? Looks grand. I did some wangling for you this afternoon; telephoned Ned to bring Charlie along for you. You can start your career of crime with *the* younger generation novelist, if you're still going in for it. Are you?"

"I don't know. I still feel outstandingly broken hearted, and I want to make Pete seem a long way off since I can't have him close as I want."

"The middle distance *is* neither this nor that. Like pink roses, isn't it? Well, try Charlie. You'll have a chance. He's like that. . . . I'll be interested in watching the fireworks, if you've really made up your mind to snatch a few opportunities. To date, you've just been sufficiently good-looking so that the men I've introduced to you haven't minded—much—the fact that you've been inert as a sofa-cushion. I see you've brought down your bright red dress."

I had not worn it yet—had bought it because the colour was heavenly. But it was, a bit obviously, a dress one wore to be stared at in. Tight across the hips, and no back.

Lucia wore a bouffant gold thing that made her look like an angel, only more sophisticated.

Ned and Charlie turned up with a flask of cocktails already mixed. Ned was a publisher. He had never paid any attention to me before, but the red dress changed that. However, Lucia soon absorbed him. Charlie turned out to be a commonplace, medium-sized young blond, who would have looked better if he took up squash rackets. But he wore his consciousness of success like his very perfect dinner coat, a trifle flamboyantly.

"Another woman with exquisite hands," he said, second or third sentence.

"Your shoulders—would make a man forget every disillusionment he'd ever had," he said, fifth or sixth sentence.

Then we went to dinner at the Ritz. Lucia was taking care of Ned, in undertones, so I talked about Charlie's books. Fortunately I had read them, but I read a great deal anyway. I said they were poignant, which seemed to please him. I had not tried to please anyone in a long time. This man was quite easy.

When we got to the party, we found the woman who knew all about Arab love lyrics, ten years too old to be decorative while she sang them, yet she *would* sing them.

I let Charlie take me upstairs to find drinks. He talked about women, and love, and snatching the unrepeatable golden moments as they came, else the champagne grew flat. That was the general tenor of it, anyway. I let him kiss me.

He was technically expert. One knows about things like that, from sophomore year at college on. He said he had not been so stirred in years. I knew that was probably what he always said next. But I was entertained.

In the dressing-room (Charlie and I were going taxi riding in the Park, of course—"away from all these stupid people," he said) I met Lucia, putting fresh lipstick on.

"Look here," she said. "Do you want to do this? Charlie admits himself he's one of the town's great lovers, and he's gone head over for the moment, but what is all that to you?"

"I don't know that I want to. I don't want not to." I tried to think what I did want.

"Lucia, I'd like to be harder, inside. To try to take all this sort of thing as men are supposed to take it, for the adventure, for the moment's gaiety—perhaps for warmth and friendliness and anaesthesia against—against feeling so alone. I know I shan't be sobbing about Charlie tomorrow morning. He won't matter enough. Damn it if I cry over this fresh make-up—

"Lucia, it might be fun . . ."

"All right. Don't cry. Sit still a minute; you may as well make him wait a bit. Better take my wrap, it's warmer than yours, and the gold's good with your dress. And this is my last protest; I act like a maiden aunt about you anyway . . . Pat, can you dash off with this spoiled young novelist, remembering that you spent last night with Peter?"

"Yes, because if this Charlie person can make me feel last night was a month ago, or even a week, I'll—I'll send him gardenias."

"Finish your cigarette and run along. And if you can really adopt the alleged masculine attitude toward sex, you've got all of New York to console you for Peter. New York on a short term lease, while you have the looks and the clothes for it. I'm betting you can't though. Not many women can."

Charlie was pacing up and down drinking a highball in enormous gulps. We went riding in the Park. I recognized a couple of things he had used in his books, among what he said, but he was pleasantly flattering, and not so conceited but that he implied gratitude, even surprise, for my manner of acquiescence.

We went to my apartment. He was unhurried. He said, "Strange little flower-face with a Mona Lisa mouth." I wanted him to kiss me, and stop talking. He did not know it, but he might be going to do me some good. I kept remembering Peter walking up and down, the night before, and I wanted that ghost exorcised fast.

Finally Charlie did kiss me.

He left when it was growing light. I slept.

In the morning Lucia and I breakfasted together hurriedly. She asked no questions at all, but talked about going to the circus that night, with two men from the "Tribune," "unless your new boyfriend is taking you places, Patricia."

"He's going out of town this afternoon, Lucia. I wouldn't have been so reckless yesterday, if I hadn't known that."

"How my protegée grows up," Lucia said.

We walked down the Avenue a little way together, laughing at things, in the Spring sunshine. Then I went on alone. I was neither happy nor unhappy. Peter seemed a fairly comfortably long time ago. I thought how to write the After-Easter-Sale-of-Millinery ad.

VII

When Charlie came back to New York, I said that I was ex-tremely busy, the three times he telephoned.

After that, when we met occasionally at parties, we smiled at each other in passing on to territory not already explored. Several successors to Charlie went the same way, during weeks that slipped past as swiftly paced as moods.

Moods—of anguish about Peter, that lessened, and was bitter-est in its lessening, for hope about Peter lessened with it—of fatigue, when the effort to work, to dress, to think of things to say to people was just less than the effort necessary to face an evening or a day alone. Gay moods, when New York was glamorous from the jungle sweat of Harlem dance halls to the cool lights on boats beyond the Battery, glimpsed as one drove through empty echoing downtown streets at dawn. Moods of tranquility, when a sense of unreality slipped between myself and any aching, and the people and happenings of crowded days were people and happenings of an unimportant dream, and my whole life with Peter was a dream fading, growing remote as the remembrance of sunsets over snowy marshes, watched through a window, when I was a child.

There were men. When, as occasionally, their desire was sufficient to break through the defence of my indifference, I was neither glad, nor very sorry. Hoping some time to wake and find I had slept beside a lover and a friend, I slept to wake beside a stranger exigent, triumphant, or exasperated, or perhaps as bored and as polite as I.

Spring passed, and I wrote ads about clothes to take vacationing; and bought a few of them; and went for a fortnight with Lucia to Maine—two weeks spent swimming and sleeping, and feeling healthy, comfortable enough lying on sand in the sun, without thinking.

Midsummer heat enclosed New York like a fog. In printed silk frocks that, damp and mussed and dusty, I flung into a hamper to go to the cleaner's at each day's end, I wrote ads about Apparel for the Beaches, and the August Sale of Furs. In flowered chiffons and pastel-coloured slippers, Lucia and I danced on hotel roofs, or drove out to dine at Long Island roadhouses.

One day, when a sketch of a diving figure, drawn for me by an artist to illustrate an ad of men's bathing suits, made me remember, suddenly, vividly, a day two summers past, when I sat on the edge of a raft swinging my legs and watching Pete do swan dives, I telephoned him.

"Oh, hello, Pat. Anything special on your mind?"

"I thought you might think of somewhere cool, and take me there to dinner."

"There isn't anywhere cool. I'm pretty busy this week. Suppose I call you Monday or Tuesday?"

"All right. That will be nice."

He did not call.

One night at the Bossert roof overlooking the harbour, Lucia and I saw Pete and Judith dancing. We were not dancing, we were with Sam and another somewhat fat banker, a friend of his. We were both very tired, and not in form, and just said bright things to entertain the bankers, intermittently, sipping cool drinks and letting them talk about who would float loans to meet German reparation payments, most of the time.

Lucia noticed Judith first, and asked me if that was Peter, with her. I said "yes" and felt, for an instant, sick with jealousy of Judith looking gay, dancing gracefully if amorously; and then that passed and I did not look at them anymore, just bowed as we walked by their table when we were leaving, and thought that Peter was looking rather white and tired.

The next week I met Judith in front of the Library at noontime. It was a fairly cool day, and I was celebrating by wearing a silver fox that was my most recent and best beloved extravagance. Of course I had bought it wholesale, but I would be paying for it for three months more, at that. My first feeling, on seeing Judith, was just relief that I had worn the gorgeous scarf, because I could not bear to meet her in anything but the best-looking clothes I owned. Judith did wear clothes well. And I considered what else I had on, and compared it as to *chic* with Judith's clothes (it was all right, both had dresses of imported prints, but mine was a copy of a recent Vionnet, and hers of an early Spring Chanel—my wide black Milan hat was as fine a straw as hers, and we came out even on slippers—they were the same model as a matter of fact) before I realized that it was all quite funny.

"Hello," she said, "where are you going?"

"Luncheon," I said, "are you?"

"Yes," she said. "Will you lunch with me?"

"Love to," I said.

We went to the Vanity Fair tea-room on Fortieth Street.

She took off her hat, as soon as she sat down, saying she was hot. I noticed there was a light over her head, and remembered what Lucia said about Judith never losing an opportunity to let light shine across her auburn hair.

Then I knew that I was being stupid. She *was* smartly dressed, just as smartly as I. She was not as pretty as I, but for all I knew she might be cleverer, and have a better disposition, and so on. Yet because she stood in my way with Peter, I could not think about her, estimate her, calmly—judge her fairly.

I gave up struggling to be civilized about her, and ordered some fruit salad, and wondered whether she felt about me as I did about her, or whether, because I was Peter's past and she was Peter's present, she could be detached and contemplate me as just a sort of relic.

We talked about how hot it had been and what clothes for Autumn would be like, and where we had spent our vacations. She mentioned Peter first, when we had reached the iced-coffee and sherbet stage.

To be precise, she did not mention him. She implied him.

"I suppose you'll be getting your divorce this Fall, Patricia?"

"Oh, I don't know. I'm in no hurry."

She hesitated. I did not help her out. So she generalized. "Not much sense hanging on when a man's through."

I thought for a second. She did not know me well enough to be personal. I could shift the subject and she could not go back to it. But, if I let her go on, I might find out how things were going with Peter and her. I did not know what good that would do me, if any, to be sure. Still—I sipped my iced coffee. Then I said:

"How do you know Pete's through, Judith?"

"You've been separated nearly six months, haven't you?"

"Yes."

"Did you know Pete's taking an apartment, September first?"

"All by himself, Judith?"

"He and I are taking adjoining apartments in a house on East Tenth Street."

She had courage, or she was desperate, which?

"How very nice for you both."

She tried again. "Patricia, I'm not trying to be catty. I mean, I thought you and I might both be better off if we talked this out."

"What? Where you live? That's your affair, Judith."

"You know perfectly well that Pete and I are in love with each other."

"I know nothing of the sort, Judith."

But why should I be unduly disagreeable? She was making something in me hurt, about Peter, as it had not hurt in months. But she might not know that. And she was being candid, to a degree. Candid about herself, and optimistic about Peter, probably. Well—I was optimistic about Peter myself, with less reason, nowadays, than she had.

"Are you asking me to get out of your way, Judith?"

"Yes."

"Why should I?"

"Why not? Pete will never go back to you, anyway."

"I'm not so sure of that."

Her expression was suddenly anxious.

And I was sorry for her, and myself, simultaneously. She was playing her hand, I was playing mine; what was the difference?

"Listen, Judith, I'm still crazy about Pete, myself."

"Oh. I thought you were getting over it. You go about a lot."

"That doesn't mean anything.

"Judith, Pete hasn't asked you to marry him, you just think he might, if he had a divorce."

"All right. Put it that way."

We were talking round and round the thing, and I was feeling worse every minute. Better finish it.

"I don't know anymore, why I want Pete back. But I do. I'll divorce him, if and when he asks me to—we've had that arrangement for months. Until then. I'll play for time."

"That's that, then."

She picked up her gloves. I felt a little apologetic, somewhat as if I had bumped into someone going through a door.

"Sorry, Judith. But after all I didn't cut in on you, you cut in on me."

"Not on you, on Hilda."

That was casuistry, but maybe she believed it, so I let it go.

We walked down the Avenue together, talking about clothes again, and I left her at the door of Franklin Simon's. It occurred to me afterward that it was a curious conversation.

It seemed matter-of-fact enough at the time.

VIII

It was Saturday and September and half-past seven at night, and my birthday. I remembered all that. It was easier to remember that, than to think which way the stairs curved.

Kenneth had given a cocktail party for me. I had come home on a bus to get some air. Now I had to dress for late dinner with Bill. It was just a pause in the day's hard drinking. Before I dressed, I was going in to tell Lucia what it felt like to be me. Lucia could not go to the cocktail party. She had to see Sam off somewhere. Sam was getting pretty incessant. Too bad. Lucia should marry someone who looked more like Apollo than Sam. But she had once. Arch looked something like Apollo. Lots of other women besides Lucia had thought so too, from all accounts.

Well this was the last flight of stairs. I stepped through the hem of my dress, and got my foot out again, somehow, and stumbled against Lucia's door. It opened, so I went in. Lucia was lying down reading. She sat up and began to laugh.

"Patricia, my darling, *what* an edge!"

"Celebrating . . . celebrating being twenty-five years old. Sit down and tell you about it."

"Do you want some hangover medicine?"

"No. Want to talk."

"All right. How does it feel to be twenty-five? I forget."

"You got over it, I expect I'll get over it, give me time. Got over being twenty. Lucia, I'll be thirty-five, like as not, some day."

"Then you can settle down in life and let your hips grow."

"I can't eat as much now I'm twenty-five as I did when I was twenty. I used to call chicken patties, and chocolate layer cake lunch. Now I have an endive salad; I guess that's the biggest difference."

"What else is there, Pat?"

"I'm just as good-looking and I'm thinner and I certainly wear my clothes better. Used to wear floppy hats with flowers on them and Pete'd tell me I was dewy. Used to be a dewy girl but now, by gosh, I don't. Is that funny, Lucia, or am I drunk?"

"Both," said Lucia, politely. "Go on."

"Oh yes, when I was twenty I planned to have a Great Romance. Well, did I *not? And* marry it?"

"Talk about something else, Pat. What presents did you get?"

"Men used to bring me violets and now they bring me Scotch. Liquor isn't a gift to a woman, it's just an investment in her. One's Great Romance—"

"Oh dear," said Lucia. "Well if you must, you must. What about it?"

"One's Great Romance . . . Passion, Memory, Dust . . . Lucia, I have a literary edge. . . . That's Galsworthy. Isn't it funny how tired my Great Romance got of me? If I'd known as much at twenty as I do at twenty-five, maybe I could have kept it, do you think? . . . Never have another Romance like it, him, Peter . . ."

"That's the everlasting mercy of the Lord, I expect," said Lucia.

"Yes, another Great Romance would be the death of me. One gets the same feeling, or near enough, on four Manhattans if they're good; and that failing, one can see what five will do. The hangover from Manhattan's shorter'n that from Romances. . . ."

"Tell me more about the Manhattans," said Lucia.

"Manhattans, they're good. They'll never turn you into lady-entering-room-preceded-by-diaphragm, either, if you don't mix 'em with bread and pastries. The way to look at one's Great Romance is . . ."

"Oh Lord," said Lucia.

"It's very grand to get it over young. And no one's got tired of me since. I get tired first. Once or twice it's been just about one date first, but that's adequate isn't it, Lucia?"

"Entirely adequate, dear."

"The air is one of those things that it's more blessed to give than to receive. Also the Lord giveth and the Lord taketh away—smaller and less troubling Romances. Lucia, it's a *Biblical* edge I've got."

"Fine. What do you want, now you're twenty-five?"

"I don't know. But then I never did know what I wanted, except Peter, and that was very little help to me wasn't it? I guess I want to make eight thousand dollars next year and buy a couple of bonds for my old age."

"You'll buy three fur coats, a darn sight more likely, Pat."

"Maybe. Anyway I shan't make eight thousand—too lazy to get that much freelancing. Make about six and spend about seven. Oh I forgot. When I was twenty I wanted to write, and now I do fashion copy."

"Did you accomplish everything else you set out to do in life just like that, Pat?"

"Hell, no, but I'm a Futilitarian, so it doesn't matter. I am futile, you are futile, we are futile, they are more futile. But we two have a nice time at it. We don't get so bored that we have to talk about sex."

"Don't you start talking about sex now."

"Of course not, why talk about it, better put up with it in a cheerful way."

"Like a brave little woman," said Lucia.

"I feel horribly dizzy, Lucia. Listen, do you suppose I'm going on all my life, waiting for Peter, when I'm twenty-five and thirty-five and forty—Lucia. It's so *long*—"

"There, darling. Think of something else quick. Look at the newspaper. Here's a Graphic. See the pretty picture of the oldest divorcée in New York State. (I bet it's a composite photograph.

They probably used her granddaughter's legs in it.) There. See, you have lots of time. You may summon enthusiasm about being a divorcée yet."

"*Isn't* she old, Lucia. Poor thing, do you suppose she was ever bunned in her life? Lucia, *think* of the old women who were never bunned, poor dears. . . ."

"Think of all the middle-aged females who never were—all the feminists, Pat."

"How few, Lucia, how melancholily few, ever knew that beautiful swinging-of-the-spheres sensation, toward the end of a hard-drinking evening . . . when one could pass out, or laugh rather noisily about divers absurdities that occur to one . . . but does neither, just breathes very evenly, and goes on talking in a low voice about the sources of anti-Ku-Klux feeling in the South, or some such subject . . . and feels on the edge of knowing what one really thinks about everything. How few, how sadly few. . . . Oh, Lucia, the new freedom for women came just too late to save the old saloon."

IX

October's the pleasantest month of the year, in New York. Cool days succeed one another *crescendo,* like states of mind in convalescence after fever. The air is so clear that edges of tall buildings are etched against the sky, sharp and clean as lines in Chinese paintings.

On sunny days the warmth of furs and Winter tweeds is just outrageous luxury, and Fifth Avenue's a fragrance blended of furs and tweeds and boutonnières and new leather gloves and French perfume—and the underlying scent of gasoline belongs there definitely as the smokiness in Scotch.

Evenings sparkle with a feeling of things-about-to-happen-fast-again, many theatres opening, everyone giving parties to people back from Paris with gay or ridiculous stories about everyone else who was there.

One may live October through, and never see scarlet-stained Autumn leaves, except as centrepieces on tearoom tables. Yet the fires small boys build in obscure streets at dusk—fires of three barrel staves and a soapbox—have somehow a pungency that's reminiscent of heaped Autumn leaves burning on well-kept suburban lawns.

I went to a gymnasium most afternoons between half past five and dinner time, because exercise kept me clearheaded writing copy in the daytime, and fresher-looking through the evening. The gymnasium had a running track on the roof. Going 'round and 'round it, regarding the view of upper Broadway electric light signs, or thinking that the person who invented the sweat shirt had no sense of design, or just counting off twenty laps to the mile, and debating detachedly whether to be energetic and run three miles, or lazy and stop at two, I felt very contented. Thump, thump, thump, around a board track. It was a simple occupation, but an absorbing one.

That feeling of running, of having been running endlessly, so that I was breathless, yet must go on running forever, seemed to sum up my life. Running through days of posing as an efficient young business woman, through nights of posing as a sophisticated young woman about town. Running from the memory of Peter, toward something or nothing, it did not matter which.

"You're a success," said Lucia, one day. "Three times out of five, when the telephone rings now, it's for you. Ex-wife Grade A, you turned out to be."

Ex-wife Grade A, I was. Sex-appeal, dresses well, looks young, dances lightly, can make wisecracks, and is self-supporting. Lets a man talk. Does not gold-dig, except for another round of liqueurs after dinner. Never passes out or gets raucous, or gets sick. Not susceptible to the "I want you, I want you, I want you" attitude, but likely to succumb to "pity me, my life is lonely"— once with any man.

Three men came to be fixtures among the transients.

The first was Nathaniel.

At a large and stupid tea, given by a woman in the agency for which Lucia wrote copy, I noticed a tall young man wandering about looking as if he wished himself elsewhere. I wished I were elsewhere too. The room was crowded and hot, and everyone was talking advertising shop-talk. Eventually someone presented the tall young man, and I recognized his last name as one seen frequently on signs on skyscrapers in process of construction.

"You don't have to talk," he said. "You look like a Drian drawing."

That was so nice of him that I tried to talk as amusingly as possible. But he continued to look as if he wished he were somewhere else, so eventually I asked him what he was doing at the tea.

He explained that his father was a client of the agency, asked me how I got there, and I explained that I was a friend of Lucia's, who was a friend of the hostess's.

"Lucia," he said, "is gorgeous but decadent looking. She hasn't your obvious wholesomeness."

"Wholesomeness" was a term that had not been used frequently in connexion with me, of late. It left me somewhat startled actually, but pleased.

"Let's go take a cab," he said, "and drive right around the city. I hate hot smoky rooms."

Because he was such a nice scrubbed-looking young man, and also because I had nothing to do until eight o'clock anyway, I went.

By "around" the city, he had meant literally that. —West Street by the docks to the Battery, and up the far East Side, where bits of the river showed at the street ends.

I thought he himself was about the most "wholesome" looking person I had seen in months. He had brown hair that would have curled untidily, if it were not so close-clipped, wide-set gay grey eyes, a curious sensitive mouth, a good chin, a beautiful vaguely striped suit, and a necktie I did not like. It looked a little consciously vagabondish. To offset that, he had enormous, well-shaped muscular hands.

He was fun. He talked about the shapes and colours and flavours of things. I knew in half an hour that he had a passion for beauty beyond anyone I had ever met—an impersonal sort of passion for line and form and tone. He talked about the curved hulls of ships, I remember, with a warmth I had heard in other men's voices when, over wine, they remembered some woman whom they had loved very much.

I had decided that this Nathaniel person was altogether engaging, when suddenly he took off his hat, bent down, kissed the corner of my mouth, let me go instantly, and without drawing breath, announced, "You kiss very badly. I shan't kiss you again."

I laughed and laughed and laughed. He grew embarrassed; he blushed beautifully; I kept on laughing. When I could breathe I said, "Do you always make that speech?"

"Tell you sometime," he said. "There's a marvellous show of modern French painters at the Dudensing gallery. Could you leave your office a bit early tomorrow and see it?"

"Love to," I said.

Months later he told me about the speech in the cab.

The day before he met me, his roommate at college had been jeering him about his lack of "line" with women, and had recommended kissing them within the first hour of meeting, telling them they kissed atrociously, and watching them prove how wrong that statement was. Nat said he had felt the speech might also serve to indicate that he was enormously sophisticated, and then he could go on taking women to art-galleries and Russian restaurants, without bothering further about personalities.

However, since I did not react as he had expected, he dropped the line from his repertoire.

By the time he finally explained "how badly you kiss," I knew a great many other things about him. He was the only surviving son of a man who had gone from small job contracting to skyscraper building, and from an Allen Street tenement to a residence in the East Sixties, in the course of twenty-five years or so.

His older brother had died in an automobile smash-up to which the chorus girl with him contributed a flavour of champagne and scandal, when Nat was twenty.

The father turned white-haired overnight, blamed himself for having allowed the boy too much money to spend, and thereupon brought Nat home from college, put him in the business, allowed him fifty dollars a week and a charge account at a tailor's, and administered lectures to him at intervals on the evils of drink and women.

Infrequently the old man went on Gargantuan benders of his own, locking himself and a half case of Scotch in the library his dead wife had acquired, and telephoning for meals to be left outside on trays. He was discovered usually, when Nat and the family physician forced their way in on the second or third day, sullen, silent, holding in shaking gnarled hands a silver cup his dead son had won at tennis, or some casual letter about football and the necessity for an increased allowance that the boy had written him.

When Nat was summoned home from college, at the time of his brother's much-publicized passing, his father's physician had told him that his father was likely to die suddenly of heart disease, at any moment, or perhaps not for twenty years, depending principally on whether he had any further shocks. He was not to be irritated or opposed in anything.

So Nathaniel grinned at the fifty dollar salary that never was increased, charged clothes nonchalantly at the tailor provided for him, and threw overboard ideas of studying architecture in Paris. He wanted to travel, to see paintings in Florence, hear Wagner in Bayreuth, feel the sun blaze down on the pyramids. He never went farther from New York than his father's country place on Long Island.

He took me to art exhibits, concerts and concerts and concerts, beer-gardens where the Kapellmeister alternated the hilarity of "Ei, du Schöne Schnitzelbank" with the poignancy of "Nur eine Nacht." He took me to the only Chinese restaurant on Pell Street where the chef had been trained to cook for a Mandarin. He took me ten blocks out of our way to dinner to show me the design on the wrought-iron doors of a new building on Madison Avenue. And to the Lido and Montmartre to dance, and to Pierre's to lunch, and to speakeasies where he who had never seen France, moistened the labels of cognac bottles, hopefully, to see if the Hennessey water-mark showed through.

Once he talked to me about women. Like this. "Patricia, I'm conscious of possessing a very unfashionable virtue."

"What do you mean 'a very unfashionable virtue?'"

"I'm lightly sexed or something. Women don't bother me a bit. I should rather go to bed alone at ten o'clock on Saturday night, so that I can get up at six Sunday and go riding in Westchester, than spend the night in the arms of any women I ever saw. Do you suppose there's something wrong with me? Should I try to set up a coat model on Central Park West, with my fifty a week spending money, to prove I'm virile?"

"No, what for, unless you feel like it. . . . But why do you spend so much time with me, if you don't like women?"

"I don't think about you as female. You're decorative, like a well-bred young collie pup . . . and besides you laugh at things and like to look at pictures."

"You're a comfort, Nathaniel."

He was; he made me feel peaceful, usually. Rarely, he irritated me, with his habit of averting his gaze from the emotions and desires and struggles of people. He was always overlooking the ugliness of passersby, to get a better view of some tower looming black against a background of scudding clouds.

Yet he was the only practising Christian I knew. I discovered accidentally, after I had known him a very long time, that, most weeks, half of the fifty dollars which was almost all his father's fortune that he was permitted to handle, went to an old chauffeur of theirs, who had gone half blind from drinking wood alcohol.

Nat thought it was very funny, to be the poverty-stricken heir to a million or two.

I said that fifty dollars a week was almost all he had. Besides that, the family doctor gave him a hundred dollars occasionally, adding the amount to his bill to Nat's father. The doctor suggested that method to Nat, as preferable to endangering his father's heart by making scenes about money. So, when Nat ached for an Anders Zorn etching or something of the sort, he got the money for it from the doctor.

Nat worked quite faithfully at the skyscraper-building business from nine to five, disposing of steel and masonry by the ton, while dreaming of skyscrapers all of glass and coloured tile, with terraces to make New York look like a taller version of the hanging gardens of Babylon.

He never asked what I did with my evenings when I was not with him. I suspected him of preferring not to know.

There was also Kenneth.

One day, lunching at the Algonquin with Lucia, I stared at the back of the head of the man at the next table, and wondered why it should remind me of Boston, and my half-forgotten cousin Roger who had gone to war and death with the Twenty-Sixth Division. The man at the next table had the most completely golden hair I ever saw. Roger's hair had been very dark.

Roger was the first man I ever loved, I suppose. He was at Harvard Law School when I was a freshman at Radcliffe. He wanted to be a lawyer en route to being a statesman; because, he said, America needed more statesmen and fewer politicians. I was sure he would be a statesman or anything he wanted, because he was so good-looking.

When he went to Plattsburg, I took a course in the Principles of Government, so that I could be a help to him when he became a statesman. He had said, gaily, that he would marry me after the war, if I would promise to grow up nicely for him while he was gone.

The Twenty-Sixth left from Framingham, and I drove up alone through a dripping August dawn, wearing my best rose-coloured organdie dress under a raincoat, to say good-bye to him.

I was sixteen.

He kissed me in front of a whole battalion. I had never been kissed before, and was so proud, and so worried lest the organdie dress would be completely rain-soaked (I had left the raincoat in the car, of course) and I would not look pretty. He kissed me again, as he went past with his company to the train, and after that I could not see any of the soldiers marching by because the rain splashed on my face and was mixed with tears.

He was killed at Château-Thierry. I had not thought of him in years; except for an instant, if, unexpectedly, I smelt the fragrance of tea-roses. That made me remember him because I was opening a box of tea-roses, sent me to wear to a Saturday night officers' dance at Ayer, when the telephone message came that he was dead.

"What are you remembering?" said Lucia, and I came back to the Algonquin and the eggs Benedict on my plate, and the view of the Round Table that had already seen its best days, and the golden-haired man who sat between me and it.

I told Lucia about Roger, and then we talked about Boston and Portland, Maine, where she was born, and agreed that one could not go back to either place to live, at least while one was young, although they both were pleasant cities. And Lucia said that New York's a jail to which, once committed, the sentence is for life; but that it is such a well-furnished jail, one does not mind much.

Intermittently, I continued to stare at the golden-haired man. When he stood up, I remembered him. Roger brought him for a week-end's swimming on Cape Cod, on one of Roger's last leaves. His name was Kenneth, and he lived in Springfield, Massachusetts. My aunt had known his step-mother and so she had liked him.

That week-end I had thought his golden hair was very wonderful with the sun shining on it, but thought also that dark hair the shade of Roger's was really more distinguished, and that Roger was handsomer on the whole, and I had wished this man would go away, so that Roger would have more time to talk to me.

At the next table, Kenneth glanced at me, and then he stood talking to someone for a minute.

I had heard things about him since the war. My aunt had said something—story of his marrying a dancer in vaudeville, and then going out to Hollywood to be an art director, much to the disgust of his family who wanted him to be a lawyer in his father's firm in Springfield. They had been quite formal about disowning him.

He turned to leave, and looked at me again. He was very tall indeed, and extraordinarily thin. He had forget-me-not blue eyes like a little boy's that looked strange in a face so dissipated. He would not remember me, of course.

But he did.

He came over, and said, "You used to be a child in a scarlet bathing suit; and besides, Roger carried half a dozen snapshots of you through the war." I had never known that.

"You're Kenneth," I said, and introduced him to Lucia. He sat down. . . .

Once he read me three sentences of Galsworthy's, from "The Forsyte Saga." They were, "All are under sentence of death: Jolyon, whose sentence was but a little more precise and pressing, had become so used to it that he thought habitually, like other people, of other things."

Kenneth had travelled a little too swiftly and too far from the tranquil sort of life to which he had been born. Had the Love of his Life been a serene-eyed New England debutante with a cool voice, as she might well have been, Kenneth would be practising law in Boston, with the proper connexions to do well at it, the next forty years, and satisfying his interest in art by the purchase of a Sargent, occasionally.

But the Love of his Life turned out to be a little Hungarian dancer, compounded of passion and beauty and viciousness in equal proportions. She fled to him from the beatings of her dancing partner, and Kenneth married her because she thought she was with child. In Paris, she left him for an Argentine; and came back, because she had pneumonia (and a more lasting illness, as it developed). She recovered from the pneumonia. They went to Algiers. She had a relapse, and coughed out her life against Kenneth's shoulder, protesting bitterly to the end against the necessity of dying—with no apologies for having sentenced him also to death.

Whatever she was, he had endowed her with all the illusions of a romantic young man. She was to him pure high romance. He said he would not have missed it. When he spoke of her, as one speaks of a dead child, gently, things young and ardent stirred behind his tired face, and I remembered how alive he had looked that summer week-end nearly ten years past.

He was to die, in two or three years, because to his illness was added the complication of an old lung trouble caused by gas in the Argonne. They told him that if he went West to live, that if he stopped drinking, the two or three years might be prolonged to six or seven.

"But I should be so bored and lonely," he said. And he stayed in New York.

He knew no women, except me. He spoke to me that day only because I had made him remember Roger, whom he had loved, too ("in another life," he said).

He asked me to dinner, because he had a sudden desire to talk to someone once more about Roger and cool New England summers, and the sedate streets of little Massachusetts towns.

But something in his unhappy face, that first night we dined, stirred me to talk, not of Roger, dim figure on the far shore of youth, but of Peter. I never spoke of Peter to any men I met, nowadays, usually.

Kenneth looked as if he would understand about Peter, and the men one kissed to cure one of the memory of Peter, and the little hope one cherished about Peter, in spite of judgment and the common sense and the well-meant advice of one's friends. He looked as if he understood that one did not love a man because he was worth loving, or because one felt worthy of his love in return, or for any reason that one's acquaintances would think was sound.

I did tell Kenneth about Peter, not in one evening, but over many evenings. He could not help me. I could not help him when he talked of that girl dancing in the moonlight of a garden in Algiers. But we were curiously happy together.

He had a little money; enough, he said, to last his lifetime, an inheritance from an uncle who seemed to have felt that Hungarian dancers are among men's inescapable destinies.

He spent it on theatres and the merrier nightclubs. He went to every new moving picture from Germany, and was fascinated by the technique of their photography. That was a single interest surviving from the four years he had dreamed, between the dancer's kisses and their consequences, of directing a moving picture that would be a really significant contribution to modern art.

So near the end of dealing with things significant or not, done with ambition and desire, he was sometimes completely gay.

Then we went to Harlem. Not the Harlem of the big Negro cabarets frequented by whites, cabarets notable principally for good orchestras, indifferent chow mein, a carefully sinister atmosphere, and a general air of everyone self-conscious except those who are so drunk they should go home, but the Harlem of the little unpretentious dance halls.

There, the very few white people who enter are ignored more or less, are given service no better and sometimes slightly worse than the service given negroes. Whites are not particularly wanted. But, if they are unobtrusive, they can travel a thousand miles south in latitude and as many years back in time, while a bass drummer remembers his ancestors who rubbed the tom-toms calling the tribes to war, and a girl dancer struts muscles no European woman's used since Rome was old.

There, Kenneth woke to animation over absinthe, and discoursed on Stravinsky's music or Mussolini's future, the style of Marcel Proust, or the eyes of his lost dancer, or the meaning of love and death.

He bought his absinthe from an Italian boat. For a long time, he would not let me drink it. Then one night, with him, across a theatre lobby I saw Peter and Judith, looking happy, looking absorbed in each other, not seeing me. Kenneth watched my face change.

That night, and on rare nights after, he gave me absinthe. At first, he was dubious as to whether I was a type that would re-act happily to it. I was.

Drinking it, I could summon to life and warmth days, incidents, moments out of other years when Peter loved me. I could go farther back, and summon the look and the voice and the laughter of Roger. Even live again the gay breathlessness of tobogganing, and the exciting feeling of skating along a shining river as the stars came out, while that child who I had been knew guiltily that she should have started home an hour before.

Sipping slowly, slowly, watching Kenneth's gold head droop above his glass, listening to saxophones and drums and shouting of dancers that seemed very far away, there was neither pain nor regret nor weariness. I sat wrapped in peace as in a Spanish shawl.

Kenneth asked me to promise not to drink absinthe except with him; a long time afterward he asked me never to drink absinthe at all, because I was not as nearly freed from life as he.

I never have, since.

Besides Nathaniel and Kenneth, there was Bill. On a night soon after I went to live with Lucia, a night when nothing was happening, Lucia said, "Let's summon Bill."

"What is it," I said, "a bootlegger?"

"It's a gentleman of the old school, darling, and a great help in small doses." She telephoned the Racquet club.

In ten minutes Bill appeared, with Scotch and soda and Racquet club cigarettes, and three medium grade club stories he told before he had his coat off.

When he looked at me, he said, "Lord, you remind me of a woman I knew in Honolulu in 1906. Damn nice woman too, she was." He sighed, gustily, sat down, and talked to us about how he made gin, where he bought Scotch, how far and how fast he had driven through Rhode Island the Sunday before, the condition of the stock market, and how pretty we both were.

He was bald and pink-cheeked as a baby, had a smile that must have been irresistible in 1906 and thereabouts, and manners as nice as his manicured hands.

After an hour, Lucia stifled a yawn. He got up, kissed us both matter-of-factly, thanked us for letting him call, and trotted off.

"It's all right, but I don't see exactly why—" I began.

"Oh, he's as comfortable occasionally, as an old rocking chair," said Lucia. "There's a man who never got lost among the nuances, for he wouldn't know a nuance if he saw it. His life's been good wine and good food and a good-sized quota of pretty women, and the code of a gentleman of his time, defined as paying his card debts, carrying his drinks well, and never letting his wife and his current mistress meet."

"What would he do if you began to talk to him about the single standard—or the single tax for that matter?"

"Pat me on the head, and say a girl as pretty as I shouldn't bother her head with nonsense. If I kept on, he'd go to sleep. Bill's grand and healthy and simple."

"What does he think about modern women?"

"Never heard of 'em. Thinks women are three sorts, the women one marries and keeps, the women who should have got married and kept, but gummed their chances somehow, and the women one likes to bed for a night and pays well."

"Is he ever interesting?"

"Yes, he was being up to date tonight to impress you, that's why he was so awful. Take him back thirty years, and get him to tell you how the young bloods rode to the Brevoort Sunday mornings, and tied their horses outside while they breakfasted on a magnum of champagne and a beefsteak apiece. On things like that he's good."

In time Bill told me that story. He told me also the story of the woman in Honolulu in 1906; also of a Chinese girl he bought in Shanghai, in the course of that trip to the Orient that summed up far horizons for him. "You know," he said of her, "she couldn't speak a word of English, yet I felt always she was the best-bred woman I'd ever met in my life."

Some men at sixty are the total of experiences had and philosophies considered. Bill was the total of recollected meals and wine, and of women kissed. Now, contentedly, he surveyed other people's youth.

Among complex and tiring and tired men, he was solace to the heart, asking no more of me or Lucia or any woman, than that she be pretty, and speak in a "lady's" voice.

Nathaniel, Kenneth and Bill were my three friends. Stepan was a man who hated me.

He was handsome, if you like the heavy-jowled, close-clipped black-moustached type, that is so stockily built it looks lumbering, but walks, disconcertingly, like a cat. He was a Russian, obviously—Russian Jew, perhaps. His last name was not revelatory, neither was he. I heard that he had a good deal of money—he was seen about at theatres and good restaurants and the more conglomerate parties.

I met him at one of those. He was quite drunk, but that was not apparent as he circulated about a room full of guests. He was introduced, danced with me in a manner too intimate, but difficult to protest against, and took me into an empty room adjoining, on the pretense of finding cigarettes.

There, with no preliminaries, he enclosed me in arms that felt strong as an ape's, kissed my shoulders, and said, "You were made to my measure. You're going home with me tonight."

I said, "How do you get asked to places anyway? I suppose you bribe the butler to let you in, and trust that the hostess will remember your face, without remembering that she saw it in some inferior speakeasy."

"Don't underrate me, stupidly," he said. "I am cosmopolitan. I have no illusions about you American women with your pretence of superiority. Like any women, you have one function. What do you make a month . . . in your silly job? Two hundred dollars? Three hundred dollars? I will pay you that. I can pay for my satisfactions. Get your wraps."

"I know now," I said, "what they mean by 'scratch a Slav and find a Tartar.'" And then I wished I had not said that, for it flicked something in him, and he regarded me with such hate in his eyes I was frightened.

A man and a girl came in looking for privacy. I walked past Stepan and said, softly, "If we meet in some theatre lobby, please don't bother to bow," and found Lucia.

Later that night he came to me for an instant, while I was waiting for the men who were taking us home. "You will come with me, I am very sure," he said, "but, perhaps not this week."

Thereafter, he watched me, on the occasional evenings when we met.

I thought him absurdly melodramatic; forgot him when he was not present; and tried to ignore him, when he was. Yet, he affected me for months with a sense of uneasiness.

Then, one night, a man named Henry decided to devote himself to me. I had met Henry a dozen times. People told unpleasant stories about him, to the effect that he had been kept by a succession of women approaching dowagerdom, while he was in process of writing a novel still unfinished. He was a pretty-faced, curly haired blond boy, with something rather tragic underlying the obvious weakness of his mouth and hands.

On the evening when I noticed him following me about like a helpless sort of pup in search of ownership, I was feeling very tired. I had an especially trying week at the office. Nat was on Long Island, and Kenneth had vanished on one of his occasional three-day absinthe binges.

Henry progressed to: "You are so warm and clean looking, and young. You can't imagine how it helps me to talk to you."

That was average inanity, yet he was the sort of young man most women would pity. That trait must have been very useful to him, on many occasions beside this.

"I'm staying alone in a friend's apartment for the week-end," he said. "If you would come there, for an hour—just let me talk to you, it would be kindness more than you could guess."

I was appallingly tired and thought he was innocuous, and went. At the door of a rather magnificent apartment on Madison Avenue, it occurred to me that Henry was curiously nervous. I wondered if he expected either a telephone call or a personal descent by some woman or other; decided that if it happened, at the worst it could only result in an amusing tale to tell Lucia, and took off my coat and hat.

I laid my gloves and purse on a desk, glanced down, and was confronted by a snapshot of this man Henry, and Stepan. I felt as if a little cold wind had blown, suddenly, across the back of my neck.

"Is this Stepan's apartment by any chance?"

"Yes, he's gone to Chicago for two or three days."

I wanted to go home, instantly. I thought then, that I was being silly. Ultimately I stayed with this man Henry. Because he had said: "If I could hold someone clean and strong and young in my arms, I believe it would make me feel clean and strong and young, again."

No one was any good for me. There arose, occasionally, the desire to be good for someone.

I woke, to find the bed empty beside me; thought Henry had gone to get himself a drink; and slept again. I woke to strong arms around me, a mouth kissing mine, a horrible hard voice saying, "It's just Stepan, don't be frightened, lie still." He put a heavy hand across my mouth.

I thought I should die of terror in the dark. I bit his hand, I struggled. In the end I lay still.

He brought me some brandy. I blinked at him in the light. He was wearing a red velvet robe with ermine on it, and I thought that he had bought it among the bloody loot of some old-regime Russian palace, and it made him more dreadful than he was.

"Now we can talk," he said. He talked. "You young women think you can be, in the American phrase 'hardboiled.' You don't know what 'hardboiled' means. I do."

I did not answer him.

He rubbed his finger across my cheek, and I knew that if I winced or screamed it would please him. So I did not wince or scream.

"You are very pretty," he said. "I like your type. It is near enough the type of superior Russian women, whom I used to watch, from far off, when I was a boy . . . and with whom of late years one can have dealings."

He sat in gloating reverie, and I wondered, if I *did* scream, whether the elevator boy would hear me. But Stepan probably paid the elevator boy well.

He spoke again. "A pretty woman, but a fool, to set herself up against the strength of a man who knows what he wants. I will tell you a story, so that you will know you are a fool, and we shall understand each other better."

I said nothing.

"In Russia, in the village where I was born, there was a pogrom, when I was six years old. My father drove my mother and myself to a hut in the forest, for safety, and went back to look after his affairs. He came, by night, to bring us food, until for three days it snowed, and he could not come."

He paused, and smiled at me with wet red lips.

I thought, "He is telling me this story to frighten me. He's inventing it. It's going to be frightening, but I must remember he's just inventing it."

"For three days we had no food, and it was silent in the forest, and I cried with hunger and fear. On the third evening we heard a scratching at the door—"

His eyes had a strange green light in them. He sat, heavy and savage and amused—

"My mother said, 'who is there?'

"There was no answer—but we heard something sigh.

"'It will be a messenger from your father, Stepan,' my mother said. But she got the revolver he had left with her.

"There was another scratching at the door. She opened it— and a black wolf leapt at her. I lay on the floor. My mother fired the revolver into his open jaws, and he dropped, writhed a moment, and was dead. She barricaded the door, while I lay screaming.

"'Never cry again, never scream, Stepan, my son,' she said. 'The wolf is only food from the forest.' She got a carving knife from the dresser, and cut the dead wolf's throat and said 'Drink, my son. His blood will make you strong.'"

He flung back his head, and laughed deep in his throat.

"I remember how warm and good the blood tasted. . . . Does the story amuse you—little girl who thinks she is 'hard-boiled?'" He ran his huge hand through my hair.

I thought, "He is insane, and I am going insane . . . his green eyes are like a wolf's," and I broke. I said; "Can't I go home now . . . please let me go home now, and I will come back, if you want me to . . . but let me go now . . ."

He laughed again, "So polite the independent little girl grows . . . but you can't go home quite yet . . . I will tell you more stories."

I covered my face from the sight of those shining eyes. He snarled and tore my hands away.

He slept, panting a little, panting like a wolf. Slowly, inch by inch, I moved away from him; got up, and found I could not stand. It was cold. I wrapped the velvet robe around me, sat down on a chair beside a table; remembered he had left brandy on the table, and groped for it. There was no sound in the room but that faint sound of panting. The brandy steadied me, and I dressed, thinking, "If I had a knife . . . to slide across his throat as he sleeps, so soundly—"

Dressed, I crept to the door in the dark, closed it as softly as possible, and rang for a sleepy, insolently grinning elevator boy.

It was only two blocks home. I wanted to walk; the cold air made me sane. On the first street-corner, a policeman was yawning.

"Isn't it late for a young lady like yourself to be walking about?" he said.

"I've been seeing a sick friend, officer . . . and I'm only walking two blocks home."

"I'll put you on your doorstep then, if you'd like," he said, and talked cheerfully, about the cold, and his wife who did not like his new hours of work. And I was grateful for the sound of his comfortable Irish voice.

Next morning, making up my face, I thought: "It was a nightmare. It couldn't have happened. I must have dreamed it." But there was a blue bruise on my throat where Stepan had gripped it, and my hands were shaking, still.

Lucia came in, looking very fresh. "Pat, my child, if I take an extra day off to go to Portland and see the family for the week-end, would you go as far as Boston with me? You haven't seen your aged parent for months, have you?"

"Let's take the five o'clock tonight," I said.

X

Between rows of syringa bushes that, notwithstanding weight of recent snow, and starkness of bare twigs, were faintly redolent of blossom scent from all the Springtimes of my childhood, a stone pathway led to the door.

I was less real to myself than the recollection of a plump little child who had run up that pathway; less real than the memory of a girl who had walked ever so sedately to conceal the fast beat of her heart, beside a man named Roger.

Father opened the door himself—yes, of course, it was eleven and the housekeeper and maid would be in bed. I kissed him, holding my breath to conceal the scent of my last cigarette in the cab.

"You are looking well, my dear."

"So are you, father. How do you feel?" He was looking appallingly fragile and tired. We talked for a little, courteously, about Lytton-Strachey's "Eminent Victorians," and of how modern biographies were written with the dramatic pace of first rate novels. Then he told me that Nellie, the housekeeper, had said she would sit up to see me, and I climbed the curved stairway. It had a balustrade that had been fun to slide down, before I was fifteen and grew dignified when I heard someone say I was going to be pretty.

I left father sitting, reading William de Morgan's "Alice-for-Short," which intrigued him because it was a novel written by a man nearly seventy—and he had always planned to write a novel when the profession of medicine left him leisure. Father was past seventy, now.

I remembered while washing and freshening myself before I went to see the housekeeper, hearing that I had been because of my sex the greatest disappointment of my father's life. And I considered, dispassionately, the fact that he was not as aware of me, as a person; as he was aware of either of the women who had been his wives, women whose portraits hung in the long living-room. I could not be as real to him as either of those women.

He grew up, finished medical college in a year when the man giving the Commencement address to the young doctors (address on "The Necessity of Keeping a Sense of Proportion"), illustrated it with the awful example of certain physicians who were going mad, contemporaneously, about things called "germs."

Two or three years after, father and other impecunious young doctors in Boston pooled their small funds to import from Philadelphia one of these "madmen" who believed in germs, and had him lecture to them.

A man lives through so much and no more. Father had lived through years when Darwin and Huxley were gods of his young generation; through a grand passion for a wife who died young; through a felicitous second marriage with my mother, who was to him, probably, like a delightful young daughter. He lived to be a successful physician. He lived to grow old and tired—too tired to keep up his practice, except among charity patients who would have had most difficulty in finding a successor to him. It was unreasonable to expect him to have interest or understanding left for a daughter who had grown up in a generation which discarded the ideal of "service to humanity" for the working philosophy of, "let us enjoy ourselves by the way for the end may prove disappointing."

He was polite to me; was sorry for the catastrophe of my marriage, sorry with the detachment of a man whose seventy crowded years have left him with no sense of importance in anything, save the problem, growing immediate, of—"and after death?" That was a problem that absorbed him the more intensely now, because his life had been too occupied to consider it.

In my childhood, a younger, more vigorous man that he had been, used to say to mother, that exquisitely dressed gay young figure that vanished before I was twelve, "Take the child to church—religion's a great solace to women, and they need it in this world."

That was a sentence vaguely remembered, with the sound of mother's deprecating laughter, the odour of Eau de Violette, and light that came through stained glass windows so beautifully it made up for the heaviness of the preacher's voice.

Nowadays, father urged me courteously to come home to live; and I knew that my presence in a household, slow-moving as his old footsteps, would be disturbing. I knew that he knew that, but felt it his duty to urge me. And I could not live at home anymore; for I was not, even yet, sufficiently tired, or sufficiently old to live solely by remembrance.

I knocked on the housekeeper's door.

Her name was Nellie. She came to us as cook thirty-eight years ago, the year father and mother were married. She came out of the Canadian backwoods, via three years in a German family, and four years in a French one, wherein she accumulated the technique of making complicated sauces and an impatience with alien (meaning non-Canadian-Irish) viewpoints.

They said she was a handsome rosy-cheeked slim girl, but she had weighed a hundred and eighty since I could remember. Four or five years after her advent, a housemaid, also named Nellie, was brought in to help her. The two became known as Big Nellie and Little Nellie. They never got on. Mother said that they would get used to each other, but they did not—not in thirty-four years.

Little Nellie decided to retire (as father had written me some months before) and go to live with a cousin in Braintree. Four days after her retirement, she began dropping in for tea with Big Nellie, though there had never been an hour's civility wasted between them. She confided that Braintree, a country town near Boston, was dull, and that the pastor of the church was not like "our own Father at home." After a week, Big Nellie spoke to my father.

"Doctor," she said, "I think you should ask the poor thing to come back. She looks very bad, and I'm sure she's not getting enough food." He did ask her back. She came forthwith; and, within six hours of her return, was quarrelling with Big Nellie as to whether or not she wiped dishes thoroughly.

Big Nellie's public vocabulary, the one she used to father and guests, was most proper. Her private speech, used occasionally with me, since I postdated her arrival in the family by so many years, was more picturesque.

I knocked on her door. After an instant of being touchingly pleased to see me, she summed up the departure and return of Little Nellie.

"You know," she said, "that devil I'm cursed with went away, but she came back."

She was in bed, a huge brass bed she begged from mother thirty years or so ago, when brass beds went out of fashion. She had commanded supper, just "something light and tasty," brought up to her by Little Nellie. In her large lap was a tray containing half a duckling, a pint or so of her own applesauce (made with cinnamon and lemon peel) a generous amount of oyster stuffing (tour de force of hers, stuffing duckling with oysters, and making the result delectable). On the tray, besides, were a quarter loaf of nut bread, two bottles of her home-brewed beer, and a large slice of apple pie.

She began by saying that her rheumatism was bad, and "the doctor" thought she should diet; but after all she had to keep her strength up to look after him. Then she told me I was thin, and should come home and have some proper cooking for a while. Afterwards, shyly, she asked about Peter, and "whether he'd got over his foolishness, and showed any signs of coming home to his own pretty wife, like a Christian."

And I was carried back to years in my 'teens when she had probed to find the facts behind any of my misdemeanours at school, that she might stand staunchly between me and the anger of a maiden aunt who was determined I should not be "spoilt."

She thought she might have distressed me about Peter; so she changed the subject. "You can have a cigarette in here, if you want to," she said. "I know smoking doesn't mean you're bad, it's just foolishness you picked up from that husband of yours." She put her empty supper tray aside.

I lighted a cigarette, and walked about and examined the photographs that were the only decorations on her walls. Photographs and daguerreotypes. One was her brother and her lover, who "took the shilling" together some fifty years ago when times were hard in Canada. They died in some forgotten British border war, in Her Majesty's colonies. The daguerreotype was a faded picture of two young men looking solemn and uncomfortable in old-fashioned regimentals.

Nellie stayed "faithful to a memory" apparently. Father used to tell me that, when she was young, he hoped she would marry because she was so mad about children. But, every "First Friday," through forty years she had gone to communion for the repose of her brother's and her "young man's" soul. She often told me when I was a child, that she was happy looking forward to seeing them again in Heaven.

She had, besides their picture, photographs of mother, and of the babies who died, and at least eight of me because I was the last child and was "her" baby.

I walked about the room, regarding the photographs; and stopped, suddenly, before one I had not seen.

It was a mother-and-child picture, of me, looking very overwhelmed, and of that baby Patrick. I had forgotten about that.

When he was two months old, Nellie persuaded me to have his picture taken. The proofs of those photographs came after he was dead. I had never looked at them. I did not want to.

Her old voice was gentle. "You don't mind my having that, do you, lamb? I found the proofs, and had them finished up; he was such a beautiful little boy."

I threw my cigarette away, and hunted for my voice. "It's all right," I said. "That was a pretty dress he had on."

"He'd be two years and two months old," she said.

He was a picture of a baby with fuzz on his head, and a smiling toothless mouth, and unbelievably little square hands. His enormous eyes, and the length of his lashes, showed in the photograph.

I looked at it. There had been a year when I looked at babies in carriages in the street—most of them were fat and healthy but none of them had eyelashes that really curled like his. I had stopped looking at them, long ago.

"Nellie," I said, "babies two years old can talk and walk, can't they. What do they talk about?"

"Indeed they can talk," she said. "I remember I taught you a poem out of a book, to tell your mother when she came back from a trip. You weren't much more than two. It was part of 'The Wreck of the Hesperus' and you didn't know what any of the words meant, but you said them off as nice—"

I stared at the photograph. Young woman who had been me—need not have been so bewildered, the baby was not a problem long. Baby in an absurd full frock—with his toes showing under it, if one looked for them carefully. His name had been Patrick. He used to feel warm to hold.

I had got over any grief for him.

And then, because I had got over losing him, and could not remember very well what he had been like, I went and sat on the edge of Nellie's wide bed, and I cried against the cleanness of her cotton nightgown.

She patted my head, with rough old hands. "There, child," she said. "You mustn't sorrow over him. He's a little angel in Heaven and I often think your mother must be glad to have him to keep her company. He might have grown to be a disappointment to you—and now he's safe with God. In His own time you'll see him again in Heaven. . . ."

The gentle voice was altogether cheerful. Heaven was to her as real a place as was to me the advertising department where I spent my days.

I grew calm, under the ineffably kind touch of her hands.

I wished that Heaven were real to me, and wondered why it was not, to me or any contemporaries I knew. The Victorians had been able to leave things to God—or the next generation. But the sound of guns and the knowledge of the immediacy of death and the desire to live as swiftly as possible, in the little time that youth and capacity to live swiftly, lasted—had got between that next generation and any whispering of angels. Perhaps that was it—it did not matter why, really—we had to get on without Heaven as best we could.

Nellie had found a way of changing the subject again.

"Patricia, I wish you could advise me. I've done something I think is very wicked."

She had never done anything more wicked in her life than beg a prescription from father, for wine to use in making *sauce madère*.

"What is it, Nellie?"

"I've taken out naturalization papers."

I did not see why that was wicked, but I thought it surprising; because father had tried for years to get her to become an American citizen, since she had lived in the United States most of her life, and had bought property here with her savings. She had always refused. "Forswear my allegiance to the crown my brother died for?" (that was just about her phrase) "never!"

"How did you happen to do that, Nellie?"

She reached for a box, that held money, a rosary, a prayer book, and snapshots of her nieces in Canada. She extracted after some search, a newspaper picture of Al Smith, coming out of a Cathedral after his daughter's wedding. She showed it to me.

"There," she said, "doesn't he look like a good pious father and husband? The doctor says he'll be running for President next year, and I got naturalized so I can vote for him! He looks like an honest Christian, and I thought I should."

She sighed a little. "I do feel dreadful though, because it's as if I were throwing my allegiance in the face of my brother and that friend of his, in the picture over there. It makes them seem away off somewhere. That I should live long enough to give up my allegiance to the crown—Do you know, Patricia, if it had been in the Old Queen's lifetime I could never have done it."

"Nellie, Nellie," I said, "the story should be captioned 'Queen Victoria's Death Gains Al Smith One Vote.'"

She did not understand me, but she smiled. "Now don't you be making fun of me, child; it was a great difficulty I had, deciding. You go to bed, and rest, and I'll send that Little Nellie up with your breakfast in the morning."

I had a week-end of conversation with father about Massachusetts politics, and about his difficulties with the real estate on which he depended for a competence, now that he was old, and retired from active practice; a week-end of too many and too elaborate meals thrust at me by Nellie, who produced in swift succession every dish I had been eager for when I was young.

Sunday afternoon (it was Nellie's "day out" and Father was resting), I sat by a window of the long livingroom, and read "Vanity Fair" (Thackeray's not Condé Nast's), and had tea; and watched the dark grow. From that window I could look down the slope of Milton Hill, and see the reflection of the sunset dim on the icy river.

Roger had taught me to skate on that river, a lifetime ago, or the day before yesterday; some indeterminate time past. I thought about the Heaven that Nellie was so sure about; and tried to imagine Roger going on to be a statesman of some other country beyond that winter sky outside. It seemed conceivable. Perhaps it would seem more real someday, if I grew to be very old.

Meanwhile there was New York and the advertising business.

While a cab waited at the door, and I said "good-bye" to father, who was not well enough to go to the station, and to a wet-eyed Nellie, who urged me to write him more often, I wished I did not have to leave him.

Families—strangers who knew one well when one was a child.

In the cab, I lighted a cigarette, and wondered if Lucia's train from Portland would connect with the five o'clock to New York.

XI

I was assistant advertising manager, within one step of having a secretary of my own. I had, already, a private office with a desk and a rug and a typewriter and a window and a telephone that rang twenty times an hour.

It was the fifth anniversary of my marriage. I was sad about that for ten minutes, in a cab on my way to work; and I might be sad about it again on my way home from work. In the interval I was very busy answering the telephone, and hoping I would be an advertising manager and have a secretary to answer it, soon.

It rang. The millinery buyer wanted extra space on the Friday page. I said I would let her know definitely later.

It rang. The typographer wanted to know where the cuts for the rotogravure page were, because the *Times* had called him to find out when it would be ready. I told him to telephone the engraver. I told someone in the department to telephone the engraver and rush him.

I began an ad on "We are seventy-four years young." It was a "prestige" ad. A "prestige" ad is a thing on which store owners spend money, sorrowfully, because other store owners spend money on "prestige" ads, sorrowfully.

The telephone rang. The lingerie buyer wanted extra space on the Friday page. I was inconclusive about whether or not she would get it. The telephone rang. A printer wanted to tell me that he could not match paper on the folder of which we needed five hundred extra copies for mailing by noon. I encouraged a young copy-writer who was ambitious to be an assistant advertising manager, to run around in a few circles over that.

The telephone rang. The shoe buyer wanted larger space on the Friday page.

I wrote a little more copy on "We expect to be young for seventy-four years more." (We were going to have an anniversary sale soon.)

The telephone rang. The *Times* announced irritably that our rotogravure copy was already three hours late, and they could not hold the space much longer. I was wistful with them. I sent someone to quarrel with the engraver about the missing cuts on that page. The engraver telephoned me, that there was so much etching on those cuts he could not deliver them to the typographer to "prove-up" and send to the *Times*, for three hours more. I was wistful-with-an-undertone-of-rage, with him.

I wrote a little more copy. The ambitious young copywriter came in to demand praise for having solved the printer's difficulty. I praised her. The telephone rang. The glove buyer wanted more space on the Friday page. I was pessimistic with him. The telephone rang. The advertising manager (in conference with the FIRM) told me to cut the Friday page to six columns, and cut every department's space proportionately. The telephone rang. Lucia wanted to know "how about lunch?" I said I was having a sandwich sent in.

The telephone rang. The jewelry buyer wanted more space on the Friday page. I sympathized with him. I told the layout man to cut everyone's space on the Friday page. I wrote a little more copy. The *Times* telephoned. I said, "Just this once . . . give us a little more time . . . it will never happen again." (I said that every other week.) The beauty shop telephoned to say I was ten minutes late for my shampoo appointment. I told them to cancel it.

The advertising manager telephoned to say they wanted the copy on "We have been young seventy-four years," upstairs in an hour. I turned it over to the ambitious young copy-writer who was thrilled. I knew I should have to rewrite her version, but that would be faster than doing it myself.

The telephone rang. The millinery buyer wanted to know definitely, how much extra space she was getting Friday. I sent the fashion copy-writer down to persuade her to run her ad on Sunday. The typographer telephoned to tell me he had not got the *Times* cuts yet. The printer telephoned to tell me the paper the ambitious copy-writer had sent him from our other printer's was the wrong stock.

The telephone rang. The shoe buyer wanted to know about extra space on Friday. I called in the layout man and told him to combine the spaces planned for millinery and shoes and give it all to shoes. The advertising manager's secretary came in to tell me the millinery buyer was outside in a rage, because she could not have more space on Friday. The advertising manager telephoned that he was going out to lunch, and would be back at four, and to settle everything myself until then. The telephone rang. The *Times* was irate with me. The millinery buyer came in, weeping.

The telephone rang.

"Hello, Pat?" I did not recognize the voice. Mine was cool. I did not like men to call me at the office. The telephone rang too much anyway.

"Yes, this is she."

"Many happy returns."

(For what? Oh yes, it was my wedding anniversary. But who knew that?)

The millinery buyer sniffed.

"Who is it, please?"

A chuckle at the other end of the telephone.

"It's Peter."

I said, "Good God, I mean how marvellous."

The millinery buyer sighed impatiently.

"Are you busy being the important young executive, Pat?"

"Yes—you talk."

The millinery buyer began to drum her fingers on the desk. Oh, to hell with her. I could feel myself getting ecstatically pink.

"Something reminded me of to you today, Pat. Will you go to dinner with me tonight?"

"Yes, what time?"

"Seven?"

"I'll be working late, Peter darling—could you meet me here? They'll let you in at the side door if you ask for me."

The millinery buyer walked out. Something would have to be done about her, swiftly, but not instantly.

"All right, I'll do that, Pat. Seven o'clock."

The desk and the window and the rug and the typewriter spun around gaily. I assumed a formal expression, and called the ambitious copy-writer. "Take care of things here, for ten minutes, will you please? I'm going down to the millinery department. And telephone the shoe buyer. Be very sweet to him and ask him to please come see me as soon as possible. Tell him I want to consult with him about giving him adequate representation on Sunday, instead of inadequate representation Friday." The child beamed. She would be an assistant advertising manager yet, God help her. At my office door I collided with the layout man coming in with the Friday layout.

"Listen, Milt," I said, "take out shoes and give all that space to millinery."

"God damn," he said, "I've made over this page four times. Millinery has to go at the *top*."

"There, there," I said walking past him.

I heard my telephone ring. The young copywriter called me back. "It's the *Times*, *very* mad about the rotogravure ad. What shall I tell them?"

"Give 'em my love and tell them all will be well ultimately."

I went to placate the millinery buyer.

That afternoon I charged myself a Chanel red velvet dress and a hat shaped like a Dutch cap, that matched it. I sent the young copy-writer for suède shoes (her feet were the same size as mine) and gloves and stockings and a handbag. (She had excellent "style sense"; she would have my job someday no doubt.) The child was very pleased, because she had to go to another store for the shoes and would have a chance to buy herself tea and cake en route. I bribed two girls in the beauty shop to stay after the store closed, to give me a facial and manicure and shampoo.

At five-thirty, I had a shower in the employees' "recreation room," and the shampoo, manicure and so on. At ten to seven, I was back in my silly private office, revising the child's copy on "perennial youth." (It had turned out much better than I had feared. The FIRM was fairly well pleased with it. I had only to incorporate such of their suggestions as they would remember having made.)

I finished the ad, and telephoned the typographer to send a boy for it. Then I went outside, into the long empty advertising department, and put on my hat, in front of a small cracked mirror. It was seven o'clock. I remembered that Pete was usually late. I lighted a cigarette, and went back to my own office, smoking it.

I was not particularly excited. If Peter wanted me back, and said so, something in me that was quite comfortably dead would resurrect and start singing paeans. If Peter did not want me back, and had just telephoned on an impulse, I would dine with him; and get up next morning and go on to breakfast and to work, and to whatever developed for the evening, just as on any other day. . . . If Peter wanted a divorce, I would go see Lucia's lawyer. . . . If he did not, I would let things drift, and go right on living in the hope of a miracle. Why not? There was nothing else I wanted as much as that miracle. Perhaps that proved I was a fool. I did not care if it did. I had been over all that ground with myself so many times before. . . . There was nothing to be excited about, now.

It was five minutes past seven. I went again into the department and brought back with me the last month's files of Pete's paper. I could talk to him at dinner about some of his recent stories. Up to this instant, I had not read one of Pete's stories since he had left me. I knew that it would trouble me to find phrases in them that I had heard him use. I knew, though, that he had covered the Doane electrocution. (Mrs. Doane was that young woman who killed her sleeping husband with such cool-blooded deliberateness that the jury convicted her notwithstanding her ingénue face.)

I turned over the files, looking for his signatures. There were a good many of them. Pete was turning out to be a good newspaperman. Once, I had clipped every story he wrote, in the days when his stories were three paragraphs buried on an inside page. Recollection of that fact distressed me; gave me the flat feeling of I-used-to-be-much-younger-than-I-am.

I began to read his account of the electrocution, and could not tell whether it were good or bad. Remembrances of Pete kept getting between me and the sense of it.

A phrase toward the end did catch at me, though. It made me laugh. He said, describing the entrance of Mrs. Doane into the electrocution chamber, "She looked so very small." I laughed, because Pete always said that, or something like it, about every woman who ever stirred him for a moment.

I heard the door at the end of the department outside open and close, softly.

And suddenly, I had the sense of something dreadful about to happen. I heard steps, the familiar tread of someone drunk, walking steadily by an effort, coming closer across that long dark room outside. The sound of footsteps stopped.

I looked up and smiled.

Peter leaned against my office door, smiling with his eyes. He was very drunk.

"'Lo, Pat, still working? Looked at a paper this morning and saw by the date it was our wedding anniversary. Brought you a present. You 'n' I haven't been on a long, hard-drinking evening in years, and it's damn well time we went on one. Brought you a quart of Scotch."

(While I remember the last six months that we lived together, I shall be afraid of Peter drunk. . . . Think fast, think fast. . . . Hell! that is just a line from "What Price Glory?")

"Thanks for the Scotch, Pete. Bet you had a pint yourself, where you bought it." (Think . . . where is Judith? Oh, manage him yourself; you have, before.)

"Pat, you're looking lovely. You look frightened though. Don't be frightened. I'm drunk, but I'll behave. I just thought it would be nice if we went on a party . . . sort of friendly."

"Grand idea, darling. There are two glasses in that lowest drawer. Let's have some Scotch, straight." (And if the night watchman comes in, and finds me drinking here, I shall lose my job. I do not care. I can get another.)

"Kiss me, Pat . . . because you married me once . . . and because you're lovely-looking . . . that doesn't make sense, does it? Kiss me because I'd like you to."

We kissed. I had kissed a good many people since Peter. And so, no doubt, had he, since me. That did not mean anything. Neither did this, perhaps. "Peter, pour me a drink while I put my coat on."

We had three drinks fast. "Down the hatch, Pat. I taught you to drink. Be a credit to me. Drink even, kid."

(This Scotch is raw. I shall get horribly drunk, if I do not eat soon. I must keep my head. Oh, what does it matter, whether I keep my head or not.)

He talked about Mrs. Doane, dying. "She looked so small, Pat, and so blonde. When they wheeled her past us, after, one of her little hands swung out from under the blanket that covered her, as if she wanted to clutch at one more man before they buried her. God, Patty, it was brutal."

(His friends have kept asking and asking him about that electrocution, and no doubt he has been posing as being hard-as-hell about it, and getting more and more jumpy. Pete is not hard at all, really. Or, at least, he was not hard, when I knew him first.)

"I brought you up right, Pat. We've killed a pint, even. Let's eat."

Some vague restaurant in the Forties. Highballs. He talked about newspapers, Judith, Hilda, London, myself and himself, and how poor we had been.

I did not care what he talked about. He disturbed me. No other man disturbed me much, or long. Pete made me think of things it was no use thinking of. Still, it was nicer to be dining with him, than with anyone else.

I had three highballs. (Thank Heaven for Scotch. Everything swims gorgeously, not real anymore. Vistas in hell, but a well-anaesthetized hell.)

"Remember, Pat, when you bought a jar of French mushrooms for my dinner on my birthday. They cost a dollar and a quarter, and you dropped the glass jar on the way home. . . ."

"And when you came in I was crying, Peter, and you insisted on knowing why. I was crying because I didn't have another dollar and a quarter, and nothing else in the house to eat but canned beans and a birthday cake."

"We always had canned beans for dinner the night before pay day, didn't we, Pat? But, that night we washed the glass out of the mushrooms and ate them. They tasted good."

(I suppose we make twelve thousand a year between us, nowadays, and we lived for two years on something like forty dollars a week.)

He talked about going to hell gaudily, in the tropical tradition, via some Central American Revolution. "When I have been drinking five or six more years, Patty, I'll get out. Buy me a sombrero with silver coins jangling, and a sash and two pistols, and end up merrily on mezcal. You're the only woman I'd ask to come, Patty. But you wouldn't. You haven't the courage to be really disreputable, even. You have a flower face though, damn you. Flower face and hands and a two-for-a-nickel soul."

He talked on.

Once I said to him, melodramatically, "I'll be sitting right beside you, in whatever gutter you choose to die. I plan so to live that we may be reunited in hell forever." (Applesauce! Live alone and die alone, like as not. And nonchalantly, too. He taught me to be nonchalant. I may be grateful someday.)

He is getting pretty profane—be obscene in a minute. Influence of Judith. Oh, that is damn unfair. He used to do it, in the Hilda era, to shock me. Try and shock me now. He is as unhappy as I am. Curious.

If I can start him off on poetry . . . try "Shropshire Lad" . . . that's sure-fire.

"Pete, how do the verses go that begin, 'When I was one-and-twenty—'"

"'When I was one-and-twenty—I heard a wise man say—give crowns and pounds and guineas, but not your heart away. . . .'"

There, he will go right straight through. How I am drunk!

"Pete, let's go taxi-riding."

"All right. Where's the check?"

"Taxi, go up the Drive to Grant's Tomb and back."

He put his arm around me. I clung to him. It did not mean anything, but it was friendly. The taxi was cold. . . . Animals huddled together for warmth.

"It's snowing, Pat."

"That's nice."

"Listen, Peter. Do you want to marry Judith?"

"Hell, no. I don't want to marry anybody. You cured me of that. How do you feel—very dizzy?"

"No, getting soberer now, the air's grand."

"You drink well, Pat, for a girl . . . I drink pretty well." He laughed. "It's a good thing that child of ours died, he'd have turned out just the prize drunk of his generation, probably."

"Go to hell will you, Peter."

"Sorry . . . I'll talk about something else. Do you honestly still give a damn about that baby?"

"And I still give a damn about you. . . . I'm that kind of fool. Will you light me a cigarette?" His face, when the match flared up, looked hard. It was not much like the face of a boy I had known. . . .

"I suppose you consider me 'the man who spoiled your life,' Patricia."

I thought about that. "Everyone spoils his own life, given time, probably."

"Well, what you did to mine, little girl, was plenty. You taught me a lot though."

"No doubt. Haven't you heard any good stories lately, Peter? You aren't being outstandingly entertaining."

"You are a very beautiful young woman, Patricia. Is that better? Do I get a kiss for it?"

"Why not?" It means nothing; but, for its duration, I may pretend it means whatever I wish.

"Pat, Judith's away. She has the apartment next to mine, you know. Would you like to come down and see my place?"

"Very much."

He had written me a note, when he rented the apartment; and I had sent a letter to the storage people, to permit him to take out such furniture as he chose.

He kissed me again. Well, he was my husband, and it was very respectable to kiss one's husband. I laughed and told him that. He thought it was amusing, too.

His apartment had etchings we had bought together in France, and curtains and a new rug that represented Judith's taste, not mine.

We talked about the etchings. I took off my hat and coat, and he said my red dress was a gorgeous shade. He brought me a glass of cognac. It was good, much better than the Scotch had been.

He said, "You never were, Pat. I invented you."

I said, "What does that mean?"

"That I shouldn't damn you as much as I do."

I said, "I suppose I am as responsible for the sort of person you are, nowadays, as you are responsible for the sort I am. I never thought of that before. There just are no villains in the piece."

"Patty growing philosophical. Don't. I'd rather you kissed me than talked."

"As you wish." He was right. It was better to kiss him than to try to talk to him. It might mean something to kiss him. How could I tell?

It was pleasant, too, to go to sleep with my arm slipped through his arm. It meant as much as anything else did, certainly.

His voice waked me. "Pat, do you plan to stay all night? It really isn't very comfortable, for two."

I wished that I had never married him, never kissed him, never met him, never heard of him. Also, that I had a revolver and could shoot him.

He said, "If you like, I'll dress and take you home."

I said, "Thank you, I should hate to put you to such great inconvenience." I took my clothes, and went into his bath to dress, and stopped to take a shower.

Standing under it, it occurred to me that I should write ads for plumbers, because I seemed to take a shower at every crisis of my life. Or a bath.

Dressed, I went back to get my coat. He was sitting up in bed, smoking.

"Peter, tell me, just to placate my curiosity, why do you do things like this to me? I don't believe you handle your other women by the same system . . . I hear too often that you are successful."

"Oh hell, must we go into that, Pat?"

"I'll simplify the question. Do you love me, or do you hate me?"

"That's no simplification, and you know it."

Both our voices were indifferent.

"Well, Patricia, if it will do you any good to know—before I kiss you I think of you as you used to be, and after I've kissed you I wonder how many men you've slept with by now."

"The other women you know aren't exactly without pasts."

"It doesn't matter about them. You are handicapped by dating back to the time when I was so full of ideals about the faith and constancy of women that I had no room for any sense about them.

"Yet, still, Patricia, you remain . . . a little different from the others. . . . You'd better get out. I must be tight, still, or I wouldn't talk so much."

I put on my coat and picked up my gloves. I felt that this really was the end for Peter and me. Yet I knew that I had felt that before, and it had not been so. I put on lipstick, carefully.

"Peter, will you kiss me 'good-bye,' as if it were the year 1922?" (Damn it, why did I ask that? He'll present me a cheque for it as ghastly sentimentality. It was . . . but I am pretty sure that this *is* all, for me and Peter, and I wanted to end with a friendly gesture.)

He put out his cigarette, and lighted another. "You are a young woman whom it's not easy to satisfy, Patricia."

I detested him. Well, I could make him wince, too. "Why, Peter, my lovers are always complaining that I am frigid."

"Get to hell out of here, will you," he said.

I went out, without turning at the door to look at him. It was snowing hard. I said to myself, "Here am I flung out into the traditional snowstorm, isn't that ridiculous?" And began to laugh. I came to Sixth Avenue, and must have turned south, instead of north, because I came to the door of "Dave's Blue Room" which was a large all-night restaurant. I had been there often for sandwiches, and I knew that it was further south than the street where Peter lived. When I got to the door, I felt that I could not walk any farther. I thought some black coffee might be good for me. So I went in.

Bill was sitting with three other men of his own age, eating scrambled eggs and bacon. I supposed that they had been play- ing bridge somewhere.

He got up when I came in. "Come here and sit down, Patricia. What *are* you doing wandering about alone at three o'clock?"

He introduced the three men. They regarded me a little strangely, and I knew that I probably looked awful. I had not noticed, in Pete's mirror.

Better make some explanation. In a minute, when I could manage my voice.

"I am *so* glad that you happened to be here, Bill. I felt unpleasantly conspicuous, coming in alone, but I *did* want some coffee. I've been having a rather distressing evening, as it happens."

Bill ordered coffee, and recommended the scrambled eggs. I let him order them, too.

"You see, I've been arranging with my husband, the details of our divorce, and that sort of thing is always trying, I suppose."

The four old men were immediately sympathetic, sufficiently so to change the subject. They said kind jovial things to the effect that it was delightful to have a young and pretty woman walk in upon their boredom.

I knew after a minute, and a sip of coffee, that I was not going to faint. But I could not do anything about the scrambled eggs. Bill took my hand, and held it hard, under the tablecloth. Well, he had known a great deal concerning women in his time.

Bill took me home, and left me at the door, after suggesting that we see three musical shows the next week.

I walked upstairs, thinking that Bill was a very nice man.

Outside her door, I decided to wake Lucia, and tell her that I was going to get a divorce. She would be sufficiently interested so that she would not mind being waked.

"Lucia, I'm going to get a divorce from Peter."

"I'm glad, Pat. I'll take you to my lawyer tomorrow at lunch time." I sat on her little couch. I was too tired to go upstairs.

"Talk if you want to, Pat."

"All right. I held on because I couldn't let go. Now I'm letting go because I can't hold on anymore."

"You'd better sleep down here, Pat. Sit in a chair, while I fix up the couch."

"What is it like to get a divorce, Lucia?"

"Like having a tooth out. A wrench, and you feel better the day afterward."

"My Great Romance threw me out into a snowstorm, Lucia, so I decided he'd had enough of me."

"Patricia, darling, pull yourself together. Think about tomorrow being another day; or if that's no good, remember that nothing ever in your whole life will hurt you very much, after this."

"Is that true, Lucia, or are you being kind to me?"

She laughed, and put a cushion behind my head, and told me to take off my shoes, because they were soaked through from walking in the snow.

"This is true, Pat. It is unlikely that any other man will 'desert' you . . . any man you want to hold. Because, when first you suspect he's ready to go, you'll pack his baggage and buy him a one-way ticket anywhere he likes, so fast that he'll leave reluctantly. You'll never hold on again. It's the holding on that hurts. Difference between sudden or long-prolonged dying. Do you think you could sleep now, if you went to bed? It's four o'clock."

"I think so."

Next morning Lucia brought me my breakfast in bed, and was very entertaining about the virtues of Sam. That noon we went to see her lawyer.

XII

Sam gave Lucia an Orthophonic Phonograph for a birthday present. Gershwin's "Rhapsody in Blue" was almost the only record we ever played on it. We turned that on, about once an hour when we were at home.

"The tune matches New York," Lucia said. "The New York we know. It has gaiety and colour and irrelevancy and futility and glamour as beautifully blended as the ingredients in crêpes suzette."

I said, "It makes me think of skyscrapers and Harlem and liners sailing and newsboys calling extras."

"It makes me think I'm twenty years old and on the way to owning the city," Lucia said. "Start it over again, will you?"

Seven in the morning.

Lucia was calling from downstairs. "Pat, did you have a good time last night? I brought some food in; come down and have grapefruit and eggs with me; I have something exciting to tell you."

"All right, but it's so very early, Lucia."

I got up. My mouth tasted of too many cigarettes the night before. But after a few minutes (and the calisthenics and a shower) I felt all silkily smooth and fresh. There was a gay February sunrise outside.

I put on a dull green jersey dress and beige stockings and brown alligator shoes; and put my money and makeup and a green handkerchief, in my alligator purse; and fitted a beige hat down over my right eye and up over my left. I tied a beige and green scarf around my throat, and got out fresh chamois gloves, and carried them downstairs with my green coat and my purse.

Lucia was looking very beautiful in the same sort of clothes. "Your grapefruit is over on the mantelpiece," she said. "There wasn't room for it on the coffee table. Eat it while I finish the eggs."

"Why did you get me up an hour early, darling?" I said.

"I woke up early and felt conversational."

"That isn't why," I yawned.

"All right, look at this," she said. She had on a gorgeous new emerald ring.

"Oh, Lord," I said. "You *are* going to marry Sam!"

We both laughed. "And I was expecting felicitations, Pat."

I felt somewhat apologetic, and said that Sam was a grand person.

"You mean," said Lucia, "that he is forty-five and not svelte by fifty pounds. I'm glad of both those facts. I'll be the Last Woman in his life, with any luck at all. If I were a prize fighter, I'd want to have a chance at the main bout of the evening, sometime—not spend my whole career getting knocked around in the preliminaries. Besides, did you ever hear of the fifteen gold pieces? It's a philosophy."

"Tell me."

"Every attractive woman has fifteen gold pieces to spend, one for each year between the time she is twenty and the time she is thirty-five. She may squander the first ten or twelve if she likes, but she damn well should invest the rest of them in something safe for her middle age."

"Who told you about the gold pieces?"

"The woman who washes my hair. She used to be a model for magazine covers."

"You could marry plenty of younger and gayer people than Sam," I said.

"I don't want to. I tell you I want to be the Last Woman in someone's life."

"Do you like listening to discourses on the new trade markets of the world, and how much oil they expect to find in China in the next ten years?"

Lucia beamed. "I love it. I am thirty years old, and I have spent five years listening to discourses on new books and new plays and new clothes . . . and wisecracks . . . I never want to hear another wisecrack until I die. I adore hearing about the glamorous future of South America, and how the rate of foreign exchange affects . . . I am not sure what it affects, yet, but I shall find out. . . ."

"Good Lord, Lucia, you expect to be happy."

"Of course, happy and settled and as protected as my grandmother. I plan to make Sam happy, too. I would marry him if he were relatively poor."

"How do you feel about sleeping with him?"

"I'd rather sleep with him the rest of my life, for the sake of having his kindness and good humour and honesty around; than put up with the selfishness and vanity and casual, heartbreaking infidelities of any 'attractive' man I know, for the sake of occasional golden moments in bed."

"Do you want to have children, Lucia?"

"I'll have them if he wants them. Some women who've been self-supporting do seem to acquire a permanent feeling that we should earn our way. Have some more coffee, Pat."

"Oh, dear," I said, "I shall miss you like hell, and I do feel you should marry someone you are crazy about."

"You can come visit me on Long Island every week-end, darling . . . and I did marry someone I was crazy about, once. . . . I'll find you a nice banker, younger and thinner than Sam, if you like."

"I don't like . . . I don't want to marry again."

"You'll feel differently, after your divorce goes through next month," said Lucia. "Run along to work. I have an appointment outside the office and I don't have to start yet."

I put on my coat. "Lucia, is Sam really what you want?"

"Not much like what I used to want. And much more than I ever expected to have, now."

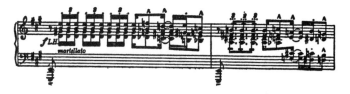

Half past eight.

My cab was held up in traffic. I lighted a cigarette. Everyone kept saying to me, nowadays, "You'll feel differently after your divorce," or "You'll feel better after your divorce." Just as they say, "You'll feel better after you have your tonsils out," or "after the baby is born," or "after you eat."

I wondered if doctors said to the very old, "You'll feel better after you're dead."

Committed to divorcing Peter, with the suit filed, and the lawyer's retaining fee paid, I knew no more whether I wanted to divorce Peter, than I know what sort of coat I should want for the Springtime of 1940.

If I had held on, for six months more, or six years, would Peter have come back, ultimately? And would I have wanted him, or not?

The traffic signals changed. I told the driver to hurry.

Eleven o'clock.

The ambitious young copy-writer, who would probably have my job someday, knocked on my office door.

"Things are quiet today, aren't they," she said.

"Yes, thank God."

"I wanted to ask you to luncheon," she said shyly. "You see—you are older than I, and married, and a successful business woman; and I wanted some advice."

Well, I was twenty-five, she was probably twenty-one. I myself had thought twenty-five a fairly advanced age, four years before I reached it.

"I am sorry I can't lunch with you. I have an appointment with the misses' dress buyer. But why don't you sit down now and tell me about it."

She stumbled about for a beginning.

"Your work is going very well these days. I have been meaning to tell you so," I said.

"It isn't that. Thanks awfully, though . . . I want to get married."

"How very nice. I can arrange for you to get a leave of absence whenever you want it," I said.

"No. The thing is—the man I'm thinking of marrying insists that I give up my job. He doesn't want his wife to work. He hasn't very much money, but he will make more all the time . . ." She stopped.

"Same old marriage versus career problem?"

"Yes."

"How old is this man?"

"Six months older than I. He's twenty-two."

"Do you care very much about him?"

Tears filled her large innocent blue eyes. "I love him *terribly*," she said.

I was surprised by my own enthusiasm. "My dear child, marry him—and if you have to get a job someday you'll get one. If there's anything I can do to help—I mean I can give you notes to people who will sell you your furniture wholesale—do tell me about it. . . . Tell me some more about your fiancé."

She talked and talked. She said she would be leaving in two weeks.

She had not needed my advice—she would have married him anyway, probably. She would have done well, in advertising.

Instead, she would eat canned beans the night before her husband's pay day, or something of the sort, I supposed. And I would have to teach someone her job.

I wondered if I meant the rhapsodies in which I finally told her that she must not let love go by, or words to that effect . . . and decided that I meant them, in some moods.

Five o'clock—telephone ringing.

"Pat, it's Nathaniel—I'm celebrating—have you a dinner date?"

"Yes, I have a dinner date, but I should like to celebrate, briefly."

"I'll meet you at the side-door at five-thirty."

End of the day. Hands-and-neck bathed. Face cold creamed, lipsticked, rouged, powdered.

Nat waiting at the side door.

"Hello, small girl. You're looking lovely. My aged father up and gave me a raise. He made two hundred thousand in the market last week, so he raised my salary from fifty to sixty dollars. Let's have cocktails."

Giacomo's bar. Clover Clubs cold as ice cream, and pink as fingernail salve.

"Nat, where have you been all these two days?"

"I forgot to tell you—so excited about my raise—I've been on a trip—longest trip I've taken since my brother died sudden— I've been to Philadelphia—papa's building a bank there."

He looked worn, and dismal.

"It's grand about the raise, Nat. . . . And some day, some day you'll go places . . . and see all the lovely pictures in the world."

"Yeah—some day when I'm fifty and my eyesight is so bad I can't see anything smaller than a twelve by twenty foot mural."

I felt sorry for him. He had spent seven years paying the cheque for the brother who had died gaily via the alcohol-chorine route. But everyone paid the cheque for everyone else, after all. And some day his father would leave him money to go places and see things.

"Darling . . . if you want me to cut my dinner date, I'll try to, and we can go riding about until you feel better."

"No, Pat. You are a dear, though. You're always cheerful. Did you have a hard day?"

"No. Advised a young woman to choose love before the advertising business—and marry a man who makes fifty dollars a week."

"You are a reckless girl. You should be married yourself, but not to anyone making less than fifty an hour. Your taste in clothes is too subtle."

"How percipient you grow, Nathaniel."

"Well, I like to look at pictures, and so I notice you."

Nathaniel's efforts at compliments always embarrassed me. They were so solemn.

I told him the story about the farmer's daughter who had a grandmother, and I told him that Lucia was really going to marry Sam, and I told him that he (Nathaniel) was an ever-so-bright hour in any young woman's day—and then I said I must go home to dress carefully, because I was dining with Horace.

Nathaniel was impressed. "America's greatest portrait painter.—Pat, will he do a picture of you? I'll borrow money from the doctor to pay for an option on it."

"I doubt if he paints me—he's not definitely through with his Spanish girl." And then I wished I had not had four Clover Clubs so fast, because Nathaniel hated to hear things like that about people whose work he admired.

"His sense of colour is marvellous, Patricia."

I talked to him about colour—of paintings, of skies, of buildings—and had him happily stirred about the possibility of making New York the most colourful city in the world by the time I left him to go home to a sombre silent dinner with his father.

I met Lucia coming downstairs as I was going up. She was wearing a white and gold dress, and a wrap with a white fox scarf. "Lucia you look heavenly. Is all this in honour of your affianced?"

"Yes, darling, in honour of him and his brother from Chicago, and dinner at the Ritz."

"I never knew Sam had a brother from Chicago."

"The brother has four children dear, and a healthy wife. No good to you, in the soon-approaching days of your freedom."

"Not having any, I told you."

"We'll see about that, Pat. Speaking of men you are not going to marry, has Kenneth got keys to your apartment?"

"Yes, I forgot to tell you. I gave him keys some time ago; so that he could sit about and wait to take me to Harlem, if he turned up late."

"Well, he's been poking his once beautiful head in and out of my door for an hour, demanding you. He is very drunk. Poor Ken, he looks like the wandering Jew gone Nordic. He left some time ago, though. I heard him falling downstairs. Were you dining with him?"

"No, dining with Horace."

"What are you doing, trying out all the self-advertised Great Lovers in New York, one after the other . . . or do you want a sketch of yourself? He never makes them until afterward. Says it's not anatomically possible . . . I suppose it's all right for you to amuse yourself though—and you have been cutting down on adventures recently, haven't you?"

She sat herself in the niche by the landing, where once, I suppose, before the house got remodelled, a saint or a bust of a statesman or perhaps even a virgin had sat.

"Pat I have a minute to talk. Are you very unhappy about divorcing Peter?"

"I don't think about it. I *have* cut down on what you call adventures—they are no good to me. At first, I thought I could take them as easiest way to forgetting Peter, but that doesn't happen. I'm not designed for a just-for-the-fun-of-it woman, perhaps."

"Never mind—I couldn't make that grade, either. I'll find you a husband. I'll have lots of spare time after I'm married. Meanwhile have fun with the Great Lovers."

"Horace is no Great Lover so far as I know—and he's ages old, Lucia."

But Lucia stood up, and started downstairs. Her voice floated back with her perfume. "Great Lovers—men who've 'known a hundred women,' and boast of it—they remind me of the man who wanted to be a musician and so took one lesson on each instrument in the orchestra."

I called downstairs.

"What happened to him, Lucia?"

She put her face against the balustrade below. "He couldn't play a tune on any of them in the end, Pat."

Eight in the evening.

Horace was almost as broad as he was long, physically. I met him at his studio, as he had asked. I had wanted to see the things he was working on; because they would be worth seeing, and because Nathaniel would love hearing about them.

Horace had half a shaker full of Martinis before I turned up. He kissed my hand, poured me a Martini in a tumbler, and began to talk. He admired my frock—I had worn my sapphire-blue taffeta, because it was a "picture" dress, and, while I did not plan to go to any great lengths to get Horace to paint me, still one never knew.

If he wanted to, the picture would hang in some gallery where Pete could go to see it, when he was old, and it would help him to remember how I had looked. (I could not "sell" myself that pretty idea, with any conviction. I was sure that Pete would remember me, if at all, as just one among the errors of his youth.)

Horace was entertaining. He had kissed and painted his way from Soho to Manila, and his reminiscences of the pictures and ladies he had made in his day were almost as good as the pictures, and probably much better than the ladies.

He told me a story about a woman who had sent for him (from St. Louis to Honolulu) to be the father of her son. The child turned out to be a daughter, though—and besides, the date of its birth was only six months after Horace reached Honolulu. The rest of the story was romantic though.

When he went from that to a monologue about the amount of savoir faire young women could gain from association with older men-of-the-world, I sighed and recognized that he thought of me as a bedroom, not gallery, adornment. Pete would have to get along with a photograph, if he had kept one.

My retreat, for the moment, was easy. It always is, with men who are really beauty-mad; if a woman will be humble enough to realize that they rate her as somewhat less exciting than a sunset, and nothing really to be compared with a good piece of pottery.

Horace had, in his studio, the most exquisite maple lowboy I had ever seen. Its proportions were heavenly, and its patina was that cross between velvet softness and satin sheen that is never actually achieved in fabric.

I began to admire the lowboy. I was as intelligent about it as possible. Soon, Horace was regarding it with love and absorption, and patting its surface with the regard he had bestowed ten minutes earlier upon my shoulders.

When his concentration upon the lowboy was complete, I said that I was painfully hungry. The man had good manners. He took me to eat, stopping to swear at the unfinished portrait of his Spanish girl as we went out.

One in the morning.

I had had a lovely time so far. Horace was a genius, and I had met so few of them among the semi-celebrities. He had talked five hours straight, with time out for consuming a Gargantuan dinner, and endless drinks—about painting and women, and art and women, and life and women designed for the solace of men.

I was trying to remember everything he had said about painting, for Nat, but I could scarcely keep my head up. He was thirty years older than I, but had four times as much energy.

Nevertheless, I felt that just a little more to eat should certainly put him to sleep for the night, so I dragged him to Childs, on the way home, saying that I ached for some of Childs' coffee. If Horace reached my apartment still able to manage himself, I could not depend on Lucia for assistance. She might not turn up until dawn. So I tried ordering an omelet and buttercakes and pumpkin pie for him. He enclosed them all, with no apparent difficulty.

Ten people bowed to me, but not one came over to join us. And Horace had discovered that I was utterly voluptuous. (No one else had *ever* said that, and I doubted his judgment. I weighed only a hundred and five pounds now, and that is not voluptuous by most standards.)

I looked about, but there was no maple lowboy in Childs for Horace to examine instead of examining me. So I let him call a

cab, suggested a taxi-ride, discovered within five minutes that I
might as well let him take me home, and said, "Let's go home."

Two in the morning.

As I waited, while Horace paid the cab, the night air blew
clean and cold and fresh against my face, and a winter moon
that looked very remote and detached, shone down on the tall
dark buildings, and the quiet grey street, and on Horace and
the taxi-man and me. And I had, for an instant, that feeling
that New York was an altogether beautiful place to live, no
matter what happened to me living in it—a comforting feeling
that had come to me sometimes, of late, when I stopped looking
to people for comfort.

Horace trotted energetically up the stairs behind me. I felt
worse, every step I climbed I did not want him to stay, could
not think of any good reason I should ask him to go, and un-
locked my door.

I sat in a small chair, so that Horace would have to sit on
the couch, opposite; lighted a cigarette, and wished I could go
somewhere to sleep for a month.

Horace sat down heavily.

I waited for him to begin whatever he planned to begin.

"Young woman," he said. (Probably he was near enough
drunk now so that he did not remember my name.) "When I
met you, I thought you were intelligent, because your head is
the right shape."

I grinned. He was going to be original—well I might have
trusted him for that.

"You are not intelligent, though, else you would set higher
value than you seem to set on the admiration of a man like
myself, who is a connoisseur of women. Perhaps you prefer
callow and pretty boys—"

(Oh, he minded being old, did he? Now I could not send him home. He would feel so—done. It was not fair for an assistant advertising manager to make a great painter feel—finished.)

"I'm extremely flattered that you should have devoted an evening to me, Horace."

"Don't say words that mean nothing, young woman. Listen to me, please. I have something to say that may interest you."

He was a bit arbitrary, but if he felt like it, I did not mind. I was too tired. His huge head was framed against the whiteness of the panelled door behind the couch. I wondered if he had ever done a portrait of himself—that grizzled head was marvellous. I wished that door led somewhere I could go, instead of leading just to the bath. I could not spend the night in the tub.

"Young woman," (I thought that if he called me that again I would fling a cushion at him. There was no reason why I should let people sit in my own apartment and say "young woman" to me, whether they could paint beautiful portraits or not.)

He went on. "You have a body that is delightful, whatever you may lack in intelligence. And since you seem to set no value on me, personally, I will give you the maple lowboy you had taste enough to admire, if you will let me stay here tonight."

That means the Spanish girl is not coming back to have her picture finished, and the man is offering me the successorship. He can stay, unless I think of a method of getting him out that is more subtle than saying, "You are rather a disgusting old man; please go." Because he is not disgusting, he is just candid. Wants what he wants and will pay a price for it.

Oh, I suppose I shall have to let him stay, but he can keep his maple lowboy. The only thing I have left to cherish is my amateur standing. (Did that door behind him move? I'm so tired I am seeing things. Of course it did not.)

Horace had not finished talking, quite. "Permit me to light another cigarette for you, and take five minutes to consider the lowboy. There is not another like it in America."

He lighted my cigarette. Then he took out his watch.

"It is twenty minutes past two. I shall ask for your answer at twenty-five past." He stood staring at the watch.

I laughed. He ignored me. I looked at my own watch. I knew I should say something to stop this absurdity, but I could not talk, I could only laugh.

"It is two twenty-five," he said. "Do you want five minutes more to make up your mind?"

There was a sound of glass smashing, in the bathroom. Horace turned. The bathroom door opened a little. A voice said, "For God's sake, Pat, take him or leave him, *now,* I can't live five more minutes without a drink."

"Kenneth!" I said. The bathroom door opened wide. Kenneth staggered out and leant against it. His opera hat was on one side of his head—his tail coat was crumpled. He stood, tall and golden-haired and dreadfully thin, grinning down at us both, looking like a cartoon of a Young-Man-About-Town.

Behind him, I could see a bottle smashed in pieces on the floor.

Horace had got his breath back. He roared—at me. "Who the hell is this?" He lost his breath again, after the roar.

Kenneth answered.

"Sir," he said in the more severe of his Harvard voices, "If you are inquiring about me—I am the young woman's—manager. I agree with you that she is charming, but she has the annoying habit of going out to get business for herself occasionally, in spite of our arrangements. Now—if you will discuss things with me. . . . You were saying something about a lowboy. We don't usually take furniture—but if it is accessible for evaluation—"

Horace got his breath back, permanently, as far as I was ever to know. He got his breath and his hat and coat and gloves and stick. He began roaring.

He roared all the short Anglo-Saxon words I had ever heard, and a few others whose meaning I gathered by his tone. He walked out. His roars could be heard receding, as he stamped downstairs.

I wiggled about in my chair. "Kenneth, you idiot," I said. "Did you ever hear so many synonyms for slut as that man used?"

But Kenneth did not think it was funny.

"Damn you, Patricia," he said, "You would have let him stay—that horrible old man. 'Let me stay and I'll give you a lowboy.' Christ—let *me* stay and I'll give you—"

"Kenneth, stop please—I've had a damnable hour and I can't stand any more. You had better go away."

And then that tragic young man, whose gaiety was perennial as the blueness of his eyes, began to sob, and sob, and sob. He sat on the floor, and took a ruffle of my blue frock in his hands, and shook with sobs.

I patted his hair a little. I could not think of anything else to do for him. I said, "Please stop, Kenneth, dear. I am not important enough for anyone to cry about."

He grew steady, after a little while, but he still kept twisting the blue ruffle in his hands.

"Patricia," he said very softly, "so little and so nice—too nice to get mauled by all the fools in New York."

"Please don't, Kenneth," I said.

"You stir me too," he said, "didn't you know? I am no different than the others."

"No, I didn't know."

"Damn them," he said, "and I can't ever touch you."

"Kenneth, my dear, my dear."

"Patricia, if I never touched you, would you marry me and go away somewhere? I have enough money left so that you could live a year. I shan't live a year. We could go to California, and you could swim in the Pacific."

It sounded pleasant.

"But what's the use Kenneth? Isn't your favourite aphorism that there's no sense in going other places if you have to take yourself along? Thank you, though."

We sat quiet for a little while.

He looked up and smiled, and I knew he was all right again.

"Car's around the corner, Pat," he said. "Want to put on something warm and go for a drive in the fresh air?"

"Let's," I said.

"Bring a volume of Swinburne along, like a nice girl," he said. "I'll make you read aloud to me at breakfast, if we stay out that long."

Kenneth liked me to read poetry to him—quite old-fashioned, romantic things. Perhaps they were things that had pleased him when he was in school, or perhaps his Hungarian dancer had liked them. I never asked.

Seven in the morning.

The sun was rising over the East river. We sat, Kenneth in his crumpled evening clothes, and I in my blue frock that just would not ever look fresh again, under an old fur coat, in his car at the foot of Beekman Place, by the river. We were quite warm and happy and sleepy. I was reading aloud to him from "The Garden of Proserpine."

From too much love of living—
  From hope and fear set free
    We thank with brief thanksgiving
Whatever Gods there be
    That no life lives forever—

XIII

"Taxi!"

"Go to the courthouse on Center Street, one block above City Hall."

"There are lots of courthouses there, ma'am, which one?"

"I don't know—never was there—drive down and we'll see.

"This might be it, driver; stop and I'll ask that policeman.

"Officer, is this the courthouse where they hear divorces?"

"No, lady, this is worse; this is the Tombs prison. Go on another block."

The taxi-driver went on another block. When I got out, he said, "I wish you good luck, ma'am," so I gave him fifty cents for himself instead of twenty-five.

The courthouse was a handsome new clean building. I climbed the wide steps to the entrance slowly, feeling surprised more than anything else. I had not ever planned to get to a divorce court; I did not want to be a divorcée; yet, there I was on my way to meet my lawyer and my maid who was witness for me, outside a room numbered 238.

The entrance hall of the courthouse was a great circular space. The marble floor had brass animals set in it. Probably they were signs of the zodiac. I remembered that the hall of the Boston

Public Library had brass animals set in it, too; and that I had liked to walk on the animals when I was a child, because they felt so cool and slippery under my feet.

This courthouse hall was filled with men who wore dark clothes and secretive expressions, and smelt of cigar smoke.

My lawyer, who had been Lucia's lawyer, had told me to wear black. Mr. Charles Marshall Henry was the sort who would think of things like that. It was my own idea though, to borrow the ensemble; so that I should not have to appear in it again. I had been sure that I would have a miserable time, anywhere I ever went, in the clothes in which I became a divorcée.

I borrowed it from Helena, who had just brought it back from Paris. Helena was going to take over Lucia's apartment, when Lucia married. Helena painted; did gorgeous fashion drawings, like a realist—and played around in her spare time making masks. She sneered at those of us who got involved with men; made three times as much money as Lucia and I; was always disposed to lend it to friends that were hard up; and had a passion for reading Greek dramatists in the original. She had a plain face, a supple figure (she played tennis with cool fury) and had an absolutely perfect taste in clothes.

The coat and frock and hat she lent me, made me look like a young widow discreetly inviting a future.

I tried to keep thinking of Helena, and whether Helena were really happy, and what Helena valued most in life, as I climbed the stairs to Room 238, so that I should not think of Room 238.

My maid was waiting outside the court-room door. She was a calm, competent taciturn coloured person. When I asked her to be a witness, after my lawyer said I must choose people who had known both Peter and me during our marriage, she told me, matter-of-factly, that she had started life as personal maid to an actress, and had been a witness in three divorce cases already.

"Good-morning, Nora. Do you remember everything that you have to say?"

"Yes, ma'am, I do."

"Let's wait for Mr. Henry inside, Nora."

I felt glad that she was calm, because my other witness had gone to Chile for the Guggenheims, leaving nothing but depositions behind him.

I was quite calm, myself. Lucia had been afraid that I would be disturbed, and had wanted to come with me; but a conference with one of her clients prevented. I thought about Lucia for a while.

"Mis' Patricia, is this what they call the non-combated court?"

"I don't think that's *exactly* the name for it, Nora. It is the court for non-contested divorce cases."

"I knew it was something like that. Here's Mr. Henry, ma'am."

"Good-morning, Mr. Henry. No, I'm not at all nervous, thank you."

"Court will open immediately. Your case should not take more than twenty minutes."

Someone, long before had said to me something like "your case should not take more than twenty minutes." Long ago—in a taxi—Oh, yes, that almost-forgotten doctor of mine.

(What did I have to think of that for? I have stopped being detached. Something begins to ache horribly, in my heart. I had better look around and not think.)

Nora is sitting up very straight, looking pleased and important. The room is full of little groups, each composed of one lawyer, one woman about-to-be-a-divorcée, one or two witnesses. They are just like the little groups arriving in the waiting room of a maternity hospital. One doctor, one about-to-become-a-mother, one anxious husband. But there are no anxious husbands here. That's a help.

The about-to-become-divorcées have the same tense expression that the about-to-become-mothers had. . . . Well, I lived through that, too.

It is so *silly* to mind. Just an incident in the career of a Modern Woman. What the hell!

But I never expected it to happen to me. Neither had any of the other females assembled, perhaps. I inspected them.

One was all dressed up in purple silk and purple rouge and hennaed hair. The corners of her purple mouth kept twitching. Another looked seventy years old, and wore a beaded bonnet and black silk gloves. I wondered why divorce came to her so late. I thought she might well have put up with matrimony for the little time remaining.

One woman wore a woollen shawl and another wore sables and Le Début perfume.

"The referee is coming in; one stands up," Mr. Henry said. The referee was a very old man with an altogether gentle face. I thought that he must have forgotten passion and anguish and ecstasy, twenty years before I was born.

Mr. Henry explained that the clerk was reading the calendar, and that mine was the second case.

I thought, "What do I want this for? Why don't I walk out, here and now? What would Peter say if I walked out and telephoned him that this was a preposterous thing to happen to the nice young people he and I had been? . . . Peter wouldn't say anything, probably. He'd just hang up the receiver."

I thought: "Probably *all* these cases are collusive. I must remember when I am asked that question, to say 'Yes' because it reads, 'Was this adultery committed *without* your knowledge and consent?'"

I remembered hearing someone say at a party, that the only grounds for divorce in New York state were adultery or perjury—usually perjury. I wished that perjury might have been one of a few things I had missed.

They were hearing the first case. I tried not to listen. I looked about, and remembered that divorce courts were supposed to be funny, so I tried to be amused.

The room was clean and bare and furnished in walnut. Bleak sunlight drifted in . . . but March sunlight was usually bleak, and I had lived long enough to get over being sentimental. At least I should have got over it.

(I loved you so, Peter. Well, I do not love anyone else *so*.)

The witness testifying said, "and a woman was in bed, and she covered herself up with the blanket."

(*Do not listen to it.* Where else should she be? Every co-respondent's place is in a bed.)

I tried to pull myself together. I watched the sunlight slipping across all the ugly faces. I thought how Cabell would describe that court-room. . . . Something like:

"to this dreariness comes high romance, and that gay challenge that once, when she was twenty, she flung at time and habit and poverty and all the other women who would love his handsome face and cool voice, in the end comes just to this."

(Ours was to be forever and ever, on those summer evenings when we sat on a roof and never saw surrounding smokestacks because we were looking at the moon; and did not mind the street noises, because, in an apartment across it, a man was playing Chopin. . . . But that was ages ago. . . . Five years. . . . His fault, my fault, it does not matter now. We were both too young, we were both spoilt. It does not matter now. All there is left of the power we had to stir each other, is a wonderful ability to make each other wince.)

I felt that I never wanted to see Peter again. If I never saw him, perhaps, when I was old, I would only remember things like the Chopin music.

On the witness stand, someone stopped talking.

Mr. Henry said: "Remember to speak slowly, so that it will be easy for the referee to hear." The skirts of Helena's black ensemble swished as I walked up to the witness chair.

"Do you solemnly swear . . . the whole truth . . . and nothing but the truth?"

"Yes." (First lie. My divorce is costing me four hundred dollars and four lies. I am glad that my voice is steady.)

"When were you married to the defendant, Peter—"

"December 27, 1921."

(We eloped . . . our families thought we were too young, but they sent us wedding presents afterward. We were married on Peter's pay day so that we had money to celebrate. He made thirty-five dollars a week on the "Telegram." We went to dinner at Mouquin's. There is no Mouquin's anymore.)

"Where were you married?"

"At the Municipal Building in this city."

(The deputy city clerk stood on a red dais between two palms and said, "God bless you both, *NEXT*" all in one breath. I carried pink roses the cleaning woman in Pete's apartment gave me. She pressed a white organdie dress that had got mussed in my suitcase on the way from Boston, so that I could wear it to be married. I wonder what happened to that woman. She used to smoke cigarettes while she scrubbed floors.)

"Adultery, on January 12, 1927?"

"Yes." (Second lie. Not with that poor little unwashed wench. She was probably so glad to get the fifty dollars Pete paid her . . . and she looked so horribly scared.)

"Without your knowledge and consent?"

"Yes." (Third lie. Peter and I spent two hours arranging it the week before. It would not have taken so long, if we had not quarrelled most of the time.)

"And you have not voluntarily cohabited with the defendant since that date?" (How dirty the formal phrasing sounds . . . Peter came, very drunk, to see me later that same night. He said I had looked so disturbed. Poor darling, he looked disturbed himself. That was the only time in years that we have been friendly. . . . That is as much of a happy ending as we shall ever have.)

"Asking no alimony?" (He does not have to pay for refusing to live with me.)

(Mr. Henry is bowing me off the stand. Now it is Nora's turn. I do not have to listen. It takes so much longer than getting married. Damn it, I am going to cry. That will probably please Mr. Henry . . . it looks so authentic. I shall weep five minutes for Peter, because I loved him all of five years.)

Nora: "He had on a blue silk dressing gown."

(I bought it for him just before he left me, when I was trying to prove to him that I could be nicer to him than Hilda. It was a good-looking dressing gown, and undoubtedly it has been much admired. Nora looks as cheerful as can be. This is probably the big day of her year. She will tell all her Harlem friends about it. They all will hear that *this* "lady" wept. I wonder how her others took it.)

Mr. Henry read Dudley's deposition. I hoped that Dudley was having a nice time in Chile. I thought that I would probably never see him again. I remembered Peter and Dudley and a girl of Dudley's and myself, having breakfast-and-bridge parties on rainy Sundays. We played excited bridge for a tenth of a cent a point, and I felt adult because we had cocktails from breakfast time on.

I thought that it had been very nice of Dudley to be a witness for me.

"I am quite all right, thank you, Nora. It was just for a minute."

Mr. Henry swore to something or other.

Then it was all over.

Mr. Henry said: "I am so sorry that you were distressed. The interlocutory degree will be mailed to you, shortly."

I wondered if I were supposed to frame it.

He said, "You will get your final decree in ninety days. Then you will be just as if you had never married."

"Yes, Mr. Henry." (Enclose with that decree a complete assortment of young illusions, a beatific confidence, an entertaining lack of common sense, and an innocent expression—and I shall be—just as if I had never married.)

I said "Good-bye" to Nora.

I walked down the stairs, and across the round hall and decided I had time to go home and take off Helena's black ensemble before I went to my office.

"Taxi—drive uptown."

XIV

I bought a rose chiffon frock and a wide-brimmed transparent hat to wear to Lucia's wedding, and went home to take her to dinner.

Lucia was sitting on the floor, surrounded by strapped trunks and bags, and a half-packed suitcase, reading. She looked up and smiled. "I have found a motto for you, Pat—*the* perfect motto for any young divorcée. Listen—

'Live thou whom life shall cure
Almost of Memory . . .'"

"Who wrote it?"

"Kipling."

"I don't think it is a perfect motto—the 'almost' ruins it—and why read poetry the day before your wedding anyway?"

"The 'almost' makes it accurate . . . Arch sent me this (it's 'The Years Between') when he went to France. We were engaged then. I believe he thought he was going to die fast and heroically—and he marked those two lines in the book, to be consolation to me if he did die. Do you want the book—I am not taking it along to Sam's house."

"Thank you. . . . Where do you want to dine?"

"At the Waldorf—if you hadn't planned anywhere else. We can get a table by the Fifth Avenue windows, and watch people go past. Sam wants to bring over some relatives at ten tonight, and I said he could, Pat, do you mind? I had planned to save this whole evening for you."

"That's all right. Kenneth may be turning up later anyway—he is dining with that mysterious friend of his on the *Times*—the man he doesn't want me to meet—Noel Something-or-Other. You must have heard Ken talk about him."

"Yes." She got up and began to comb her hair.

"I'm going upstairs to dress, Lucia."

"No, wait a minute. When is Ken going to California?"

"The first of next week."

"He won't be back, Pat, you know."

"He knows that himself. But when the weather began to grow warm he developed a sudden ache to see the Pacific again before he died. I shall miss him. I shall have a dismal summer, without you, or him."

"I'll send you a postcard from every fjord in Norway, Pat. . . . Tell me something—were you ever in the least in love with Ken?"

"No, really."

"That's good—I wondered, because you have been seeing him so often."

"He and Nat and Bill are the only men I know who want nothing of me but my waking hours."

Lucia laughed, and I went to dress.

At the Waldorf, I wanted to tell her that I had loved sharing an apartment with her, and that I liked her better than any woman I had ever known—but Lucia and I were inarticulate with each other about things like that. So we talked of places Lucia and Sam would visit, and things I wanted her to get me in Paris, and ate tomato en gelée, and lobster, and alligator pears—the preposterous sort of meal women order when they are dining together. Warm summer dusk deepened along the Avenue outside.

Lucia began to talk again, of Kenneth. "Odd that one doesn't feel very sorry for him. He has, so obviously, had his quota of golden moments."

"Yet you wouldn't say he had a happy life, precisely."

"Well, who has? You? Or I?"

"Not happy, but certainly not boring. We have come a long way from a couple of simple New England girlhoods anyway— have seen so much more than if we had married stability when we were seventeen."

"I told you that you'd become reconciled to being an ex-wife, Pat."

"I am reconciled to it when I have a new dress, or am eating the kind of food I like, or dancing to good music. Let's talk about something else. I'm reconciled only when I don't think about whether I am or not."

Lucia said: "Pat, how often do you think about Peter nowadays? You have stopped talking about him at last."

"I think about him often—almost all the time when I am not occupied. But, I think of him as someone I used to know—not, anymore, as a person of importance to me in the present. I don't know what he is like now, really. Judith must know that much better. I know what he was like when he was younger. . . . It is a little as if he were dead. . . ."

"Well don't try to manage a resurrection some time that you are bored."

"No chance, Lucia. Even I can learn—"

We drank iced coffee and looked out at the Avenue.

"There's Kenneth," said Lucia. He was walking very slowly, with a man I did not know.

Lucia knocked on the windowpane with her ring. Ken saw us, seemed to hesitate, then waved his arms to indicate that he would join us.

After a minute, Kenneth and the other man came into the dining-room. As they crossed the room toward us, I said to Lucia,

"Isn't he attractive?" meaning the other man, not Kenneth.

"All right if you like the red-haired type. I don't, because I belong to it."

Kenneth said something to Lucia, to the effect that she looked like a hybrid between a bride-to-be and a healthy angel, and introduced the man. It was Noel about whom I had been hearing for so long.

Lucia thanked Ken for the cigarette box he had sent her, and everyone began to talk about marriage and Norway and California and the Black Hills. The Black Hills were included because Noel was leaving to spend the summer there, reporting the summer holiday of Mr. Coolidge.

After five minutes, Noel and I began to talk to each other. I cannot remember at all what we talked about—I can only remember three things he said, and those were inconsequentialities.

The first was: "Marriage is like war—an experience that no adventurous man would evade, and no sensible man repeat."

The second was: "Coolidge is the best living demonstration that, if you keep silent long enough, something fortunate may happen to you."

The third was: "Your voice is like a 'cello."

Those statements were not extraordinary—they were just the sort of thing men say. They had nothing to do with something that had happened when he sat down, and began to talk.

When he sat down and began to talk, I said to myself: "This is why I have powdered my face, and bought pretty clothes, and done calisthenics, all the long time since Peter stopped loving me. I always believed, in a corner of my head, that someday, somewhere, something lovely might happen to me yet. This is it."

He had dark red hair and eyebrows. He had a warm gay voice. He had beautiful broad shoulders, and a strong chin with an incipient dimple in it. All that did not matter.

He looked as if he found women interesting, but not a bit as if women were the major pursuit of his life. I began to wish that I had behaved better, in the last years. Then I remembered that he was going to the Black Hills next day, and knew that it was unlikely that I should ever see him again. I decided that would not have happened to me if I had behaved better.

He said that he had known Kenneth since the war, and I asked him if he had been in the Twenty-Sixth Division, too; and when he said that he had, I asked him if he had paraded in Boston with the Division in the Springtime of 1919.

He said, "Yes."

I said, "But *I saw* that parade. I watched it from the front row of a grand stand on Commonwealth Avenue. I was seventeen years old." I was thinking, "Why could I not have met him then?"

He seemed to understand the implications. "I rode on a white horse," he said helpfully.

Then we laughed.

I remembered for a minute that we were being extremely rude to Kenneth and Lucia. She was gathering up her gloves and things. Apparently they were talking about Life.

(*Life* had suddenly a warmth, a feeling of importance, significance again that evening.)

"It's a gorgeous procession to watch from a decent seat in the shade," Lucia was saying. "But such a tiring parade for the marchers."

"But marriage does not mean retirement, Lucia," Kenneth said.

"In certain cases it may be considered as securing a very advantageous grand stand seat," Lucia said; smiled, and stood up to go.

"Stay here, Pat. I have to meet Sam and I'll see you later tonight."

She said to Noel, gravely, "Patricia is a very lovely girl. Good-bye."

She said to Kenneth, "I shan't be seeing you again, my dear. No, don't come to the door with me. I have a desire to walk home alone and contemplate—whatever I happen to contemplate.

"Kenneth, it has been so nice to know you. Whenever I see a portrait of any of the younger, more-reckless-and-braver-looking Cavaliers, I shall be reminded of you. Good-bye."

He said, "Thank you. Have a happy life, Lucia."

She smiled at us, and walked out alone, between the rows of tables, a slender, red-haired girl, in a yellow-flowered dress. I thought, "There goes my dearest friend." I thought, "I wonder what Lucia thinks about, really." I thought, "I shall miss her acutely."

And I turned back to Kenneth and Noel.

Noel and I talked, and Kenneth listened, and looked amused.

After some time Kenneth said something about "seeing them off," and I realized that Noel and Kenneth were *both* going to Chicago the next day.

It developed that Kenneth had decided to start to California a week earlier than he had planned, so they might make that part of the journey together.

"Oh dear," I said, "This is just my evening for bowing people out of my life forever," and then realized that was a tactless thing to say to Kenneth; and, to compensate, I devoted myself to him as we all walked uptown together.

Noel left us, on the corner of Forty-Third Street and Fifth Avenue. He had to go to the *Times*.

He said, "Will you be seeing Kenneth off?"

I said, "I can't. I have to go to Lucia's wedding."

Kenneth waited, politely.

Noel said, "May I telephone you when I get back to New York this Fall?"

(I thought, "I shall never see him again; he won't remember my name.")

I said, "Do, by all means. I am in the telephone book. Have a nice summer with Mr. Coolidge."

Kenneth and I walked on uptown. After two or three blocks he said, "Let's go to Harlem. I should like to see the lights swing 'round at Small's. Or do you think it is too warm a night?"

"No, let's go . . . it might be fun."

We danced a little, and sat down and drank cold drinks. We did not talk much. I wanted to say something that would make Kenneth feel happy—but there is very little to be said to a young man going to California to die, very swiftly, of lungs and complications.

After a rather long silence, he said, "Noel will telephone you when he gets back."

"Why should he, Kenneth?"

He ignored that. "I never meant him to meet you, Pat."

"I know, Ken. . . . But I don't know why."

"Because you have had your major catastrophe, and what you need now is a little tranquility."

"He made me feel nineteen years old, and as if nothing had ever happened to me, but as if all sorts of marvellous things were going to happen, instantly."

"I noticed," said Kenneth.

We had some of our drinks. Then Kenneth went on talking.

"He is a grand person. I always had an idea that he and you were made to finish each other's sentences."

"Well, then—why didn't you have us meet last year?"

Kenneth had some more of his drink.

"You needn't tell me, if you don't want to, Kenneth."

"Oh, he will tell you himself, but his version will damn him too much. You may as well hear the by-stander's account."

"Forget about it, Ken. Let's talk about you."

"Thank you, no. I'll make Noel's story as brief as possible though. It won't amuse you.

"He made one of those just-before-the-battle marriages, before he sailed for France. His wife was a delectable young blonde thing, with no more sense than a kitten. Naturally, while he was gone she fell in love with someone else. When Noel came back, she wanted a divorce.

"Naturally, also, he was somewhat disturbed. They discussed the situation over a good many highballs. He started to drive her home. It was a rainy night and he was fairly drunk. He ran the car into a tree, or perhaps it was a telegraph pole. I don't remember."

"Was she killed, Kenneth?"

"No. The whole left side of her face was smashed in, and she lost the sight of one eye. I believe she wears some sort of black patch over it, on the rare occasions when she comes to New York. She had been a very lovely-looking young person. She was twenty, when that happened to her. They say she is a shrew, now, and her main interest in life is reminding Noel of what he did to her."

I felt a little sick.

"What happened to the man who had wanted to marry her?"

"He changed his mind about that, the first time he saw her in the hospital. She is still married to Noel. She lives upstate with her sister, and Noel visits her every other week-end; brings her books and things.

"I believe that sometimes, she seems glad to see him, and that sometimes she rails at him for two days on end. When she was convalescing from the accident, she begged him to promise not to divorce her—he had plenty of grounds at that time. He promised . . . well, Pat, does that explain why I didn't want you to meet him?"

"Yes, I suppose it does. I am not husband-hunting, though."

"Now that you know—you can do what you please. Let's dance, Pat."

We danced, as if it had been any other evening. We were quite gay. When we left Small's, we found a Victoria wandering forlornly through Harlem, and hired it, and drove home at snail's pace through the Park.

Kenneth talked happily about his Hungarian dancer, as he had talked on so many other evenings.

Then he said, "You know, Pat, you shouldn't go adventuring in bed among the portrait painters and the Russians. It isn't any fun, is it?"

"I've stopped. I thought it ought to be fun, but it was always dreary . . . like prospecting for gold and finding a coal mine. Coal has its uses, but if it isn't what one wanted to find. . . . The whole show, kisses and the rest, was once so tied to the beauty-and-sweetness of things. . . ."

"It is for me, still," said Kenneth. "You know, Patricia, my wife was the only woman with whom I ever slept, in my life."

I said, "Oh Kenneth, darling . . ."

He said, "Have a cigarette, Pat."

And we drove on through the warm summer night.

At my door, he said, "I'm not coming upstairs. It's so late. And don't try to think of any parting speech, child. Pretend I'll be coming back, in September, and wish me a pleasant vacation."

So I wished him a pleasant vacation, and we shook hands, and said "good-night" to each other.

XV

July—The first heat wave of summer sent the store's advertising manager to a sanitorium, with a thorough nervous breakdown. I inherited his problems and his secretary. Every day, all day, I planned pages of advertising of "Vacation Necessities" and "Week-end Accessories" and "Hot Weather Comforts." Then I went home to swim with Helena in the pool at the Shelton, and dine with her, discussing "art moderne" languidly. Or else I drove out on Long Island with Nathaniel in a hopeless search for coolness, and discussed languidly over lobster and sauterne, his father's lessening health. Occasionally, I went with Bill to a relatively cool roof garden and discussed liquor and women, of recent and other vintages.

I had a letter from Lucia:

"Pat Darling,

"I am happy or I am resigned or I am content. I have gained seven pounds. Sam is the most thoughtful man I ever knew. Paris is hot but exciting. Shortly I shall become one of those women, who, over multiple chins, emit 'my husband, my husband, my husband,' in doting accents, at five-minute intervals, as punctuation to all conversation.

"I plan to find you a banker, and convince you that the substance is more satisfactory than the shadow. (Bankers' shadows, even, are substantial.) Meanwhile I have found you a heavenly gold-and-silver negligee. It will make you regret that you have gone in for celibacy. Or have you? Did the beautiful red-haired Noel really depart within a few hours of his first appearance? How are you and Helena getting on?

"Though the road may be long, we arrive at respectability in the end, my child. I now own a sable wrap.

"Love . . ."

August—The apartment downstairs was redolent of Helena's paints and oils, instead of Lucia's bath salts and perfume. In the evening, when I came home, I watched Helena decorating amazingly realistic masks, instead of watching Lucia decorate her own lovely face.

I had a letter and a package from Kenneth. I opened the letter first:

"Patricia, my dear—

"I've given instructions about having this mailed. By the time you read it, I shall have found out whether they keep Hungarian dancers in heaven. (If not, I plan to fling myself over the golden bar forthwith.)

"If you were fond of me, Patricia, as I have sometimes—conceitedly—thought you were, in memory of me drink no absinthe, anymore, all the days of your giddy life. Do you mind?

"I may or may not have presented you with something, in flinging Noel into that life. Whether he turns out to be a present or not, I am sending you another—a string of amber beads, to warm the throat of a young woman who managed to warm my heart.

"Until we meet again, my dear—(that was a war song, or were you too young to remember)—

"Affectionately—"

September—Heat seemed to have lasted, immemorially.

I wore Kenneth's golden amber beads over summer frocks that were, after an hour's wearing, wilted as four day old roses. Helena took her painting to the Nova Scotian coast. I missed her cool comments on people as they passed.

I had a letter from Peter. For a minute, when I found it in my mail box, my heart beat faster than ordinarily. I bathed, and put on a cool negligee, and made myself iced tea; and then, when I felt very calm, opened the letter.

"My Already Some-time Legally Departed,

"Would you risk dining with me once more? Positively last appearance—genuine farewell tour and so on. I have something to tell you that I should prefer to tell you, rather than have you hear it, fourth-hand, in a speakeasy.

"How about telephoning me at the office? It would be pleasant to see you, Patricia."

Two days later, I telephoned him, and arranged to dine with him on Sunday. Until then, I did not speculate about his "news."

Sunday was the first cool day in weeks.

I dressed carefully, for the sake of years in which Peter's opinion of my appearance had seemed important. I wore a dress with bright pink rosebuds printed on a deep blue background, and a deep blue velvet hat, and carried my beloved silver fox.

We met at the Brevoort; decided not to dine there, and went to Giacomo's, because it was a restaurant with a garden. Peter was looking well; looking a little older, weighing a little more.

On the way to dinner, we talked about how hot summer had been.

I wondered what he was thinking, and I thought, "It is not true that, in time, one 'gets over' almost anything. In time, one *survives* almost anything. There is a distinction."

Over the Martinis, I said to Peter, "I survived you, Peter. I never thought I could. It is surprising, isn't it, that I did?"

He said, "You look as if nothing had ever happened to you in your life."

"Nothing much has. I never swam the Channel or had twins or wrote a play or murdered a rival. I have just lived quietly, year after year, on Scotch and kisses."

I thought that was entertaining—it was the best I could manage off-hand. His face continued to be grave, however, and so I tried again.

"Tell me your great news," I said, "Have you found love at last, or have they made you an aviation expert, or have you a new bootlegger who sells nothing but genuine pre-war stock?"

I thought, "I used to ache when I looked at Peter, because I loved him so. Now I ache when I look at him, because nothing in me stirs at all. He is just a good-looking young man with whom I am dining. I wonder what he is like, really."

He said: "The damndest thing about you is that you look so virginal. You don't change at all."

"Men think a woman is just as she was, until her face begins to sag, Peter. They judge by contours, not by character. I am twenty-six—I was twenty, or was it nineteen, when we met?"

"You were nineteen."

"They say every bit of a person's body changes in seven years. . . . Tell me, did you have an exciting time in Boston?"

He had been sent by his paper to report the last days of Sacco and Vanzetti, recently electrocuted. Throughout dinner, we discussed Sacco and Vanzetti, casually, as strangers meeting for the first time might discuss any piece of front-page news.

When we had reached coffee and liqueurs, Peter said: "Come sit in my back-yard garden and talk to me. It is pleasanter there than here."

I said, "I don't want to see Judith, particularly."

"Oh, she has moved uptown. We found an amusing sort of place over by the East River. I'm moving there after Judith and I are married next week. . . . That was the news I had for you."

I powdered my face and straightened my hat and put on my gloves.

"I hope that you both will be very happy, Peter."

And some absurd remnant of belief in miracles curled up and died in me, almost painlessly.

"Must you be so damn formal, Patricia?"

I answered him quite earnestly. "Yes, Peter, I have to be formal. I don't know you very well, nowadays, and I never knew Judith well."

"Do you still know me well enough to visit my garden, and have a Tom Collins with me?"

"I think I know you well enough for that."

We walked across Washington Square, and up Fifth Avenue, slowly, without talking, as he and I might walk with other people, when he and I grew old.

The garden had a diminutive fountain that tinkled pleasantly, and painted canvas chairs, and one of those trees of indeterminate species that should be called "New York Yard Tree." I looked at the moon shining through its crooked branches, while Peter went to mix Tom Collinses, and I tried not to think about anything at all.

When Peter came back, I said, "Why are you marrying Judith?" I did not want to know why he was marrying Judith, but that would do as well, to make conversation, as any other subject.

"Oh, she's a pleasant girl and I'm fond of her. I don't want to talk about that, though. I thought we might spend an evening talking about you and me."

I felt that I could not bear to talk with Peter about him and me. Feelings, hopes, even opinions as to Peter had gone from me so slowly, so very slowly, through months and years. I did not want them back. I did not want to be hurt anymore.

"I don't think there's much to say, about you-and-me, Peter. Label us as just a couple of the minor tragedies of Prohibition, or examples of the Younger Generation on the wane, and let it go at that."

"I don't mean to go in for any lengthy analysis of who was to blame for what. But there are things I should like to tell you."

He began to walk up and down, under the Yard Tree. When he spoke again, his voice was strained.

"Patricia, I loved you very much, and I treated you very badly."

"No worse than I treated you, perhaps, Peter."

He said, "I don't remember very well what it was all about. We were young, and we loved each other, and we 'wanted to be free.' It doesn't make much sense."

"I never was able to draw any Great Moral Lesson from it, myself, Pete."

"I shall make Judith a much better husband than I ever made you, Patricia."

"No doubt. But am I expected to extract any great comfort from that? I am not old enough yet to be an altruist. Will you give me another drink?"

He filled my glass, and his own.

I wanted to go home. Peter made me feel old.

"People have no second chance with each other, really," he said. "If I were fool enough to ask you to marry me again, and you were fool enough to do it, I should strangle you within three months afterward. Whenever I came home, and found you serving some man tea, I'd take it for granted that you had spent the afternoon in bed with him."

"I know. I should never see you pick up a book, without expecting you to fling it at my head. I suppose that is funny."

"I suppose so. . . . But, Patricia, do you remember—"

"Peter, stop. I probably do remember, whatever you were going to ask, but I don't *want* to remember. I wish you would begin to be disagreeable. That makes it easier for me."

He laughed. "Darling, I know exactly how you feel. If you stamped your feet at this moment, and cursed me in Bowery accents, I could watch you walk out of my life and be glad to see you vanish. But you sit there looking lovely. . . . Curious, how distressing it is to be anything but flippant. If I said, brokenly, 'Good-bye forever, my dear young love,' I should feel like an imbecile. Yet I want to say something nice to you."

We both laughed—and Peter came across the garden, and put his head against my knees, and his arms around them.

"Patricia, I am glad I married you when I was young. I wouldn't have missed it."

I said, "Peter, my darling, damn you for making me cry. I am glad I married you when I was young, too. And I'm sorry for every stupid thing I ever did that hurt you." Tears spilt down my face, and dripped on the back of his neck, absurdly. He gave me a handkerchief, and a cigarette, and asked if I wanted another drink.

"No, I think I want to go home, Peter; and by myself."

"All right. Would you believe that I'm not trying to be disagreeable, if I tell you that I hope I never see you again?"

I could understand about that. I said, "You will like me pretty well, if you never see me for five minutes."

"That's it. . . . Will you kiss me, nonchalantly, Patricia, before you go?"

I kissed him nonchalantly. He bent his head, and put his cheek against mine, gently. It was a gesture of his that once was familiar to me. It hurt. I wanted, more than I had wanted anything in years, to find words to tell Peter how much I had loved him once, and how sorry I was that I did not love him now.

He kissed my eyelids and my mouth and my throat. He lighted a cigarette, and walked once up and down the garden. Then he said, "Patricia, will you stay here with me tonight?"

I wanted so much—to want to stay. I wanted to feel for an hour, that I loved Peter. I could not feel anything at all.

I said, "It just would be pretending; and I should cry, probably, because it was not real anymore; and that would make you cross."

"Yes, and I'd treat you as outrageously as possible in the morning, I suppose. I couldn't help it."

"I know. Better find me a taxi, Peter. I am going home."

He went to find a taxi. When he came back, he said, "For God's sake, think of something flippant for your parting speech, darling. I have thought of mine."

I powdered my face, by moonlight. "All right. Tell me yours first, Peter."

"I left you. Now you're leaving me. So you win the last battle."

"That's not very amusing, Peter."

"Probably not."

We walked from the garden through his darkened apartment to the street door. Before he opened it, he said, "What is your exit line?"

I said, "And now Lord Thou lettest Thy servant depart in peace."

"That's no better than mine," he said.

"I know. It's the best I can manage, though, Pete."

The taxi was waiting outside. He gave my address to the driver.

He said, "Well, Patricia, thank you for dining with me."

"I enjoyed it," I said.

Next day Helena came back from Canada, and she and I shopped for Fall clothes together. The advertising manager returned from his breakdown and I had a vacation.

On the first evening after I came back to New York, I was sitting alone, reading an accumulation of letters from Lucia, when the telephone rang.

A voice said, "After I left the Black Hills I had to fill in at our Washington Bureau. I got back to New York twenty minutes ago. Is it too late in the evening to ask you to go somewhere to dance? I've spent the entire trip from Washington discussing the Republicans who want to run against Smith next year, and I want to hear music."

I said, "Hello, Noel. Of course I'll go dancing. How soon will you call for me?"

"Half an hour," he said.

XVI

That telephone conversation with Noel was in September, 1927.

On a November afternoon in 1928, I was having tea and muffins with him, in front of his fireplace.

The Republicans had run Hoover against Al Smith, and the old-fashioned Americans who had been troubled by the possibility that Al might invite the Pope to Sunday morning breakfast in the White House, were sleeping again at night.

When we finished tea, Noel put on his overcoat. He said: "I shall be back in two hours or so. I have two or three rapid 'good-byes' to say to people. Then we'll go to dinner wherever you like."

"You have finished packing, haven't you?" I asked.

"Yes. When you take the papers in the desk to my safe deposit vault, be sure to take that tin box on the bookcase with them. It has all your letters in it. When I come back, I shall need them to comfort my declining years."

We smiled at each other. "Do you mind if I put your letters to me in the same vault, darling darling," I said. "It is as near as we are likely to come to sharing the same grave."

"Don't, Patricia," he said. He was not talking about the letters.

"I'm sorry, Noel. It's all right. After all, we have had so much more than most people ever dream of having."

"Sit by the fire, until I come back, Pat—and look over your letters. They won't distress you."

(Dear Noel—he knew the letters would remind me of gay evenings we had shared, and that was the best he could do for me, at the moment.)

He reconsidered, just before he went out. "I don't know," he said. "Perhaps you had better read the 'Mercury.'"

"No," I said. "I want to find out if I ever managed to write you that you were the nicest person in the world."

He went to say "good-bye" to people, and I made myself fresh tea. Before I looked at my letters to Noel I went upstairs and got his from a drawer in my dressing table. Noel and I had had apartments in the same house for nearly a year.

My suggestion that I store his letters with mine had been made on impulse, but I felt that it was sensible enough. I did not want to destroy his letters—neither did I want to keep them about to read and re-read when I was lonely—to find, possibly, in each re-reading, a little warmth gone from them.

I was twenty-seven. More than a thousand crowded days intervened between myself and that younger woman who believed she could not live without Peter. When, rarely, now, I was reminded of the Peter I had known, I thought of him kindly, as someone with whom I had shared a painful postadolescence, someone who no doubt had been as bewildered as I about most things. He and I were married and had a child and separated, before either of us grew up.

I had lived to discover that after First Love one can love again—as much—more, for one knows more. I believed that I would love Noel forever, perhaps. But I knew also that I could live without Noel; and that, as Time changed me, I should not even miss him, often, or very badly.

I opened the box that held my letters to him. There were a good many, for I had written him daily, whenever he was on out-of-town stories.

He had all the letters packed neatly, in the order in which I had written them—and I found that infinitely touching, because Noel was the sort of man who had to search through four drawers to discover shirt studs or handkerchiefs or a fountain pen or collar buttons.

The first letter was to his New York address.

"Noel Dear,
    "I remember telling you, some weeks ago, that I never stayed with the same man twice, in the years since Peter, because I never liked any of them after I had stayed with them. Therefore this—to state specifically that I liked you twenty times as much this morning at breakfast, as last night at dinner-time."

I wrote that letter two months after the late September evening when Noel telephoned. In those two months I decided that his hair was the shade of burnished bronze (and complained to him that he kept it clipped too closely—but never, to the last day that I knew him, did he wear it any longer.) I decided that I loved his voice and his smile, and the shape of his eyebrows (they exactly matched his hair) and the things he said, and the way he laughed, and the fact that he believed in taking exercise.

I knew that he was supposed to be brilliant. I heard a story about him: that several city editors, dining together, made separate lists of the five best newspapermen in New York and that his was the only name that appeared on all the lists. But I had known so many people who were supposed to be brilliant. I liked Noel better because he was so obviously sane, and stable, and well-balanced. It gave me a feeling of great steadiness to be with him.

And I had found someone to whom I could talk, after years when I had just made conversation.

I saw him nearly every evening, and saw no one else—except Nathaniel and Bill. I knew them well enough to say, "I shall be able to have dinner, but I must get home by quarter to ten. Is that all right?"

Noel worked on a morning newspaper, and got through at ten or eleven at night. We walked, danced, went to supper. We talked about politics, disarmament, the War (he had a combat decoration, but he did not tell me that, someone else did), newspapers, advertising, books, operas. We talked about his childhood, my childhood, people he had known, people I had known. We flung the patterns of our lives at each other.

I was worried, at the beginning, lest someone tell him I was supposed to be promiscuous. I thought he would not like me anymore. I was sure that I loved him, when I had seen him three times, but I saw no reason that he should ever love me. I was just a woman whose own husband had found her impossible. With other men, I had not felt as humble, but that was because I did not care whether they ever loved me or not.

I decided to tell Noel, myself. If the knowledge that I had been promiscuous was to make him stop seeing me, that would hurt less, immediately, than later. So, one October evening, when we were walking along lower Fifth Avenue, I said abruptly:

"Look here. Don't have any illusions about me. I have slept with more men than I can remember." That was exaggeration, but I had to exaggerate, lest I should understate.

He did not look disgusted or shocked or even surprised. He said, "That's interesting. What were you doing—trying to use sex as an anaesthetic for something-or-other? That can't be managed, usually."

I said, "You needn't be polite about it. If you think I am an awful person, say so."

He said, "You darling imbecile—I think you are the nicest person I have ever known. Whatever happened to you has made you poised and tolerant, and comprehending, and anyone who knows you should be grateful for whatever produced the result."

I said, "Oh." I said, "Do you mean it—you aren't just being sorry for me?"

He said, "God, no. I mean it."

Something in me that had hurt horribly at odd moments, for a long, long time, stopped hurting forever.

I slipped my arm through his. "I am glad you don't mind, but anyway I stopped."

He laughed at me. He was so friendly that I laughed, too. "There must be thousands of bitterly disappointed men in New York, Pat. You don't mind being ragged about it, do you? . . . I promise never to ask you to stay with me, if I can help it." The tone of his voice changed. "For various reasons, I don't stay with women for whom I would be likely to care. It seems somewhat unfair."

He had never referred to his marriage before.

"I know about your marriage, Noel," I said. "Kenneth told me."

"Oh," he said.

"Noel, let's stop at Childs and have coffee and butter cakes. I am hungry."

Afterwards, we talked about our marriages too, as just among the things that had happened to us.

Noel did not kiss me for another month. Once, in the interval, he did put his arms 'round me—as we were crossing Madison Square Park—because I said that, given the choice of staying with Gene Tunney or Jack Dempsey, I would choose Dempsey, joyously.

Then, on an evening when we had talked, before his fire, for hours and hours, I said, reluctantly, that I supposed it was five in the morning, or some-such hour, and he had better get my coat. He went to get it instantly. He held it for me to put on. Then suddenly he put both arms around my shoulders, and I turned and put my arms around his neck, and held up my face to be kissed.

I knew in that instant that I was to stay, and I was glad.

Very soon afterward, he was sent to Boston to cover a naval inquiry into a submarine disaster. I felt half-alive while he was gone, but used my leisure to solve the first problem in our relationship: how I was to get any sleep. I worked from nine in the morning until five in the afternoon: and Noel worked from two in the afternoon, until eleven, or thereabouts, most nights, and then we wandered about the city until four or five in the morning.

So I got myself a new job, as advertising manager of a specialty shop—where no one cared if I did not appear before noon, provided I worked until seven or eight at night.

During the week that I remained at my old office, after my resignation, the wide-eyed little girl who had been an ambitious copy-writer, until she decided to marry, came to see me. She was looking shabby, and harassed. It appeared that her husband was not getting any of the salary increases upon which they had counted so confidently, and she had pursuaded him to let her go back to work.

She wanted to know if I had heard of any vacancies, anywhere. So she did inherit my job, as I had anticipated long before.

My new one paid less money, but I planned to make that up by doing more free-lance advertising—it left me leisure to breakfast with Noel, which was more important.

Noel wrote me a letter from Boston—the first I had from him.

(I turned to his letters to find that. It was written in pencil, on a series of Western Union Special Blanks for Newspaper Correspondents.)

It began:

"The admiral of the battle fleet sits up very straight in the centre chair on the opposite side of the long table—listening, with a dark, long, weary, brooding face. A rear-admiral is reading one message after another in a huge wad, that represents the mobilization orders of the navy rescue force, after the submarine went down.

"So far, it appears these orders mobilized only ships, equipment, and crews—but not intelligence. I have come to understand that a few men design machines and a great many use them—and all seem very intelligent until an accident happens. Then the user stands helpless at the machine and waits for someone who understands it, like a banker who has dropped his Swiss watch.

"The rear-admiral reads on. . . . And it occurs to me how nice it would be if Patricia managed to turn up in Boston for a week-end."

Of course I managed it.

Noel did not leave New York again until Springtime—except for his semi-monthly visits to his wife.

He had told me during a long conversation about mutual fidelity—a conversation that I had been stupid enough to begin—that on these visits he stayed with his wife.

He said then: "I don't know, Patricia, whether she hates me—I could not blame her if she did—or is fond of me, as one might be fond of a keeper when one serves a life sentence. I mean, that I am her only remaining contact with life. She hates to go about, because of that disfigurement, and she sees no one but her sister and the maid month after month. Sometimes she makes scenes if she hears that I have been about with any particular woman. Her sister usually manages to find out."

I said: "It must be difficult, Noel. I understand though. It was nice of you to tell me."

I did understand, but that did not comfort me very much. I was older than I had been. I realized that there were women before me, in his life. I could understand even, in some day that I hoped was distant, there might be women after me. But I wished that I might have had him awhile to myself.

Sometimes I thought of his wife—as a somewhat fantastic, altogether tragic figure, hanging on the outskirts of Noel's life. In moods when I knew that I was looking particularly pretty, and feeling altogether gala, I pitied her; because Ken had said that she was very pretty, once. Less often, in moods when I wanted very badly to marry Noel and have a redheaded baby, and forget everything in my life before I had known him, I resented her.

On nights when I knew that Noel was with her, I walked up and down, telling myself to be civilized, telling myself that he carried responsibilities from his past, into his present—telling myself that it was far better to have whatever of himself a first rate man had to give, than to possess a second rate man wholly. I believed all that, but I could not sleep at all, on the nights when he was with her. Finally, I bought myself a long book, on every Saturday that he went to visit her, and read it until morning. Then I slept, Sundays.

Or, on some of those week-ends, I visited Lucia, who was back from Europe, finding surburban luxury pleasant. (It had turned out to be luxury in Westchester, not Long Island.) Lucia had met Noel again. All she said to me, was: "It's not sensible of you, darling, but if it makes you happy, why not? You're looking younger than you've looked in years."

There was a vacant apartment upstairs in the house where Noel lived. Once, when I had to go home, because I could not appear at my office next morning in evening dress, he said that he wished I lived upstairs. I said I would move. From that beginning, we became involved in a long debate on conventionalities. Noel insisted it would still be particularly inconvenient for a woman to be compromised by a man who could not marry her.

I did not care in the least, to what degree I was "compromised." Of course I wished that I could marry him—I wanted status and stability and a baby. But at least I did have happiness on a day-to-day basis. That was so much more than I had hoped to find, ever again, that I managed to be philosophical (most of the time) about lack of status.

A few days after Noel said that he wished I lived in his house, I had lunch with the girl who had been an eager copywriter, when I was assistant advertising manager—the girl who now held my old job.

She was looking completely forlorn. "I am going to leave my husband," she said. "We quarrel every day, because I make more money. He says that proves the materialism of America. Or sometimes he says that I don't understand his character." She shed a few inconspicuous tears. "Now he spends five evenings a week with a girl who's supposed to understand him better.

So I thought if I left him, for a while, he might be glad to have me back."

"He might," I said. "Where are you going to live?"

"I don't know. I thought you might know of some girl with whom I could share an apartment. My furniture is in storage—we have been living in hotels since I went back to work."

So I took the child to meet Helena, who was touched by her helpless-kitten attitude, as I had thought Helena would be. In a week, the child moved into the apartment which Lucia had shared with me, and I with Helena.

Helena said; "Well, Pat, I enjoyed living with you. For heaven's sake, come to see me often; and if anything goes wrong with your Great Love, come on back. Meanwhile, I'll teach the blue-eyed infant you wished on me, her way around the city."

On a Saturday, when Noel was out of town, I moved into his house. When he came back, he scolded me for being so reckless, but he was so pleased that he could not stop grinning while he scolded me.

In the Spring, he went to Albany, to attend the trial of a woman politician accused of mis-use of public funds. He came to New York week-ends, and I began my career as a daily letter-writer.

I took the letters I had written to him at Albany from the box, and looked through them.

"Dearest—

"I shall be so glad to see you when you do get back that I shan't be able to talk, shan't be garrulous at all, for at least five minutes, anyway.

"I see by all the afternoon papers that your lady politician's case is due to go to the jury tomorrow, but I believe the jury will deliberate ninety-eight hours; then they will disagree, all but one for conviction. The one juror will hold out for acquittal because the defendant looked like his mother, who was a good old-fashioned female who couldn't read or write . . . or manage funds, either. Then the case will be re-tried; that will take until election time; the defendant will be convicted by Christmas. People will point you out as the oldest resident of Albany, by then. The defendant will appeal; there will be long arguments; the case will be re-tried. By then, you will be growing grey-haired; and myself, sedate. After fifteen more years the defendant will die, and the feminists will work miracles of check post-dating over her grave. There will be a legend about you, too, who followed her faithfully forty years; I shall be long dead, of waiting for a telegram saying you are coming home. . . ."

After a week-end:

"Belovedest—

"I was so happy, walking down the street this morning after two whole days with you, that when I passed two truck drivers one of them said to the other: 'Jes', look at that girl *smile*.' And I didn't have the grace to be embarrassed.

"If you are permanently resurrected from Albany by the week-end, I shall just go completely joyous, and have to be restrained from singing in speakeasies, or otherwise behaving in an undignified manner.

"Noel, am I undignified? Oh darling, please am I not dignified, always or occasionally, or ever? Please, please dearest will you teach me to be dignified? All my life I've wanted to be dignified. I never thought of it until five minutes ago, though."

He was sent to Wisconsin in June, to cover President Coolidge at the Summer White House, and I saw him off at the Pennsylvania station, behaving well enough until he was gone, and then sobbing so hard in a taxi, on my way home, that the driver spoke to me when I was paying the fare. He said: "Listen, kid, I don't know what it is, but whatever it is, don't take it that way, kid."

After three weeks, when we corresponded between New York and Superior, Wisconsin, by telegraph and telephone, we decided it was not to be borne, and I arranged a leave, and went out to spend a month with Noel, living in Duluth, twenty miles away, and wandering about its main streets, contentedly, all day, while he was busy.

It appears that Noel sat down, the night I left Wisconsin for New York, and wrote to his wife, asking her if she would not be just as happy, if she divorced him. His wife did not want a divorce, however, and sent her sister to New York to inquire among mutual acquaintances of hers and Noel's, as to any new reason he might have for asking for freedom.

The sister found out all the facts there were to find, concerning Noel and me. It was much more my fault than his that the facts were so easily accessible. Noel's wife did not tell him, at that time, that she knew of my existence. She just wrote him that she could not bear the thought of being a divorcée.

After I came back from Duluth, I wrote to Noel: "Consider that I have put both arms around your neck, and my head happily against your shoulder, and have said that I believe remembrance of the lights of Lake Superior, will glow happily in my heart for all my life."

And, when I was making an effort to write a gay letter:

"I have thought of a CAREER. Plan to open a speakeasy for tired business women, where they can go alone, and have liquid dinners, without being stared at for drinking alone. . . . Come into partnership with me, my darling."

Once for three days in succession, I did not hear from him. So I wired, "How are you?" He explained later that there was no language to describe how damnably uncomfortable he was, so he did not answer the wire for a day.

By then, I had decided that he did not love me anymore. By the day's end—it had been a hot day, and I had to work very hard—I was contemplating suicide. I wrote him:

"This is a love letter for Noel and nothing else but . . . it will probably turn out full of profanity, but I can't help that. I don't know when the thought first came, to add to general hellishness of New York in the humidity, that you were annoyed with me. I suggested in my telegram that you wire me. What you should say, I don't know. 'It is cool here, I am working hard,' maybe. Well, you would take it for granted that I knew that.

"However, the thought that you were annoyed grew beautifully, grew through 'He thinks I am just bingeing about with Nat and Bill and whoever turns up, very pleased with myself' until I thought there must be a Wisconsin Wench. And I hope she drowns in Lake Superior and goes from there to hell, but I *do* hope she appreciates him, in the meantime.' Is that my maternal instinct?

"Then I tried to be philosophical, and steady. The Philosophical Effort may entertain you. It amounted to this:

"In a friendship, *affaire* or whatever inadequate label one affixes to the things you and I share, a greater trust of the other person is implicit than in marriage, or any arrangement where one can lean on organized status.

"In the Love-Outside-Marriage that is so commonplace, now, what with new freedom and old divorce laws, there are no fences to enclose two people, and very few cushions against shocks. That's all right. I don't mind. We have discussed that.

"Candour has to do, instead of fences and cushions. If you were annoyed with me, if your feeling toward me changed, I believe that you would let me know, specifically and immediately.

"Generalities. . . . Adult women who try to 'understand' men, make no effort to enclose them. But women (in love) can put up with being enclosed, well enough. If you said to me, 'Sorry but it makes me dismal to think of other people holding your hand, and what-not, and would you mind not going out with other men at all?' I would stay at home.

"You won't say that, though. You believe in this freedom more than I do. I just believe in it for men. Nevertheless, I do accept dinner dates, don't I? . . . Not as I used . . . I don't ever try to acquire any new men. . . . But I did go out with three people this week, and two of them made love to me. (The other was just a couple of lunch dates.)

"My grandmother would have mourned your absence—I mean your grandfather's—in tears over her embroidery, perhaps. I bet I mourn yours more violently, in a cab with the wrong person, or in a speakeasy over a drink that I'm not having with you.

"I go to dinner, and I try to be amusing . . . sing for my supper, why not? And if there is a dreadful instant, when I think, 'I wish I would find a telephone message from him on the switchboard when I get home,' I am more likely to say, 'yes, I'll have another, thank you,' than to look bored and sleepy. There is nothing to go home for—no message will be on the switchboard.

"As for the rest—on its merits. I don't row if I get kissed once in the course of the evening, or so. I don't invite it, and I make it obvious that I'm damn well not reciprocating.

"The only person *I* want to kiss is wandering around the Great Northwest—and I wish Coolidge would get nostalgia for the sight of the dome of the White House.

"Footnote to all this. . . . You said once that you thought incidental necking was awfully boring. So do I. But that is one of the things about which you are extraordinary. Most men do seem to feel they've achieved something, in a minor way, if they succeed in touching their lips to a woman's chin or thereabouts, a couple of times in an evening. It makes me feel slightly like riding in a crowded Subway, but it's nothing to make a scene about. Just part of all this damn freedom.

"Finally, about the possibility of your Wisconsin Wench. I hope not, but I don't care except with those instincts that can't be helped. Shan't ask, want you always to do what you want. *But,* any Wisconsin Wench will have to be just miraculous, to be half as good, or nice-tempered or angelic to you as I plan to be when you come home at last."

That night, an hour after I posted that letter, Noel telephoned from Wisconsin, and we spent ten extravagant minutes talking gay nonsense. I told him I had written an outstandingly dumb letter that he might as well tear up unread.

But he answered the letter, this way:

"Patricia—

"I miss you steadily. I have not taken to wenching. I have sat around talking politics with the old men or listening to young men (the photographers) talk of their probably fictitious dealings with the local virgins. I have a memory of you that seems undiminished in warmth, with which I go tranquilly to sleep, alone.

"This summer will end. And, darling, darling (as you say in your 'cello voice) I am closer to you at two thousand miles distance, than I could be to any other woman in my arms."

I wrote him, later:

"When you come back, pack me in a suitcase, and haul me off to Vienna or Buenos Aires or Leningrad, and whenever you want conversation you can take me out of the suitcase and sit me on a chair and we'll talk very merrily. When you want solitude I'll fold myself in the suitcase uncomplainingly, for days at a time. And we'll never be bored or hurried or under pressure to do anything ever, we'll just be gaily disreputable until we die. Except that you will get famous, and women will make pilgrimages to see you, 'specially after they have learned you are handsome. I won't let any of 'em in, except the very loveliest ones . . . I'll let those in so that you will admire my taste.

"I send you a kiss-at-great-length."

He wrote me apologetically, that if it weren't too much trouble, he would like me to send a heavier overcoat, and some other things, to him. I wrote:

"You must know that I adore doing small things for you. It damn well isn't modern, but I damn well can't help it . . . so I shan't pose about it . . . don't have to pose with you about things."

He sent me some Scotch from Canada, via a photographer who came back to New York.

"Noel Angel,

"I shall save the Scotch to revive me, when I finally see a newspaper headline reading 'President Returns to

Washington.' I expect to be found clutching the newspaper, muttering things about our chief. You've led the paper with your Kellogg treaty stories, three days in succession. Did you know it? *Such* a bright young man."

He was coming home in two weeks! I wrote:

"Noel: When you come back I shall telephone you . . . and suggest we go swimming; I shall telephone you, and ask to be taken to dinner . . . I shall telephone you, and demand to be taken for walks. I shall invent excuses to telephone you. I shall telephone you daily, hourly, incessantly. Will you mind?

"I feel that all sorts of lovely things will happen instantly, as soon as you're home, and that you and I shall spend our old ages happily (over drinks) in front of the same fireplace, regarding a long row of books, written by you. And the old ages are so nice and far off.

"I'm looking handsome, what with sunburn turning brown, and I hope you'll be pleased with the effect. I remember how you look in all sorts of moods. I have a whole collection of snapshots of you, inside my head. One of the nicest is Himself, asleep, with a pleased expression, looking ten years old or so.

"You wired—when a letter of mine missed a mail two or three days ago, asking if I had taken up with a blonde. Of course not—blondes are an adolescent taste.

"I had a 'orrible thought . . . you might have to stay in Washington, covering the President, until election. . . . Noel, a nice old-fashioned female (meaning myself) would then go modern. *Nice* old-fashion whatnots don't *ever* pursue a man, they guard their reputations . . . they are patient *forever*. But if you get stuck in Washington, I go to Washington and get a job waiting on table in a restaurant, and the only thing that separates us, hereafter, is your wish to be by yourself.

"I want to know (if I met you in Washington as you suggest), if you'll take me to see the Washington Monument, and give me highballs, and talk to me hours and hours and hours about politics and the Kellogg Treaty. I don't care what you talk about. I just want to hear your voice. And will you pick me up and carry me about the room, but *not* muss my hair, and take me for a little walk about Washington. And if I'm *very* well-behaved will you kiss me once or twice?"

He answered that by wire.

"I shan't mind being telephoned at twenty minute intervals stop will take you up Monument stop don't guarantee about your hair stop yes yes yes."

I wrote him once more, to Wisconsin.

"After my shameless correspondence, I shall probably be so shy that I'll insist on sitting eight feet away from you, staring at you with an imbecilic look of content. . . . Let's go for a week-end to the shore where I can fall asleep on the sand in the sun with my head on your shoulder. I shall feel that I've reached Ultimate Truth, like a Russian at the end of seventy-two hours conversation."

He wired:

"Arranged going straight through to New York stop expect to enter city shouting love love nonstop reach Penn Station seven five P.M. Wednesday stop might I be met."

He was met.

We had days and weeks of high felicity. Sometimes, as I walked along the street, remembrance of years when I had been unhappy, came to me; and they seemed an infinite distance away, and altogether unreal, like stories one hears about a friend of a friend of a friend.

He had a rather extraordinary offer made to him—to go to Yokohama as head of a Far East news bureau. He would have liked to go. He had been a foreign correspondent on the Continent, and he spoke Russian, which would be useful in the Far East post, but he had never been to Asia.

He broached the project to his wife. Part of the terms on which they had arranged their lives was that he was not to take a post outside New York, because it would be too embarrassing for her to travel. She refused to hear of the Asiatic scheme.

He spoke of it to me, and I was entirely willing to fling the advertising business overboard, and go. We had often talked about the places we'd see, and how I would occupy myself learning Japanese, while he covered Chinese wars and Indian border uprisings. But neither Noel nor I took the project very seriously. We did not expect that his wife would let him go.

During the conversation, when he told her that it was an extraordinary opportunity, and that he wanted very much to go, she told him that she knew all about me. He was startled—and even more surprised to discover that she had nothing more to say than that she knew about me.

He asked her to reconsider agreeing to let him go to Asia. (He had three months in which to make up his mind—someone was filling out a term of office in the meantime.) She said she would not agree to it, but that he could ask her again in a few weeks, if he chose.

Noel was growing a little restless on the *Times*. He felt that, on the New York staff, he'd gone about as far as he was likely to go, and he didn't contemplate with much joy, the probability that he would spend the next twenty years, doing the same sort of stories, over and over.

Most of the time that we were together, though, we were too pleased with the world in general to worry about things like that. I did have one acute attack of wanting-to-be-made-an-honest-woman, and wrote him about it, when he was upstate covering the campaign tour of a governor.

"Noel Dearest—

"The preface to this letter is—I am as binged as I ever was. First time in a year. Nat and I fell off the wagon with the loudest splash imaginable—that acquaintance of yours, Tony, who has had the unreciprocated 'glad' on me for so long, caused it.

"Nat telephoned me to ask me to dine at seven. (You know he's been having an attack of wanting-to-get-away-from-it-all for months. Poor child.) At ten to seven the bell rang. It was that fool Tony. His yellow hair was combed four ways at once, as usual; and he was drunk as usual, too. He had a flask, and I had a drink. Then Nat came. He was tight, too, which is extraordinary. It seems he'd just seen his father through one of his attacks. So we all had more drinks.

"We went to Delano's bar, and began drinking Manhattans. A wild rainstorm developed outside, and no cabs were to be had, so we had more drinks, and the bartenders cooked us eggs and things.

"I was feeling low, because I was tired—and Tony and Nat are a God-awful combination, although they seem to go out together frequently. I mean, Nat's likely to get dismal, and Tony amorous, simultaneously.

"They both got tighter and tighter on their drinks.

"Then Tony said to Nat; 'You're the boy Pat'll marry in the end, of course. One day she'll look at herself in a mirror and know she's not going to be an apparently-sophisticated-twenty-two eternally. Then she'll marry you, and make you a swell wife, that's the funny part of it. I'll send you a wedding present.'

"I said, 'I don't want to marry anybody.'

"Tony said: 'You'll get sense someday.'

"We had two more rounds of drinks, and I talked about the Paramount Building.

"Then Tony said: 'I shall "make" Pat, one day . . . not for a couple of years, one day when she's tired.'

"Nat said: 'The hell you will. I'll marry her some day when she's tired. You're right . . . she ought to be married . . . women need stability . . . I don't care how she occupies herself in the meantime.'

"I said, 'Stop talking about me as if I were a car that must be parked somewhere ultimately. If you want to know, I'm perfectly happy at the moment.'

"They said, jointly: 'Sure, but he can never marry you.'

"I said, 'Talk about something else, please.'

"It's all right, Noel, I probably wouldn't write you about it, if I weren't tight myself. It was a pretty disgusting evening—but not extraordinary. We are an unmannerly generation. The best-brought up man you know is likely at any moment to start shouting his sexual ambitions in a speakeasy. It doesn't mean anything.

"This means something, though. It's damnably true that I shall someday look at myself in a mirror, and know that—not in the scarlet frock I wore tonight, or any other, shall I look like twenty-two, anymore. And wish that I had stability, meaning a husband to pay for facial massages through all my middle-age. But I shan't take such a husband. It would be too great a waste of you and me and dreams and love.

"I'm asking something of you, though. I probably wouldn't ask it if sober. Because the thought of growing old, alone, frightens me, would you write me a letter and say, 'I would marry you if I could.' I know you never can . . . but to have a two-line note that said you would have married me, had things been otherwise, would comfort me.

"Your affection for me is the loveliest thing I ever found, you know, in a world-full of second rate solutions for everything, and I should rather have the off-chance of permanence with you, than nineteen gold framed marriage certificates with anyone else. Can you understand though, that a two-line note would be comforting, because it *was* a dismal evening?"

He wrote me a long letter. I looked for it among the other letters he had written me. I read it, and put it aside. That would be the only letter I would keep, because I didn't believe the warmth could ever go from it. It ended: "The thing that all men look for, I have found, with you."

I recovered from that mood of aching-to-be-a wife.

Noel and I went about through October evenings, and were as happy as we had ever been—happier, for we grew more and more at ease with each other, and closer to each other in understanding. He said that we were getting like the two ancient philosophers who sat, contentedly, and listened to each other think.

One day, I was getting ready to leave the office, and thinking that I would have time to go to the gymnasium for an hour before I went home to dress for dinner with Noel, when my little assistant-secretary came in and said that a lady wanted to see me.

"Who is it, Doris?"

"She wouldn't give her name. She said it was personal. I thought you might know her. She has a black patch covering the whole left side of her face."

"Oh," I said, "Send her in Doris. . . . And you may go home. I shan't need you again tonight."

There was an instant in which I thought, "I should have refused to see her—she wasn't ever real to me, while I did not see her." But I knew that I could not have sent her away, really. I could not have done that, to Noel.

I said: "How do you do. Won't you sit down?"

She said: "I am Noel's wife. I have been wanting to talk to you for some time." She sat in the armchair beside my desk.

Light from the wall lamp opposite, fell across her. She was a rather tall woman—with a figure that might have been good, had she chosen her clothes carefully. She wore the sort of good, country tweeds that women select for practicality, for durability, without reference to the nuances of style.

Under her tan felt sports' hat, golden hair outcropped, with an effect of untidiness, that might, once, have been an effect of splendour. Over the left side of her face—a black patch concealed what lay beneath, from hat-brim to chin. The right side of her face was composed of a large eye, of violet-blue, a graceful brown eyebrow, clear white skin and half a mouth that once, obviously, the men who knew her said was "rosebud."

Well, I should have known that Noel's taste was all right. War bride married-in-haste, she might have been—she must have been composite of cream and roses then.

She said: "I feel this is an intrusion and that I should apologize. Something has happened that makes it necessary."

Yes, it was a well-bred voice. Curiously unformed, though, like the voice of a very young girl.

"That's quite all right. I have so much admiration for Noel that I'm delighted to meet his wife."

(Being civilized means that one keeps one's words unrelated to one's thoughts, when necessary.)

She said: "It will be easier for me—I am not used to talking to people—if you will let me say what I have to say—first."

I said, "As you wish."

"I don't like Noel, usually. If you had driven, when you were twenty, with a man who got drunk, and wrecked his car, and your face, so that you went about like a cripple, all the rest of your life, you would not like him."

I said, "Perhaps not."

She said: "I have had weeks and months and years to think. I have had nothing else to do, since the summer of 1919. Sometimes I think I have spoiled Noel's life. But he finished mine."

I said, "No doubt that's true. I met him years after all that. Can you tell me what it has to do with me?"

"Yes," she said, "I'm getting to all that. Granted that I loved someone else, when Noel came back from the war. He ended that for me, too."

I said, "Yes, quite."

"He is the only person I still know," she said, "who is going on in the world where things happen. . . . My sister is a tired old maid."

"I have understood that, a little," I said. "You may have heard a good deal about Noel and me. I have never tried to take what you have kept."

"I know," she said. "I have nothing against you. I used to quarrel with Noel, because he met younger, beautiful women, while not a man this side of hell will look at me, again. But I've got reconciled to that. Only—now it's different."

"Why?" I said.

"Because Noel and I are going to have a baby, in seven months or so."

I held on to the edge of my desk. The sharp corners cut into my hands. Noel's wife became part of a picture—the office walls and ceiling—and the view of Manhattan lights outside. The picture swung, and swung, crazily.

I said to myself: "You have been rarely privileged, Patricia. You have been The Wife, and The Other Woman. You have played ball on both sides of that net, and been privileged to lose on both. That's a rare experience."

I said to myself: "This finishes you, Patricia . . . that wife that was a vague fantastic figure on the outskirts of his life—owns him now for all time. Poor Noel, poor Noel—he'll never go to Yokohama, he can never leave New York. He'll live and die where he is, tied to that half-masked figure, and the red-haired baby I wanted, that woman will have."

I said to myself: "No, one doesn't go insane, one doesn't scream—one remembers that the years taught one something. But what, after all, did they teach? Oh, yes, I remember—that all things pass—that all things pass."

I said, "Are you glad that you and Noel are having a baby?"

Noel's wife said: "Yes. He used to talk about having one—ten or eleven years ago, when he loved me. After my accident I never wanted one, for years, because I thought a child would be frightened by a face like mine—and I didn't want a baby that would be afraid of me. But—this last year or so" (this last year or so—all the time I'd known Noel), "I've thought that a baby wouldn't mind, if I was good to it. I have wanted one for a year—it didn't happen before."

I said: "I think it's very nice for you."

She said: "I came to see you, because I know you are Noel's mistress. I haven't needed him, or wanted him, often, all these years. I did not have anything to talk to him about. But now, I want him as the father of my child."

(God—that was a phrase they used in movie captions.)

"I have not told Noel," that unformed, girlish voice went on. "I wanted to see you first. I wanted to ask you to stop seeing him. I plan to live in a suburb close to New York now, and have him live with me, or at least come to see me every other day or so—so he will grow fond of his child. . . . Noel used to want a child once, when we were young . . . I hope this child is a son. . . . And I'm asking you to do this, because you are a young and handsome woman. . . . There will be other men for you. I have only Noel . . . and this child, who will give me something to live for."

I managed to say: "I understand how you must feel about it."

(She had called me Noel's "mistress." Ugly word, "mistress." He and I had loved each other so . . . Noel would want a son . . . he had wanted one of mine . . . Noel to grow old, to be bound forever . . . to end up on a newspaper copy desk, when he was tired—and through. Noel was honourable. I had so loved that in him. Noel would stick to his disfigured wife . . . who was with child.)

I said: "I had a child once, I remember. It died."

Something of animation, of sympathy, even, stirred in that half-face. She said: "I am sorry. Was it a boy or a girl? How old would it be?"

I said: "It was a son. I forget how old he would have been. Almost four, I think."

She said: "Well, will you give Noel up, so that I can have him to be a father for my child? . . . Some weeks ago he wanted to go to Asia . . . I wasn't sure about this then. . . . He won't mind not going to Asia, now."

I thought: "How little she knows Noel, nowadays."

I looked out, at the dark New York skyline, with the lights of other offices, shining. I wondered what the people, sitting in those offices, after hours, were discussing. I thought: "This finishes me . . . but it finishes Noel, forever, and he is a more valuable person than I."

She said: "Don't blame me, Patricia . . . may I call you Patricia? I have always heard of you, as that. I held Noel back from Asia . . . but think of the things his careless driving of that automobile has held me from, through nine years. . . . And I'll try to make it up to him by having a child."

I said: "I am thinking." And a most curious idea came . . . and warmed me who had felt for ten minutes, as if nothing in life could warm me again.

And I thought: "Yes—if I can manage it. (And when in some speakeasy someone who dislikes me says, 'By the way, Patricia, what happened to your beautiful redheaded boy-friend?' I shall answer, 'Oh, didn't you hear? I gave him the air—and the continent of Asia.' I shan't make that answer, though. If I manage this, I shall never tell anyone, except perhaps Lucia . . . and Helena.)"

I said: "Why don't you pack up and go to Asia with Noel? Start life over, with your child?"

She said: "I will show you." She took the black mask off her face. I looked. There was a sightless red blotch, where there had been contours that men—Noel, no doubt—had ten years ago found desirable to kiss. There was a congealed horror. . . . Whatever of hate, or resentment, I had had against that woman, died. Had I suffered that, what sort of woman would I have been, after?

She covered that twisted red scar that had been half a face. I heard her voice, saying "If you were I, would you travel among strangers, with this?"

I did not pity her, actually. One does not pity fate, when it intervenes between one's self and what one wanted most of all in the world.

I said, "No" at first "I wouldn't travel." Then I thought of Noel . . . who loved the beauty of women, and the beauty of strange places, and I said, "No, but—there are things that you could do."

"What?" she said. "After the war, I went to various facial surgeons. They could do nothing for me. . . . There was not enough left, on which to re-build."

Then, suddenly, she began to cry, out of her one violet-blue eye. And I said: "Don't cry. I am thinking about you—and Noel whom I loved so much. You don't mind hearing me say that I loved Noel so much."

She said: "No. He is, in a way, a good man. I don't exactly remember loving him. I was only nineteen then, you see. But as much as he could be, he was good to me through these years. I have often been bitter—and blamed him. I suppose no one was to blame."

I thought: "*And there are no villains in the piece.* I knew that before. If there is a God, among things so badly managed—if there is One, let Him please remember that, in this, I did the best I could. Because of a baby . . . a baby with long dark lashes that curled over his white skin . . . a baby who died long ago . . . and because of Noel who healed everything that had hurt me . . . and who thought me a generous woman, in this I shall do the best I can."

I said to her: "Noel wants to go to Asia. You go with him. If you stay around here, I don't promise to keep out of his life. I don't know that I can. If you go, you have him for all time . . . and he has the work he wants."

She began to speak. I said: "Wait a minute . . . I have a friend . . . a painter . . . a girl who paints masks . . . theatrical masks, mostly. But she did three for a girl who was going South—a girl with a specially delicate skin that couldn't stand sunburn—and that girl wore them all the time, outdoors, during the daytime. I'll get this Painter to make some masks for you. They aren't obvious masks, fifteen feet away. And you can tell people whom you meet travelling that you—hurt—your face recently, and are just wearing a mask until it gets better."

It was dreadful, to watch what waked in that half of a white, cold face. "Do you mean it?" she said. "Do you mean that I could go and see the Coast, and go on a ship to Japan, and not be pointed out, and have people shudder and turn away? . . . My sister is so tiresome; it would be such relief to see new places. And you don't think Noel would be ashamed of me?"

(I said to myself, "Since you have to do it, Patricia, do it in the grand manner. Hope that that may be some comfort to you—through all the years when nothing else will be much comfort.")

"Your name is Beatrice, isn't it?" I said. "I am going to call you Beatrice—if you don't stand in the way of Noel's career, he will become very fond of you, I'm sure. And he will love the baby . . . I'm going to take you to see Helena, now. She is the girl who makes the masks. She should get them finished for you in a week or so. Then you could come to town again, to try them on—and if you like, I'll take you about to various smart wholesale clothing houses—where you can buy quantities of things for travelling.

"You have a lovely figure—and, after the child is born, you can use these things in the East. . . . In a good many places you might find it intriguing to wear a veil, as if you were a Mohammedan woman. Let your yellow hair show, and everyone will find the effect piquant as can be."

She was shaking with excitement. "You make it seem so real." She said. "I like you. I thought I should hate you. I think I am sorry . . . that I am taking Noel away from you."

Years of practice in flippancy were a wall against my back. "Oh, don't mind that," I said. "I shall get over it. I have got over a good many things, first and last."

I telephoned Helena: "I have some rush work for you . . . client's a friend of mine . . . it's masks . . . I'll explain in detail when I see you. . . . May I bring her up, now?"

She said: "Sure. Why does your voice sound so queer? Lucia's here, visiting. Shall I tell her to wait?"

I said, "For God's sake, do, Helena. I shan't be more than fifteen minutes."

"Come on," I said to Noel's wife.

In the taxi, on the way to Helena's, she said: "Will she have to look at my face?"

"You won't mind, Beatrice. It's just as if she were a surgeon. She'll just want to know the proportions."

When we climbed the stairs to Helena's apartment I thought of divers other times I had climbed them—feeling happy, feeling sad, feeling tired. Now, for the moment at least, I felt—nothing.

Lucia was sitting, being very decorative, in a warm brown frock and furs, on the little couch. Helena was finishing a fashion drawing. They both looked at me sharply. I said: "This is Noel's wife . . . you both have met Noel. . . . He is going to take the Yokohama job I mentioned to you, and Beatrice is going with him. . . . She had an accident, long time ago. . . . And she wants Helena to make her some masks, so that she won't be embarrassed travelling."

Lucia said: "Why, that's a *marvellous* idea. Helena's masks are *so* decorative."

Helena said: "I should *love* to make her half a dozen masks . . . blend the skin tones with her gorgeous hair. She has the most beautiful hair I have seen in years."

Beatrice hesitated a moment, and then took off her hat. Her hair *was* lovely. She arranged it badly, but I could take her to a hair-dresser next time she came to town.

I walked across the room, and dropped my coat and hat on Helena's daybed.

"That's a lovely violet frock you have, Pat," Lucia said from across the room.

Helena followed me, without being obvious about it. "There's a bottle of Scotch under the washstand in the bath," she said, in an undertone. "For God's sake go pour yourself a couple of drinks. You look as if you were going to faint."

"What's Noel's wife's first name, Pat?" she asked aloud. "I always call my models by their first names."

I said, "Beatrice."

"Beatrice," said Helena, "I want to make a mould of your face . . . it won't take long. . . . Have you time?"

"Yes. . . . My train doesn't leave until eight-thirty."

"I'll leave you for five minutes," I said.

Lucia followed me into the bath. My hands shook, when I began to pour the Scotch. Lucia took the bottle away from me, and poured me a large drink.

She lighted two cigarettes; gave one to me, and said nothing, until I had finished the Scotch.

Then, "You are behaving damn well, Pat, but what is it all about?"

"Noel's wife is going to present him with a child," I said. "He has always wanted one. Isn't it an extraordinary world?"

Lucia put her arms around my shoulders, and for a dreadful instant I clung to her . . . trying not to sob, lest the sobs be heard in the room outside.

"Steady," Lucia said. I remembered that she, or someone else, had said that to me long ago.

"It's quite all right," I said. "Noel and I did manage a year."

"God," said Lucia, to the shower bath and Helena's array of face lotions. "There are certain women, under the present system who should take up professional card playing for a living. They certainly have no luck in love."

I laughed.

Lucia said: "You are wiser than you were . . . you could hold on, this time, and he'd love you a while and then hate you . . . because you would stand between him and his concept of himself as a decent person . . . I repeat, that you are behaving well."

I had cold-creamed my face. Now I was putting rouge on. I said: "Well, I doubt that it'll be much satisfaction to me in the years when Noel has Asia to console him . . . I don't know though. I never tried it before . . . but maybe the only satisfaction in anything, in the end, is the consciousness of having behaved well."

Lucia said, "The Victorians expressed that as 'doing one's duty as one saw it.'"

I said: "Some of the duties we see would just make a Victorian cock-eyed." I arranged my lipstick, as if I felt the effect important.

"By the way, does Noel know how you've settled his destiny between you?"

"Hell, no. Beatrice plans to tell him over the week-end—but I shall tell him, at dinner, tonight."

Lucia put a little unnecessary powder on her lovely nose.

"Better spend the week-end with Sam and me, Pat."

"All right," I said. "Thank you."

"I must go outside," she said. "Noel's wife will begin to suspect a conference. I see why you are doing it, Patricia. Whatever minor hells you and I have visited—that girl's lived in a major one."

"I know," I said.

Lucia kissed me, for perhaps the second time since we had known each other. "Is there anything I can do for you, child, before I go?" She asked.

"Yes, stop at a drug store and telephone Noel. Tell him I'll meet him at Dante's at ten for dinner, and that he is not to call for me. I'll have just time to dress, after I put her on her train."

Lucia put her hand on the door, and then turned back to me. "Patricia, I mean this seriously. . . . Most things have to come to an end. You know that, by now, as well as I. My candid opinion is that you and Noel might have come to a much worse end than this . . ."

I said: "Thank you, Lucia. I'll see you for the week-end." And I wiped powder off my eyebrows.

Helena had been managing Beatrice dextrously. . . . It was an excited, an almost happy, woman that I put on the train.

She chattered. She said: "That Helena girl says she'll make me masks to wear in sunlight, and rain, and electric light—and moonlight, even. She is most kind . . . I haven't been so interested in anything in years. . . . And you don't mind about Noel, do you? I mean, you'll find a successor to him . . . you are *so* pretty. Did anyone ever tell you you had a spiritual face?"

I thought: "It's got spiritual by traversing a good many beds, first and last. . . . No, Noel did that for it, if it *is* spiritual."

I said: "There are men for whom one finds substitutes, but not successors. But don't you worry about that. . . . You think of seeing Fujiyama, you know, the always snowcapped mountain of Japan?"

She said, "I hope you see it one day, yourself." I didn't mind—I was the first woman whom she had had a chance to patronize in ten years, probably.

I went home, and dressed, and dined with Noel.

After dinner, we went to his apartment. I said to him: "Go mix yourself a highball. . . . There is something that I want to tell you, and I want you to look out the windows, and think of time and space and relativity, while I tell it, and not interrupt until I finish."

I began: "You can go to Asia, after all."

When I was done, he came and put his arms around me; and I ran my fingers through his hair, and we did not talk, for a long long time. Thereafter, we had some debate as to details . . . but no man of his type is very eager to yield adventure even for a woman.

Noel was to have Asia. He suffered a good deal, I believe, at the thought of losing me. He might suffer more, as Asia grew commonplace; but, meanwhile, Asia was his other Great Desire.

We lived through a week in which we lived as if all things between us had lasted since the beginning of Time, and were to last forever. Then I had a wire from Beatrice, who wanted to know what time on Thursday she should arrive, to go clothes-buying among the fashionable wholesalers.

I arranged to take Thursday afternoon off . . . and since her sentence to wearing a black patch was so nearly ended, we went without embarrassment to various wholesale clothing places and bought tweeds, and evening frocks, and sweaters-and-skirts, and jersey ensembles, and hats to wear with them all. (Even a silver turban for dancing.)

We ended the afternoon at a shoe-shop, and I discovered with some amusement that, though she was a taller woman, her shoes were a smaller size than mine.

There was more enthusiasm in her voice than there had been the week before. She told the shoeclerk gaily that she was travelling to Chicago, to see her mother whom she hadn't visited in ten years.

(Noel was to join her in Chicago. He was leaving New York, a day or two later than she.)

Helena could not see us before six-thirty. Beatrice asked me to go to tea with her, to fill in the interval. I said: "Well, I was thinking of going to a speakeasy. I know a nice one, on Fifty-Second Street, where women without escorts are not conspicuous."

Her voice was like the voice of a sub-debutante invited to an important college prom. "Oh, *could* we go to a speakeasy?" she said. "You know, my accident was in 1919, before Prohibition, and I have never seen a speakeasy."

"That's wonderful," I said. "I have wasted my youth in so many of them." We went to Fifty-Second Street. Beatrice was stirred by the fact that she could put her foot on a brass rail at the bar. She had read about brass rails but never seen one. We had two Alexanders, and they did not seem to disturb her, unduly.

I thought, simultaneously, that this girl was only a year or two older than myself and that, except for one thing and another, she would have been much prettier than I.

(And would have held Noel forever, perhaps? . . . The chances that determine people's lives. Well, no sense considering them at any length. One accepted them. It was easier.)

Helena had made six masks for Beatrice. They were lovely things—she must have worked until dawn, several nights in succession, to finish them. Across the width of her apartment they were amazingly life-like. Even viewed closely there was nothing in the least grotesque about them, because they were so decorative.

There were full-face masks for evening wear, and a full-face mask for wear with sports' clothes. There were half-masks, too. "And how do I eat, wearing them?" Beatrice asked.

Helena explained that the half-masks were designed for that. . . . "They are cut out, a little, around the mouth. The explanation of it is intricate, but you eat a cookie, and see how simple it is."

If a woman with half a face could glow, Beatrice glowed when she tried them on. Her hands (which were well-shaped, graceful hands) looked excited.

"They are wonderful," she said. "So light, and so comfortable, and *pretty*. How much should I pay you for them?"

Helena said: "Nothing. Patricia is an old friend of mine."

Something—something vaguely familiar in the expression of the mouth and chin on the full-face masks, disturbed me. I could not think why.

Lucia drifted in, to admire—and Beatrice tried each mask on, again, for her. Then Beatrice showed all her new clothes (she had insisted on bringing them along, in a cab) to Helena; and Lucia and I went into the bathroom for a drink of Scotch.

Lucia said: "Do you feel all right?"

I said, "Yes. She is leaving in the middle of next week, you know, and Noel is going at the end of it."

I said, "Those masks *are* extraordinary, aren't they. They are not only decorative—they have a definite individuality, even a definite charm."

Lucia said: "Helena always liked you."

"What do you mean?"

"Honestly, don't you know, Pat? Was there nothing about the lower part of the face, in the full masks, that you recognized?"

"Something, vaguely, but I don't know what."

Lucia smiled—her all-comprehending smile.

"Ever see your face, Pat, when you were looking tranquil, and well pleased with life? . . . Helena has a sardonic humour. . . . She's copied that grave smile of yours, to follow Noel, all over Asia."

On the way to Beatrice's suburban train, she and I had a short conversation. "Maybe you dislike me," she said, "but I hope not . . . I feel that I owe you a good deal, and I thought . . . if my child were a girl I might name her for you."

I lighted a cigarette. "God is an ironist," I said, but that seemed beyond Beatrice's comprehension.

She said: "Anyway. I wanted to tell you . . . that I mean to be good to Noel. I know that he will have to leave me by myself, much of the time, in the Far East" (—the words conjured up pictures of the places Noel and I might have seen, together . . . the sounds and colours of bazaars, I would never know them, now. I drew a long breath) "but I shan't object," she said . . . "Now that he is going to be my husband, really officially, I mean to give him as much liberty as can be managed. After all, I shall have the baby."

"That's sensible, Beatrice," I said. "And, if he should have a brief romance with a Geisha girl, don't curse him out for it.

He'll come back, to see the baby, and to get himself a clean shirt. That's marriage."

"I'll behave, Patricia," she said. . . . Her train was leaving in three minutes. She stopped by the train-gate. "Tell me you don't hate me," she said.

"I don't hate you. I hope you work it out, Beatrice." After two minutes, now, I would never see her again. For that at least, I could be grateful.

"Beatrice—they say there are splendid British surgeons in the East, and facial surgery has been elaborated, since the War. . . . Perhaps, something may be managed for you, there."

She smiled half a smile, and *she* found a good exit line. (Peter, who was almost forgotten now, had asked me to find one, once.) Beatrice said: "Meanwhile there are the masks . . . you wear them, too, don't you?" She ran, not ungracefully, to catch her train.

I hurried home, to dine with Noel.

And the infinite time that he and I had felt destined for us, together, was determined now as ten days. They were not unhappy days. We talked to each other as if all the years we had lived were stable behind our comprehension of each other—and as if all the years ahead were ours to share.

Only once, I spoke to him, of the little time remaining. I said: "I understand better now, about the French aristos, who died serenely on the guillotine. I don't believe they suffered at the last. . . . Relieved from all concern with the day after tomorrow—they were serene. Kenneth felt like that, do you remember?"

He said, "Yes. . . . The only problem is whether one adds life to one's years or years to one's life. . . . Or did you tell me that, concerning something else, Pat?"

I said, "Concerning an Ex-wife, perhaps. . . . Noel, your hair is a colour destined to shine in my soul."

But he was thinking of Asiatic cities, where he would live his life—and I let him talk, about the possibility of learning Chinese, in five years.

"It is a five year contract, Pat—with option of renewal for the same length of time. When I come back—I may be forty-five years old."

(In ten years, I shall be thirty-seven—and whatever I am spared—I begged to be spared, meeting Noel next, when I am thirty-seven.)

Noel was still working on the *Times*. On one of his last days, there, he went to Lakehurst, to do an aviation story. I wrote him a letter—because I had written him always, when he was on an out-of-town assignment. (We had agreed, that I was not to write him to Yokohama. There would be no return-from-Yokohama, in which I would be concerned. He was to write me only in the stories . . . that the *Times* would run, about how the years went, in Asia.)

I wrote him, to Lakehurst:

"Please don't decide that I care very little—because I am taking this so calmly. I have wrung my hands over it, a good bit, first and last.

"You-and-I apparently come to an end. The commonplace and possessive and exacting and stupid relationships, into which people drift, come to *bad* ends soon or late. But what has that to do with you and me? We may yet be sitting before a fireplace, when you are eighty-seven and I am seventy-nine, discussing flavours of wines, and of adventures. Why not?"

I believed that, too, for five or ten minutes.

That was my last letter to Noel.

I put it back in the tin box, with the others, and put the rest of his letters to me, unread, in the box, too.

I went upstairs to change my dress.

And thought, not for the first time, that vanity is so great a blessing to women that it should be listed among the major virtues. Recollection that the last time Noel ever saw me, I was wearing a bright red dress from Paris, with a hat that matched it precisely, and a brand-new grey Krimmer coat, would be some comfort to me, always. That might be absurd. It was none the less profoundly true.

I went back to his apartment, and put fresh logs on the fire. He came in.

"You're looking very lovely, Pat," he said. "Have you decided where you'd like to dine?"

"Dante's, I think."

"Grand idea . . . and we'll have crabmeat ravigotte and filet mignon and Chianti and crêpes suzette. . . ."

We had an evening, and a night, and a morning, left to spend. We spent them as gaily as we had spent a hundred others. We pretended to each other that this evening and night and morning, were just like all the others.

We pretended so successfully, that, on the way to his train I felt that I was just seeing Noel off on another out-of-town assignment.

As always, he took me through the train-gates, at the Grand Central (although non-passengers are supposed to make their parting speeches outside the gates) so that we could talk a little longer. As always, I watched the porter arrange his baggage. As always, we walked out onto the platform, and Noel gave me a cigarette.

But I found that I couldn't hold my cigarette, steadily, beside this train. So I threw it away, and Noel threw his away.

I said: "How much time is there?"

He said: "Two or three minutes."

I said: "I don't want to be casual. I want to tell you that I shall love you forever and ever, whatever that means . . ."

"Whatever it means, Pat, I shall, too."

He took off his hat. He was a young man with red hair that was the shade of bright-burnished bronze, and a nice chin, that almost had a dimple in it, and a grey tweed overcoat, and a grey muffler I had given him. I wanted to remember exactly how he looked . . . I wanted to think of some words that would be significant—that would make him happy to remember.

A silly inappropriate tag from Virgil came into my head: "Forsan et haec olim meminisse iuvabit." —"And perhaps someday even this will be pleasant to remember." He had taken my hand, and was holding it so tightly that an old emerald ring—a ring I wore because Noel had admired it—hurt my finger. I tried to remember where the emerald ring came from.

Noel said: "I must go, now, Patricia. . . . Could you manage a smile in the face of a transcontinental express?" I smiled; he smiled at me.

Someone was shouting "all aboard." Noel's lips were brushing against my face, he had let go of my hand, he had gone, I couldn't see him, inside the train. I ran along, looking for him. He was there, smiling, with his face close to the train window, and his hand against the windowpane. I put my hand, on the outside of the pane against his on the inside.

He was looking unhappy, but he was smiling. He was saying something to me, but there was a noise—I could not hear. The train made too much noise starting . . . and the windowpane pulled from under my hand, and was gone and Noel's face was gone. There were other faces, all blurred together, passing, behind train windows. There was the noise of a train gathering speed. Then there was an empty track where a train had been.

It seemed very quiet.

I walked back along the platform, and upstairs, through the station, and out onto the street. There were crowds of people hurrying about as if they had somewhere important to go. I wished that I had somewhere important to go.

I had the day to myself—I might go call on Helena, and the blue-eyed child who had just discovered Broadway first nights. The child had told me, in a pleased way, last time I had seen her that she had to hurry home to dress for an "important" first night.

I did not want to go see Helena, or her. I wanted to think of somewhere important to go myself. I began to laugh at all the people running around.

I passed a newsstand, and remembered that from the day I had first met Noel, I had read every single one of his stories.

Then I was pleased with myself, because I had thought of somewhere important, to go. . . . I walked across town, to the *Times*, and bought a five-year subscription.

XVII

There remained no reason now for me to breakfast at eleven, instead of eight o'clock. I gave up my noon-to-seven o'clock job, and found one from nine to five, at a better salary.

Before beginning at the new place, I went to Bermuda for a fortnight. Bermuda—because a letter from Bill came along, while I was trying to think of somewhere that I wanted to go.

The letter read:

"My Dear Patricia,

"Over brandy flips in the morning and champagne cup at night, I wish you were here. The climate and the scenery and the absence of automobiles make me able to believe that the last twenty years haven't happened. Except when I look at the women's clothes.

"Can't you take a vacation? If you turn up, I'll take you to the damn fool race-track that reminds me of county fairs in Maryland when I was young. All your generation should go to the tropics for ten years anyway, and watch roses blooming under palm-trees. You'd all come back languid enough to be ladylike.

"I don't suppose you'll leave your silly job, but if you would I'd take you driving in a carriage, and you could pretend you were one of your own aunts, exhibiting gentle alarm at my recklessness if I went around a corner at a gallop."

I thought it might be pleasant to contemplate Bill's contented old age for a couple of weeks, so I cabled him and sailed. But I stayed at a hotel about a mile from Bill's, lest contemplation of contented old age through all my waking hours, should grow monotonous.

In the mornings I swam before breakfast, and dressed and had breakfast, and sat about languidly on the hotel terrace, looking at the palm trees and thinking about nothing, until Bill's wide sturdy figure rose over the brow of the hill.

"Well, well, let's do a bit of pub-crawling before luncheon. Cheer you up. You look as if you needed a bit of cheering up. . . . God knows why . . . you're young." Something like that was his invariable greeting. Then we walked down to the landing and took a launch for Hamilton, while Bill told me I wore white, or blue, or yellow, or whatever I was wearing, well.

In the Bermudiana bar, Bill sat with a brandy flip in front of him, his wide red kind face beaming, explaining that all I needed was a husband, and considering, in his strong loud voice, those of his contemporaries who might qualify.

"We're all too damn old for you, Pat, though. Wish I knew some younger men; wish I'd had sons." And he sighed briefly for the sons whose non-existence was the only apparent regret of his life.

Then he trotted me about Hamilton, every day, muttering, "Women like trinkets; always cheers a woman up to buy her trinkets." At intervals he vanished, briefly, into some little shop, to reappear with coral necklaces or earrings or brooches, that were not suitable for wear with anything I owned, but that I wore, with everything.

In the afternoons he played golf with men of his age.

I went alone and sat on unbelievably pink sands, and watched incredibly blue and white waves come curling in to shore, and read "The World of William Clissold."

Through long afternoons, while the shadows of the palm trees lengthened across the sands, and a small breeze fragrant of sea and palms and roses, blew gaily along the shore, I read and reread that section of the second volume where Mr. Wells considers the relationship of men and women.

I found therein solace for my resentment against the stupid jest I had long called secretly this damn freedom for women. There were sentences by Mr. Wells:

"We live sexually in a world of mixed and broken codes, and irregular and extravagant experiments and defiances. . . . Our ways of living are more provisional now than our governments. . . .

"One finds the companion-mate as a dream in the hearts of a few people here and there, as an experiment, an almost hopeless experiment, like a match lit in a high wind, or a swimmer borne away by a stream."

I read that, and looked at the shadows of the palm trees on the sand, and thought: "Noel, Noel . . . a dream made real, an experiment achieved—and a dream lost, an experiment ended forever. But it did not end in shabbiness and recriminations—so there remains, something. . . . Something . . . perhaps very much . . . a fire to warm my hands at all the days of my life."

And I was able even to make a jest to myself, about Noel and me. It was not a very gay jest. It was, "Well, we both were destined to see palm trees, but not in the same country."

I went back from these solitary afternoons to dine and drink champagne cup with Bill, and to listen to Bill's stories of the early nineteen hundreds, feeling as serene as I used to feel, on coming home from afternoons of sailing in a breeze that was strong and exciting, when I was a very young girl.

And if sometimes, I waked at night, and listened to the warm steady wind sweeping through the palm trees outside, and ached, rather horribly, for Noel whom I would not ever see again—still, I knew that ache would pass, and was quite sure, this time, that remembrance of lovely things we had shared, would long outlast the ache that they were ended.

I went back to New York, feeling that I had been away a long time.

Lucia met me at the dock. It was a great comfort to see her. I said "Thank heaven, darling, you aren't likely to dash off to Asia or South America or elsewhere, permanently, ever. I look forward to spending week-ends with you in Westchester when we're both doddering."

"Thanks," she said. "You are looking all beautifully rested. But tell me, are you convalescing?"

"I think so."

I got my baggage through the customs, and we started up-town in Lucia's car. I hauled a bottle of Crême Yvette out of my blouse, for Lucia, and said: "I've been wearing corsets all day for your sake, to keep this from falling through. I hope you are appreciative."

"Oh darling, my favourite liqueur," she said, "But I don't know whether I can drink it. I'm going to have a baby . . . I think I'm very pleased and Sam is of course radiant . . . I'm dieting like mad, though, so that I shan't permanently ruin what figure I have . . . they give you a funny diet."

"That's grand about the baby if you want it," I said.

Lucia's conversation was noticeably circuitous; her usual method of approaching some news that might be distressing in effect.

She looked out of the car window. "It always seems to rain in New York when people come back from cruises, I've noticed," she said. "Peter and Judith have a daughter, I hear."

I was not glad or sorry or especially interested. I said: "Everyone seems to be doing something about the next generation, except me."

"You're young yet, Patricia. . . . Listen, Nathaniel's staying with us. His father finally died, and left Nat all his money, with a note, saying that he appreciated the years Nat gave up to looking after him. Nat is taking it very hard . . . the note seems to have made him feel that he never was nice to his father . . . was impatient with him and so on. All that sort of thing is so dreadfully futile. . . . But Nat is in something of a state."

"I know," I said, "Nathaniel is such a dear."

Lucia looked at me for an instant, speculatively.

"No, darling," I said, "All I want is peace. I feel as old as Time, no matter how perennial I look."

"I know," said Lucia, "A comfortable fact about all of us, though, is that we have got through so much, so fast, there can't be much left. I doubt if this will be a long-lived generation. We shall reach sedateness via emotional exhaustion, by forty—and die of senility at forty-eight. . . . I was afraid that the news about Nathaniel would disturb you."

"Or was it the news about Pete you were afraid of?" I asked. "Nothing is ever going to disturb me much, again."

"That's grand," said Lucia. She looked very preoccupied. Then: "Pat, would you think me a horribly greedy woman, if I got the chauffeur to open this bottle somehow, and stop for glasses somewhere, and we drank some of the Crême Yvette, now? I do adore it . . . and I'm so afraid the doctor will forbid it. If I had a little, before I asked him, it couldn't hurt me, much."

We drank Crême Yvette all the way to Lucia's house, and were unable to eat dinner, but the Crême Yvette had tasted so good that we did not care.

Nathaniel seemed very glad to see me. He *was* looking unhappy. "He's lost his occupation in life," Lucia said, later. "He has been devoted to his father for the eight or nine years since he was twenty, and feels lost with no responsibility, now. I am going to suggest that he adopt an orphan, poor darling."

Nevertheless, Sam and Lucia and Nat and I had a pleasant enough week-end, and then I went to work.

January went by slushily and drearily, so did February. I worked very hard, and missed Noel very badly, and hunted through the *Times* for his stories as they appeared. They were not signed, and I was never quite sure whether they were his, or someone else's. They were written from so very far away.

One rainy March day, I found Nathaniel waiting for me in my hallway, when I came home from work. He was looking more cheerful than I had seen him, all Winter. When I brought him upstairs, he began flinging bright-coloured booklets, from an envelope he carried, all across a couch. They were travel booklets.

His voice was jubilant. "Pat, the doctor says I should leave the business in the hands of the office-manager—he knows more about it than I do, anyway—and go on a trip. Do you know, I haven't been anywhere for so many years, I didn't realize that I could go, now."

I took off my hat, and laid it on a table, and smoothed my hair. I should miss Nat, too, but it was nice that he should go places . . . he had wanted to, for so long.

"Where are you going, Nat?"

He began picking up booklets and waving them at me. "I don't know. Bermuda, Cuba, Florida, New Orleans."

"You blessed idiot," I said. "Why not around the world?"

He looked at me as if I had produced two full sized rabbits from the small hat on the table.

"My God," he said, "I *could* go 'round the world."

"Wait a moment, darling, and I'll mix you a drink to help you get used to the idea," I said. "You must promise to send me postcards of mosques and things."

I was tired, and had a cold, and wished I could summon more enthusiasm about it, because Nat was such a pleasant person.

"Don't mix a drink yet," he said. "I want to tell you something . . . I want you to come along with me."

I stared at him. He began to talk very fast. "I want you to marry me, I mean. Oh, I know you've never thought of that—I mentioned it just once when I was tight, I think. Perhaps I am not passionately in love with you, but if you don't mind that, we might have fun. You are very gay to go places with . . . it would be lovely to have you along on a trip 'round the world, and I should be very lonely, by myself. I *am* fond of you, you know."

I still stared at him. I said: "I am fond of you, too . . . I suppose I like you better than any man I know, nowadays."

His voice was more confident than it had been. "Better come along then, Pat. And that'll be that."

I remembered having heard someone say that his father made decisions fast.

"Nat, dear, just a minute." I felt very tired.

I wanted to say—to God or Noel or someone who would understand: "I have travelled such a long way, all the way through youth, I think, and I am so tired. You must not blame me too much, for taking what shelter offers, now."

I smiled at Nathaniel and I said, "I'll be able to talk in an instant, darling. Is that all right?"

"Of course, Pat, child," he said. "I didn't mean to startle you."

I looked at my hat, lying on the table, beside an unread copy of the *Times*. I looked at the dark outside the windows. Rain was splashing hard against the panes. I wished that I were not too tired to think.

And a wave of remembrance of Noel swept over me. Vividly, as if I had seen him an hour before, I could remember his smile, and the exact shade of his hair, and the way his mouth felt when he bent down to kiss me. Noel—who had lifted me, for a while, to the level of his strength. . . . Remembrances enfolded me warmly—ebbed, ebbed and were gone. I stood alone, in a room with Nathaniel.

I said, "Nat, how about my gaudy past? I am supposed to have had one, you know." He shrugged his shoulders.

"Would have had one myself, if I'd been you, no doubt. That doesn't bother me. I'd as soon not know the details, though."

I said: "All right. I'll marry you, Nat dear. Thank you for asking me." We both laughed; he kissed me; and we went to dinner.

Lucia was very pleased.

We were married one April afternoon at the Municipal Building, where, long ago, someone with the same name as I, had married Peter. A phrase in the ceremony seemed vaguely familiar.

"Do you promise—to cleave to him only, forsaking all others, as long as you both shall live?" Well, this time, it might be true.

Because Nathaniel's father had died so recently, we had no other celebration.

We were sailing that midnight—going around the world.

All our friends came to the boat, to wish us *bon voyage.* I said appropriate things, in answer to their felicitations, until my throat hurt from talking and talking.

Bill was ill and could not come to the boat, but he sent us a case of champagne, by his own bootlegger, a very large Italian who appeared suddenly, made a flowery speech wishing us long life, and gave us a detailed account of his difficulties in getting the champagne aboard. It was excellent champagne.

We began to drink it immediately—when it was almost all gone, people began saying "good-bye."

Lucia drew me aside, and said: "Do you like your ermine wrap? I helped Nathaniel choose it for you."

I said: "It's a beautiful one. Why did he want to get me an ermine wrap?"

"Ever since he read 'The Green Hat,' Nat thinks ermine wraps are robes of romance. Pat, he's a grand person." She hesitated, then. . . . "It's none of my affair, Pat, but are you thinking that Asia is a large place, or a small one?"

We regarded each other. I said: "It is a large place, Lucia. Still one never knows. . . ."

Lucia said: "That'll be all right, I suppose." She ran her finger down the ermine cloak. "It might be labelled 'Success in the American edition,' Patricia."

We smiled at each other. She went away. Everyone else was gone, except Nathaniel.

He said, "Patricia, I'm going upstairs to send a wire or radio or whatever one sends at the last minute, to Bill, to thank him for the wine. Then I'll come back to take you on deck, so that we can watch New York go by."

"All right, darling. I want to put on some fresh makeup, anyway."

The steward was clearing away the champagne bottles and glasses from our living room. I went into our bedroom.

Champagne bottles and glasses were all over the place. I put on fresh lipstick and powder and perfume. I felt warm with champagne, and interested in going around the world.

There was a long mirror on the door of the bedroom. I walked toward it, and stood still.

In the mirror, a small, slim young woman stood. She had black straight shining hair, grey eyes, and a curved red mouth. Around her eyes, there were faint shadows, that would be lines in ten years, but not for ten years. She wore a rose-coloured net dress. One side of its ruffled skirt swung out like a half-opened fan. She wore an ermine wrap, negligently, over her shoulders. They were creamy shoulders—that many men had kissed—and that now, only one man would kiss, probably.

She did not look happy or unhappy. She looked a little tired and a little amused.

I wondered what she was like, underneath her attitudes. But I knew now, that neither I nor anyone else would ever be sure as to that.

She and I bowed to each other gravely, and I went to join Nathaniel.

Nathaniel and I stood silent. The ship moved smoothly down the river, and we watched New York move past. Nathaniel put a friendly hand on my shoulder.

Slipping past, slipping past, the lights of city skyscrapers, and with them all my life. Peter, Patrick, Kenneth, Lucia, Noel—voices and sounds of people and things I used to know.

Nathaniel spoke. "You won't be lonely, Patricia?"

"No, my dear."

He flung his arms out toward that fantastic skyline.

"We shall come back, Patricia, and build a skyscraper or two . . . then we'll go on again . . . I want to see all the cities of the world. Capetown, and Budapest and Moscow—Canton and Calcutta and Yokohama . . . I love the sounds of their names."

His voice grew graver.

"I mean to be very good to you, Patricia."

It was easy to slip an arm through his, it would be easy to be very good to Nathaniel, always.

"What are you thinking, Patricia?"

"That I mean to make you a perfect wife, Nathaniel." He smiled down at me, happily.

I did mean it.

Yet I shall hope, through all my youth, through all my life, that in some far city I shall find my love again.

New York lights blurred behind us. . . . That was a shining city.

AFTERWORD TO THE 1989 EDITION

When the editor of this series reached me, a continent and about half an ocean away, after what she said was a hard search, and proposed to republish *Ex-Wife,* I was astounded. I did not even know I owned the copyright.

I remembered the book, of course. In my life, *Ex-Wife* has been like two images, a piece of furniture and an albatross. Countless families have owned some awkward piece, a desk or sideboard in a suspect and long out-of-fashion style, Biedermeier or Louis Seize. It doesn't go with the rest of the house, but it has a strong association with Great Aunt Tillie, who left you the object. So room is found for it, at least in an attic or corner of the barn, and the crisis, what to do with it, is postponed, at least until there are new heirs, or you have to sell off and move to the city. I was persuaded, only after a long argument, that some people would still be interested in this particular piece of Louis Seize.

I mentioned an albatross, traditionally a bad luck bird. *Ex-Wife* was that, in a way. Its *succès de scandale,* in the winter of the 1929 Crash, taught my mother, then a fashion writer and journalist, that she could make a great deal of money for that still-almost taxless day. From then on, there was practically no holding her. She became one of the chief practitioners of what's now a dead trade, in anything like the old, pre-TV terms:

women's magazine fiction, formula stuff. Other brand names of this kind of writing, most of them as forgotten now as my mother's is, were Faith Baldwin, Margaret Culkin Banning, and Viña Delmar. Kathleen Norris was perhaps the dean, the mother of the tribe.

My mother worked like a galley slave: I well recall the chaos and tension of making those eternal deadlines for *Cosmopolitan,* or *Women's Home Companion,* long gone now. She and a handful of her peers made more money, I think, than any American women could in that time, except those screen actresses in fairly steady employ. From 1930 to about 1945, her prime earning years, I guess—but it can only be a guess—my mother earned about seven hundred thousand dollars, with a few movie sales helping the total. She went through every penny of it, and more. My mother was a spender; she liked men and other possessions. She married four times, and two of the husbands cost her money.

Houses, cars, servants, travel, and the better products of Bergdorf Goodman and Bonwit's (which beautifully set off her petite, vivid, dark Irish looks) soaked up all the money. It was not a question of the meltdown of an inheritance, or a sudden fortune; she spent as she earned, or by anticipation. (My mother was a curious application of "pay as you go," which is supposed to be sound fiscal policy; in a way she *did* pay as she went.) Totally tapped out, which I remember as an almost annual event, she went to work again, and in the atmosphere of black coffee, cigarette stubs, and the clacking upright on a card table, and sleepless nights, she forged the dreams she sold to *"Cosmo"* or *Redbook,* for the delectation of 1930s housewives.

She was at all times very generous, as long as she had anything to give. My chief share of the swag was a very fancy education; my mother tried to groom me for the Establishment—a later word, not widely used in America until the 1950s. It might have worked but for two things, my lack of aptitude and the Establishment's lack of interest. Still, I was taught by some very good men, first to read and then to think about history in a rudimentary way. My mother had the strong belief, very common among Boston Irish and then Jewish people, in the talismanic, the magic qualities of Harvard College. I saw it in an era, the 1940s, when I think it had much more social variety than it does now; a curious thing, in terms of the frantic effort to democratize the place, but I believe it to be so. My mother had been a Radcliffe girl back in the First World War, and I have wondered if her showoff traits, some charming, some very dangerous, derived from the snubbing she took in Cambridge as a pushy lace-curtain Irish girl from Dorchester. But that's speculation only.

What's certain to me is: she was always trouble-prone. In the 1930s she had the strength, shrewdness, and luck to stave off the worst; even so, she had close calls. By the time I was twelve years old, I knew she had been blackmailed at least twice. Once, it was nothing: a maid, easily scared off, in those days, by a lawyer or a friendly local DA. My mother fired the girl, perhaps with a small sum to ease her exit. The next time, she was the victim of quite an elaborate scam, the other parties being a cheap writer and the man's allegedly complaisant wife. And that cost. Years later I read the ex-lover's obit in the *Times*. He had risen in the world and had been published by one of America's two or three most prestigious publishers; several titles were mentioned.

In the 1940s and early 1950s, she steadily lost control of her life, and the various personal Waterloos she suffered must still be of record in yellowing gossip columns and news stories and the court records of several states. My mother died in a charity ward of a New York hospital, of a mercifully fast cancer, in 1957, at age fifty-eight. (She lied a bit for *Who's Who* entries, but I never knew how much until I saw the inscription her sister put on her grave: she gave herself three years the best of it.) She entered the hospital, and perhaps died, under a false name; for one thing, there was still a warrant out against her in the State of New York. This tactic had one advantage; the press that she dreaded, but whose attentions she could not fail to attract, was pretty well foiled; she did not have to cope with the wolf pack at her deathbed.

Nickolas Muray, who is caricatured, rather than portrayed, in this book, did the best photos of my mother. But in the only book I have seen made from Muray's work, she doesn't figure. So, instead, I go to recapture her general style to a *Vogue* cover that has been widely sold in recent years as a greeting card. It was the "spring shopping" number of 1927. I can't make out the artist's signature—not Covarrubias, which I once thought.

The model is wearing some kind of figured evening coat with a high ermine collar, and a single strand of pearls twisted rather tightly around her neck. She has on one of those cloche hats with a long diamond spear, or arrow, stuck in it vertically, and the brim slightly turned up on one side. She's a blonde, but the short hair, the cupid's bow upper lip, and the very level look from her big eyes—those I seem to remember. Pallas Athena as a Fitzgerald-era flapper. Behind the girl is a New York nocturne, the artist's pastiche, it seems, of Broadway and Park Avenue, tall buildings and white lights; perhaps we're meant to recognize the old Woolworth Building. I like it. The girl and her setting seem very much as they should be; I can remember my mother that way; though, only four then, I have only the dimmest memories of 1927.

Somewhere in Santayana there's a kind of epitaph on my mother. We get in awful trouble, says the philosopher, because some of us are drawn to live dramatically in a world which isn't at all dramatic. My mother lived for awhile like the king in the Yeats poem who packed his wedding day with parades and concerts and volleys of cannon: "that the night come." It came for my mother, in ruinous style; but she may have felt that the day was well worthwhile.

The New York described here—and this was true, I think, for twenty years more—was much smaller, much more intimate, much safer and much cheaper than the city from the fifties on to the present. It was also cleaner. My mother calls it "shining," and once I puzzled over a passage in a Scott Fitzgerald essay because to him the city presented a radiantly white image. If the early generation skyscrapers were built in a lighter stone, the builders hadn't calculated on the vast increase in cars, or the virtual doubling of the city's population between 1920 and 1960.

People drink in *Ex-Wife*. I am sixty-four, and I do not think anyone under sixty can remember what a drinking society was, a whole society that drank on that scale. I speak of what I knew, the middle and upper-middle class, professional people and some in and around the arts of the Northeast. One of my earliest impressions, when I left my grandfather's Boston house after he died and came to join my mother in New York, was that a third of the grown-ups were fairly tight, or drunk—one did learn the gradations—by dinnertime, especially on weekends. It was pervasive. Handing around the hors d'oeuvres, I met, by the time I was fifteen, one Nobel winner and a man who later ran for President; both were drunk at the time.

John O'Hara said once that two things in his lifetime had tended to make crooks of the American people: Prohibition and the income tax. I believe the novelist was making a stab at the national character.

Confessional writing, and this book is in good part that, is extraordinarily hard to bring off, and of the good confessional books, a big percentage is religious, Augustine to Cardinal Newman. From the secular kind—and a great book it is— I'd like to borrow a blessing on my mother's little novel, republished so many years after her death. At the start of his *Confessions,* Jean-Jacques Rousseau seems worried about public reaction. He says:

> So let the numberless legion of my fellow men gather round me and hear my confessions. Let them groan at my depravities and blush for my misdeeds. But let each one of them reveal his heart at the foot of Thy throne with equal sincerity, and may any man who dares, say "I was a better man than he."

That's J. M. Cohen's translation. If it weren't too late for an epigraph to this novel, I'd pick that one.

—Marc Parrott
Honolulu,
April 1988

McNally Editions reissues books that are not widely known but have stood the test of time, that remain as singular and engaging as when they were written. Available in the US wherever books are sold or by subscription from mcnallyeditions.com.